CHARLES AUGUSTUS FENTON

ALANA WHITING

JOJO PUBLISHING

Charles Augustus Fenton
Alana Whiting

Published by Classic Author and Publishing Services Pty Ltd
First published 2015

JoJo Publishing Imprint

Editor: Ormé Harris
Designer / typesetter: Working Type Studio (www.workingtype.com.au)

National Library of Australia Cataloguing-in-Publication entry
Author: Whiting, Alana author.
Title: Charles Augustus Fenton / Alana Whiting.
ISBN: 9780987609601 (paperback)
Target Audience: For young adults.
Subjects: Young adult fiction.
Dewey Number: A823.4

AUTHOR PROFILE

New Zealander Alana Whiting is a first time novelist. She works as a nurse. She and her husband Nick live in Fitzroy, NZ. They have two grown children, Jacob and Sophie.

They often walk their Jack Russell Sumo along the black Fitzroy beach, with Mount Taranaki providing a stunning backdrop. Tom Cruise filmed *The Last Samurai* there. It is one of the rare places in the world where one can ski in the morning and surf in the afternoon.

Alana's love of writing, British history and research motivated her to write this intriguing and sometimes brutal tale of her fictional character, nineteenth century Charles Augustus Fenton.

For Nick, Jacob and Sophie

Birth

As I emerged from my sanctuary my parents rejoiced. Their precious son had arrived. My mother grappled me out with her own bare hands, eagerly drawing me near to her bosom. It was only the dour insistence of the midwife that I should be cleaned and wrapped as was proper that allowed her to relinquish me. I was repugnant, covered in white waxen vernix and bellowing to show my discontent at the new wilderness I had been thrust into. My face was contorted and ungraceful, but to my creators I was exquisite.

The midwife neatly removed the slimy coating and swathed me in delicate cloth. I squealed at her most vociferously, demanding my instant return to my former abode. Shackled in such a way I had no choice but to accept her transferring me into the arms of my mother.

My mother lay in what could only be described as the carnage of childbirth. The afterbirth and placental fluid complacently soaking the bedding between her spread legs, made her look like a ravaged Whitechapel whore. She wearily observed the ministrations of the midwife, who, after completing my return to her arms, had now begun on the task of the soiled sheets.

She looked at me as we rolled from side to side, completely absorbed with my newborn essence. She kissed me tenderly and smiled. 'Your name is Charles Augustus Fenton,' she whispered into my tiny cockle-shell ear. 'And you are my beautiful baby son.' With that, she carefully latched me onto her breast and I sucked with ravenous glee.

The midwife collected the soiled linen and handed it to the housemaid. Together they deftly sponged my mother and replaced her bloodied nightgown. I bawled angrily during the necessary separation between us and refused to be consoled until hurriedly returned to her bosom. My father was only allowed to enter once I was sated and the room thoroughly cleansed to the nurse's standard. She nodded briefly to my father before leaving them alone.

'Just look at our darling son, Charles. Isn't he adorable?'

Charles Senior stared at his fragile bundle lying asleep in his wife's arms. 'He is absolutely charming, Elizabeth. You are so very clever. You are the most beautiful, clever wife I know… I love you so much.'

Elizabeth smiled and carefully handed me to my father. He took the proffered bundle with some consternation, which made my mother giggle. As I continued my milk-laden nap, his chest filled with pride at his issue. He finally had a son.

Charles Senior

My arrival was a cause of great celebration not only at the manor but also in the surrounding community. There had been no secret that Elizabeth and Charles had been trying for some time to produce an heir. Amongst the villagers it had been offered that their long awaited success was only due to the visiting of Mistress Magda Williams. She was reputed to be dabbling in secret herbal remedies and held the reputation of being our local unofficial healing woman. The rumours continued that Mistress Magda had an allegiance with a coven of witches that met clandestinely in Warwickshire forest. These witches were members who lived in their very own town but used magic to maintain their anonymity. These whispers were mere murmurings as the Fentons were regarded highly and no one dared to face Mr Fenton's wrath if he were to hear them. He was particularly prickly on the subject of Magda. Having said that, I was reminded often when I grew older, how he was a good employer who had kept many of them from starving through the winter times when food was scarce. But you wouldn't cross him.

One of the more ancient workers remembered a time

when Joshua the kitchen hand had been caught stealing sausages. He recalled that Mr Fenton was told of the fact and demanded the boy be sent to him immediately. They dragged the trembling lad up to the office of Mr Fenton, who then told them to close the door. They waited outside the door keenly listening but could hear nothing much to their disgust. After what seemed an age, the door opened and Joshua walked out with tears streaming down his face and refusing to say a word to anyone. Mr Fenton was equally silent, though his grim face spoke a thousand words. Apparently the boy and his family packed up that very same day and left the village never to be seen again. They only took what they could carry. It was heard that they ended up at a workhouse, rambling that no one would help them because of Mr Fenton. Oh yes, he was a generous man when he wanted to be, but once you were found out you were damned for good. He had connections across the country that one did – powerful connections.

So the staff at the Fenton Manor worked doubly hard to make sure that I, Charles Augustus Fenton Junior, was kept in a manner according to my birthright. My nursery was bright, airy and warm. During the night my wet nurse would feed me and during the day my mother would insist on not only feeding me but bathing me as well. With such a bountiful supply of milk I had no choice but to grow fat and cherubic. I took to the breast with enthusiasm and vivacity and sucked them both dry. It was only the cook's constant supply of rich beef broth and milk puddings that kept them in good health. My mother grew to despise the milk puddings and once I was weaned, she refused to touch them ever again, but whilst she was lactating she swallowed the offensive pap night and day.

With such love and devotion, it was a great shock to both of my parents when I turned ill at the age of three.

Illness

The Newport Rising occurred not three months prior to my birth. Nearly 4000 Chartist sympathisers marched into the town of Newport intent on liberating fellow Chartists that were rumoured to be held prisoner. Their belligerent protest was equally fuelled by the rejection from the House of Commons for their petition and the indignant jailing of Henry Vincent. Vincent was a popular orator and advocate of not only universal suffrage but more importantly, the Chartist petition. His charge was for making inflammatory remarks and conspiracy. He was a man that fought for the workers and his imprisonment was grossly unfair according to his sympathisers. The organising for this uprising was kept secret for weeks, as they strategically planned to march in three converging main columns under the cover of darkness. However, whispers reached the ears of parliament who quickly drafted the company of the 45th regiment to Newport and prepared them for battle.

The rebels' plans fell apart because of unexpected delays when one of their armies of fighters arrived late. The men stood waiting for them in the pelting rain and watched the protective cloak of darkness soon turn into watery daylight. The wretched army marched down-trodden and bedraggled, sullen from the long delays and sodden clothing. Their vision of a strong and triumphant victory was swiftly turning into a shambles.

As they assembled in front of the Westgate Hotel, a simmering hush passed over the revolutionaries. No one knows what really happened next, but a gunshot rang out. This was considered to have been perpetrated by the rebels who, even then, were innocent to the fact of the soldiers hiding in the hotel. The soldiers, with adrenaline pumping in their veins, exploded with gunfire and splattered the rebels with bullets. They didn't stand a chance, with bodies lying covered in blood-soaked clothing within minutes. Shocked and overcome by this vicious onslaught, many rebels dropped their weapons and fled, with only the foolhardy left behind. Twenty-one people died during the revolt as they charged the Westgate Hotel. It was a massacre.

The Chartist petition had over one million signatures and it held six demands: 1) All men to have the vote, 2) voting by secret ballot, 3) Parliamentary elections to be held annually, not every five years, 4) constituencies should be of equal size, 5) Members of Parliament to be paid, and finally 6) the property qualification for becoming a Member of Parliament should be abolished.

This new law would have greatly inconvenienced my family as we had significant land and title at Wellesborne.

The Fentons therefore were entitled to vote and participate at Government in a manner ensuring our civilised prosperity should continue for generations to come. With the added protection of the Corn Law disabling any free trade, our future was assured and my inheritance sacrosanct. The working class needed to realise their station in life otherwise there would be pandemonium. It was for their ignorant benefit ultimately.

My father was a lawyer of some renown, so he was hurriedly summoned to London to assist at the trial after the Newport Rising. The audacity of John Frost and his kind was tantamount to treason and charged as such. It was only by the grace of God that they were not hanged, drawn and quartered in Monmouth. My father was an integral part in this successful resolution. However, his frequent travels to and from our estate to London fatigued him and my mother grew to despise the Chartists.

On the summer of my third year I scrambled behind my parents with nanny and pram in tow as they strolled along the River Dene. Charles Senior was finally given leave to stay at Fenton Manor with his beloved family and attend to his estate. Thinking back, I realise my father must have been weary and had probably grown somewhat withdrawn from the onslaught by these exasperating working classes continually fighting for more. Their damnable insolence was quite intolerable to both him and his colleagues. Those addlepated anarchists had no idea what it took to run a country. And yet it was becoming harder for the upper classes to ignore the growing undercurrent of disgruntled labourers. My father bore the strain on his face as he held my mother's arm and stared stoically forward. Even though I was a mere child at the time, I can still recall his frustration.

'My dear Elizabeth, you would not believe what these imbeciles are coming up with now. Some Irish protestant called O'Connor is conjuring up a crazy idea that all the poor people pool together their funds and buy some land. Just like that. Without thought for who would actually receive the land and farm it. They think they will just arrive there and the soil will be tilled and harvested magically, and all will prosper and become exceedingly rich.'

'Well, that's ridiculous, Charles. Are they thinking they will overtake the established farms and undercut our contracts? What a perfectly silly idea! Our family have been dealing with the suppliers for generations. They could hardly expect to be as highly regarded as the Fentons. What does Walton say of all this?' she said.

'It takes experience and good management to ensure that the workers are productive and efficient. They wouldn't have the slightest idea what is involved with running an estate. Walton has kept our crops and lands in good order because he is an experienced farmer

AND he knows his place. He laughed when I told him what O'Connor had in mind. In fact his exact words were, "Let them come, sir. Once they get a bit of dirt under the nails they'll be running right back where they came from." And I'm inclined to believe him. We have nothing to worry about, my dear. It's just so damned vexing to deal with.'

'The Fenton Estate has been here for generations and will continue to grow for future generations. Magda has told me so only last week. She has foretold that Charles Junior will be a most successful man and that the Fenton name will be famous for years to come.'

Charles frowned and looked around hurriedly. 'Really darling, do be careful what you say. That sort of comment could be overheard and interpreted in rather a poor light.'

'Oh pish, Charles, you worry too much. She hasn't failed us yet, has she?' And with that, Elizabeth turned to pick me up and cuddle me in her arms.

'All the same you must be vigilant to the ears around you. There are many who would like to possess our properties. The merest sniff of a scandal could be the undoing of us.' Charles Senior glared at Meg the nanny walking behind them, who blanched and stepped further back from the couple clasping the pram handle tightly.

I gleefully burrowed close to my mother's bosom. Though I was no longer suckling from her I still found great security and satisfaction close to her breast. She squeezed me tight and kissed my hair affectionately. My father's face softened at the scene and he stroked my cheek, his hand so close to my mother's breast as to make her blush and flash him an amatory eye. He caught her expression with a start and smiled bemusedly before reluctantly moving his hand away. Now was not the appropriate time. She continued to carry me as they strolled, until my robust weight caused her to transfer me to my father. Before too long I fell asleep, cocooned in my father's solid arms. He called Meg over, who hurriedly prepared the pram and tucked me in before chasing after the couple continuing on their walk.

That evening I fidgeted and grizzled as Meg tried to feed me my supper. Her repeated attempts were met with a cantankerous swipe from my diminutive hands. Each time the spoon neared my mouth I would size it up and push the offending matter back vigorously over her top. To her credit she showed extraordinary patience; that is until I successfully deposited a plop of mash directly into her face.

'Right then, Master Fenton, bedtime it is!' She stood up, wiped the muck from her cheek with her apron and fetched a hot cloth. I was then sponged and changed with professional exactness and delivered to my cot. She did not read me a nursery story as was the usual custom, but instead closed the door and stormed to her room.

I wailed and squealed but to no avail. My parents' room was in the other quarter and they were completely oblivious to my distress. In fact, they were happily occupied in each other's arms. I flailed my arms and kicked my feet outraged at my sudden abandonment and was met with silence. I was practically goggle-eyed with indignation that my usually tender nanny had left me to the darkness of the night. My vocabulary was limited so I was only able to communicate my disgust by crying and howling. And in this I was master. Her maltreatment of me ensured I remained unbendable in my goal to reach my mother and father. I knew their love was boundless and they would make me safe and happy again, and so with that in mind I was confident of their forthcoming arrival. All I needed to do was to make them hear me and they would come running; therefore I threw everything into my tiny lungs and expelled it out of my mouth. The result was deafening and if angels were watching over my bed that evening they would have flown back to Heaven covering their tortured ears.

The door to my room remained impassive. No sign of any movement whatsoever. My nanny had retired to her bed and stuffed her ears with cotton wool to drown out my misery. She had dealt with my irritated self all week and was furious with my abnormally bad behaviour. My parents didn't help with their constant fussing and cuddling of me, tending to my every whim. If it wasn't for her penurious state she would have resigned six months ago. She was categorically denied any type of physical punishment towards me, which was made quite clear when they interviewed her for the position. The merest smack on my backside or tap on my hand would be immediately followed by her dismissal. They had let the previous nanny go for exactly that reason. Therefore I knew in my own childish way that I was in charge of her and could do what I wanted, making this current situation rather untenable. I screamed and cried with baby tears dribbling down my flushed cheeks. I kicked my feet as if I were drowning, gasping for fresh air and sobbing in anguished despair. As each minute passed there became a growing realisation that I would not be saved and that my parents could not hear me. My reddened blotchy face was a picture of woe as I tired from my exertions and gradually simmered down. After a few more snuffles and whimpers I eventually nestled down to sleep, cuddling my snuggle blanket and sucking my thumb.

Doctor Greene

The next morning my nanny woke early with a guilty start. She had slept through for the first time in weeks and though she was rested she remembered our disagreement last night. She hurried to my room filled with good intentions and a desire to rekindle the friendship. She would start with a big cuddle and a nursery song before feeding me my favourite breakfast of coddled egg.

She opened the door anxiously and was met with silence. Strange, she thought as she neared the cot. She peered over and inspected me. I lay there flaccid, still blotchy from last night's events. My eyes were open but unseeing. I could notice a blob in front of me but had no clue as to who it was. Her eyes widened at my apathetic state and she speedily picked me up to cuddle me and change my sodden nappy. I was hot to touch and my bottom was excoriated from the loose bowel movement I had passed overnight. The nappy was soaked in offensive smelling faecal matter and she was filled with dreaded remorse.

'What have I done to you, my little man?' she muttered to herself whilst wiping the muck away and soothing some grease onto my burnt bottom. She sponged my face and chest, worried at how warm I was and hoping it would cool my fevered state. After quietly dressing me she attempted to feed me my breakfast. I refused again and it was with troubled heart that she now wished I would be the naughty boy I had been last night. She could not delay any longer. I had to be taken to my parents.

My mother was sipping her tea in the breakfast room and turned to smile at the nanny coming through the door. Her smiled dropped when she saw Meg's expression and she rose anxiously to see her son.

'What is the matter? What's wrong with Charles? Why he is so hot?'

The nanny stared at the floor and squirmed. 'He wouldn't eat his dinner last night, ma'am, so I put him to bed early and when I woke he was like this. He hasn't eaten any breakfast either.'

'Charles! Charles! Come here quickly. Our son is sick,' she called out to Charles Senior in the nearby room, who scurried in and scanned my face worriedly.

'Good God, woman! He's burning with fever! How long has he been like this?' he demanded of the nanny, who quailed under his ferocious glare.

'I'm sorry, sir. I just thought he was being a bit naughty. He kept throwing the food at me and he wouldn't listen at all. So I thought an early bedtime was the right thing to do.'

'Well, look at him, girl! He's burning up with fever! You should have known better and informed us last night.'

Charles Senior hurriedly wrote on a note and handed it to Meg.

'Go to Dr Greene immediately. Tell Jack to take you down in the buggy. Give the doctor this note and wait. You will be bringing him back to the house as soon as the doctor is ready. Do NOT come back without him or you will be packing your bags and leaving.'

Meg gulped and placed the note in her apron pocket. She hurried out of the room and down to the stables where Jack was busy combing down one of the horses. He looked up in surprise at seeing Meg. She wasn't usually able to visit so early.

'Jack. You have to help me. I'm in terrible trouble. Wee Master Fenton has taken ill and it's my fault completely. I left the wee bairn all night. He was being a little imp, and now he's all sick and hot. I feel terrible, absolutely terrible,' she said, wiping her eyes with the edge of her apron.

'There, there lass, the lad will be all right. He's a bonny little bugger,' Jack said, patting her on the shoulder. 'Don't you worry about a thing. He's a Fenton, made from this land and of good stock. He'll pull through.'

Meg implored Jack. 'We have to go right now, Jack. The master of the house has demanded I fetch Dr

Greene straight away and bring him back without delay. If I don't, my time here is over.'

Jack nodded and set to the task of preparing the buggy for transport. Meg fidgeted at the delay, hopping from one foot to the other and watching anxiously until he gave the nod for her to climb aboard.

She hoisted her skirts and with help from his proffered hand, she scooted up onto the buggy and stared resolutely ahead. Her hand clenched around the note checking once again that she hadn't dropped it in the process. She couldn't fail the master anymore. Her bowel tightened at the thought of being sacked from the Fenton Estate. She knew what Mr Fenton was capable of and she didn't want to be victim of it.

Jack drove the buggy speedily down the path towards the town doctor five miles away. He knew the route like the back of his hand and instinctively urged the horses to make haste. Every minute counted, of that he was sure. It wasn't long before they pulled up outside the doctor's practice. He hopped off the buggy and assisted Meg down. She smoothed down her skirts, raced up the steps and knocked anxiously on the door.

'Yes? Can I help you?' the doctor's wife enquired with a smile.

'Oh please, Miss. Could you give this note to Dr Greene? It's from Mr Charles Fenton of Fenton Estate. It's of a most urgent matter.'

'I'm afraid the doctor is out visiting a sick patient at the moment. He'll be back at noon.'

Meg fretted. 'But I need to get him to the Fenton Estate immediately. The young master has taken very ill and I've got orders to fetch the doctor to see him.'

'Oh, I see.' She frowned. 'Well that's no good. Let me see what I can do.' She fetched his appointment book and studied the entry in the diary. 'Yes. He is at Mr Kivell's just down the lane. I'll come with you and show you the way.' She fetched her hat and grabbed Meg's arm. The two ladies briskly marched towards the Kivell household, though the speed didn't seem nearly quick enough for Meg. They reached the door and knocked.

'Mrs Greene! What's brought you here?' asked Mr Kivell.

'I'm so dreadfully sorry, Mr Kivell, but I must speak to my husband immediately.'

'But he's seeing to my wife at present. Is it urgent?' he said.

'Most urgent, Mr Kivell. Mr Charles Fenton's son has taken ill. Could you please give him this note? He needs the doctor straight away,' she urged.

'But, of course. I see. I'll let him know.' He went back inside.

Dr Greene blustered out minutes later. 'What is the meaning of this? I'm seeing a patient. You know not to interfere with my appointments.'

Mrs Greene blushed and glanced sideways at Meg. Meg rallied the courage to speak.

'I'm sorry, Doctor. But it's Mr Fenton's son. He's awful hot and has the skitters. I tried feeding him last night and this morning and he won't have a bite to eat. Mr Fenton has instructed me to ask you most directly if you could come and see him at the manor,' Meg blurted, and then looked anxiously at the doctor.

I can picture the good doctor even now, frowning and rubbing his chin. It was acknowledged that the Fentons held a lot of clout in the town and he was aware that the loss of their custom would not be a wise choice. He had nearly completed his visit with Mrs Kivell and was certain that with his personal medicinal draught he had developed, she should make a full and steady recovery. As much as he loathed to be commanded, he was a pragmatic man and he made his decision as thus.

'Take me to him. Mr Kivell, please follow my wife back to the surgery. She will provide you with my tonic to assist your wife. I will come back to check on her tomorrow.' And with that, he collected his bag and strode with Meg to the buggy.

As they rode back to the estate he drilled Meg for information regarding Charles Junior. He asked about his appetite, his bowel movements, any skin rashes, irritability or signs of fever. Meg glumly nodded to all the questions, explaining that Master Fenton had seemed to be out of sorts for the last week and not really sleeping so soundly. Dr Greene frowned and considered what may have been troubling the small boy.

They arrived in a flurry. One of the house servants had been keeping a watchful eye out for their arrival and quickly ran inside to inform the master. Both Charles and Elizabeth dashed to the door, the worry and strain clear on their faces. As the butler helped him with his coat, they showed him to my room where I lay listlessly. My stomach was swollen and my chest and abdomen covered in red welts. The pungent smell emanating the room advised those present that I had yet again soiled myself with the loose diarrhoea seeping out around my pants. Dr Greene examined me after instructing the nanny to change and clean my reddened bottom. I was faced with the ignominy of having to wear a daytime diaper. He looked at my eyes, in my ears, listened to my heart and peered at the rash. I surrendered without fight, all anger dissipated after last night's efforts. My parents watched him anxiously, holding each other.

'It would appear to me that your son has all the classic signs and symptoms of typhoid fever. Not particularly prevalent usually at this time of year, but I have seen the odd case in town.' He opened his doctor's bag and fossicked around. 'I recommend you give him these powders mixed in with his milk. Keep him hydrated as much as possible and protect his skin with this unguent. The diarrhoea will burn his skin and needs to be removed immediately.' He regarded Meg the nanny. 'He must be kept clean, warm and dry. If he is feverish, sponge him with a tepid washcloth. Keep offering him small sips of boiled water, stewed apples and broth and the milk at night. He will take some time to get better, but get better he shall. As long as you do exactly as I have instructed,' he finished with a small smile to Charles and Elizabeth. 'Now if you'll excuse me I must resume my appointments back in Warwickshire town. There are people waiting for me.' He shook Charles' hand and returned to the buggy where Jack sat perched on top.

And so my battle began.

Elizabeth pleads for her son

Every morning at the crack of dawn Meg would come to my bed, remove all the soiled nightclothes and bedding and bathe me in an oatmeal soak that Magda had supplied my parents. I lay there in a trance-like state, my raw skin soothed by the tepid water Meg was drizzling over me. As she washed me she sang little ditties that her own mother had sung to her as a child. She felt genuinely distraught at my ill health and desired nothing more than a return of my usually ebullient state. She couldn't recall her last full night's sleep. Since I had become unwell she had been a dedicated night nanny on top of her daytime duties. Every three hours she wearily traipsed into my room to offer some fluid and change my frequently soiled diaper. Instead of gratefully smiling at her for all this love and attention, I would squeal and fuss, clamping my lips together tightly and throwing my head from side to side.

Both she and my parents surveyed my debilitated frame with dismay. My cheeks had sunken in and my petite ribs stuck out against the grotesque stomach. My eyes were dull, my skin pale and no matter what delicious delights they offered me, I would not take them.

I had developed a chesty cough, bringing up plugs of green phlegm and gasping for air with even the slightest exertion. Jack made repeated trips to the doctor's surgery for more medicinal tonics and powders but it was to no avail. I was dying.

Elizabeth was also losing weight at an alarming rate. She refused any visitors and the only trip she would make from the home was to the local church to pray. Charles insisted she have an afternoon nap in an effort to regain her strength. As she lay holding his hand, she spoke.

'Charles, I can't stand this anymore. We have to get Magda to come and visit again. She can make him better. I'm sure of it.'

'You know my stand on this. People are starting to talk and the words they are saying are 'witchcraft' and 'devil's work'. Why she thought it would be okay to publicly ridicule Mr Weston, I simply do not know. Since that very public disagreement, he has had no end of bad luck and he blames her. We simply can't have any further connection with that woman. It would be extremely detrimental to my business,' he said.

'Well, he shouldn't have sold her the spoilt grains. She found weevils in them! It's his own damned fault for trying to cheat her,' she retorted.

'Elizabeth! Mind your language. You sound more and more like her each day.'

'Good. I like her and I want her to come and see our son. It's been ten weeks now, Charles, and he is getting worse. Ten weeks. How can I believe anything that doctor says?'

Charles looked into the pale face of his tormented wife. She stared back with a silent pleading in her eyes. She squeezed his hand and placed it on her heart before kissing it softly. He couldn't stand to see the pain lying there before him. He was suffering too. His only son was fading before his eyes and he was powerless to stop it. He had heard many mutterings about his wife's friend Magda whenever he went to town and it dismayed him to be even slightly connected to her. He always felt a sense of uneasiness when she came to visit and made excuses to leave the room as soon as was politely possible. But Elizabeth had complete faith in her and he had to admit, the oatmeal soaks he grudgingly allowed her to provide were a godsend. Perhaps if they could sneak her in at nightfall she might not be seen by as many people. With that idea in mind, he agreed to send Magda a note requesting her presence that evening. Elizabeth smiled and drew him close to her, kissing him passionately.

Magda

Magda arrived soon after nightfall. She swept into the house with a dignified grace. Charles awkwardly thanked her for coming so quickly and then showed her to my room where I lay listening to Meg reading me a story. She startled at seeing Magda and laid the book down. Elizabeth looked up from her sewing and smiled. She ordered Meg to go to her room, which she did with alacrity. The two women looked at each other and embraced. Magda pulled away first to give Elizabeth a reassuring touch to the cheek. Elizabeth started to cry.

'No tears, my love. I'm here now. Hush now. Hush.' She gave Elizabeth her handkerchief to dab her eyes. Elizabeth sniffed and looked at Magda gratefully.

'You don't know how awful it's been, Magda. I have died a hundred deaths for not being able to see you again. Damn that cursed shopkeeper. Damn him to Hell.'

Magda laughed. 'Don't worry too much about that. He has grown to rue the day he crossed my path. My only concern is for you and your darling boy to get better. You look gaunt, my sweet. You should have called for me much sooner. But, not to bother – that's in the past. Let's look at the here and now and fix your little son.'

She drew close to my bed and gazed at me. I stared back, equally curious. She closed her eyes and began to chant softly under her breath. Her hands moved up and down just above my weakened body, gesturing and flicking away periodically. She rubbed them together and placed them firmly onto my swollen abdomen and I could feel a rising heat radiating from her as she muttered away. There was no pain, just warmth and a feeling of lightness going through my body. I relaxed immediately, cooing and smiling at her as she concentrated on her spell. Her shoulders hunched and lifted as she cupped her hands and drew them away from my stomach, flicking them towards her shoes and stamping down seven times with each foot. She did this several times and with each cupping I could feel my stomach easing and growing softer. She touched my forehead with her left thumb and drew a circle from the top of my face to the bottom going anti-clockwise. She then pressed my cheeks with her forefingers and flicked away towards my earlobes, hissing as she flicked. My mother watched her with love in her eyes as she touched my face and body, murmuring and whispering to herself. She finished with an incantation spoken so softly only the wind could have picked it up. She closed her eyes and placed her right hand on her heart and her left hand on my brow whilst repeating what she said. When she stopped the silence was thick in the air and no one moved for some time.

Unexpectedly, she opened her eyes and the mood vanished. She smiled at me and then at Elizabeth and turned to fossick in her bag, removing a small leather pouch and tucking it into my pillowcase.

'This is a little collection of herbs that will help ease your son's restless nights. From now on you will notice an improvement or my name is not Magda Williams.' She smiled and kissed Elizabeth on the lips. 'Make sure to keep it there for one week and he will be back to his happy self in no time. I promise you.'

As she spoke I drifted into the arms of Morpheus, not noticing the women in each other's arms.

'Oh Magda, how can I ever thank you? You are my saviour yet again.' Elizabeth placed her hands on Magda's cheeks and kissed her back.

'You have already repaid many times over, Lizzie. It is I that is in your debt,' Magda huskily responded, parting her lips to kiss her deeper. 'I look forward to seeing you again.'

'And you shall, my love. Charles has agreed to me seeing you. But for now, we must say good-night.' And with that, they regretfully parted, going arm in arm to the front door of the house, where Magda disappeared into the night.

Recovery

From there, my recovery was remarkable. If Meg noticed the pouch hidden in my bedding, she chose wisely not to bring it up with the mistress. Those things were best left alone she thought to herself. But she was relieved when on the seventh day her mistress came and removed the mysterious purse. It felt as if she could breathe again and she no longer dreaded coming to pick me up out of the cot.

My appetite returned with gusto. My chest cleared and the hacking cough disappeared. My stomach now filled with stew and dumplings, apple cobbler and egg custard, all of which stayed in my body and gave me renewed strength. Before long the bones became padded with flesh and my eyes sparkled. The joy it brought my parents was immeasurable as they fussed and cooed over me every day. Though Charles would never admit it publicly he realised that this miracle was partly due to Elizabeth's friend Magda and he reluctantly allowed Elizabeth to visit her weekly as she had before.

As my health improved my father was once again called to Parliament to be part of the select committee investigating the financial viability of the Chartist

Co-operative Land Company. The Chartists, and in particular, Feargus O'Connor, still held a vision of workers buying into shares of the company and purchasing estates. As ridiculous as it seemed to my father, the movement was gathering momentum and there were concerns being raised by major land owners about this new development threatening their livelihood. It was up to the committee to unofficially shut it down whilst openly appearing to be neutral. This was a delicate operation and they had to move cautiously, thus keeping my father away for long periods of time. This aggravated my mother and filled her with rancour towards those infernal working classes with their high ideas. Her only pleasures were the frequent visits to her friend Magda and playing marbles with me.

I, on the other hand, looked forward to my father's journeys. Not because of his absence, but because of the wondrous stories he returned with to fill my ravenous mind. As I recovered my strength, he would regale me with stories of mystical people he had met. Whilst ensconced with the Chartist Co-operative, he was able to have some light relief with a short visit from the diminutive dwarf called Tom Thumb. He was fourteen years old and only twenty-five inches high. He was introduced to society by none other than the famous Phineas T Barnum and made a substantial income by purely making an appearance. My father showed me where the little man stood compared to the length of his leg and I would have given my entire marble collection just to have seen him in the flesh. My dreams were filled with little people and barking Irish battling with the dreaded goblins underground.

My world seemed so dreary and protected to me compared to the bountiful discoveries to be made out there. And so the seasons passed and I impatiently became of an age to be ready for school.

School

Our cook was one of the finest in town, and I had grown to be a strapping young lad of six years. Spending time with Jack in the stables and Mr Walton out on the fields had turned my skin a rich walnut brown. My mother recoiled at every new scratch and scrape I came strutting home with, complete with yet another hole in my breeches for Meg to mend. My father would chuckle thinking of the time when he was a lad hunting down the frogs and scaling up trees. It was a carefree and happy childhood and the excitement I showed at making new friends in the village school gladdened them both. I refused to be kept at home with Meg the nanny and leaned on them until they saw my point of view.

I adamantly banned my mother from taking me there. Jack walked with me on the first day and then I declined his company also. I took to the books with avid ferocity, learning to read and write at a speed that bemused and surprised my teacher. I loved new words, sounding them out on my tongue like an exotic candy and then attempting to place them in a sentence that had no relationship with that word. I didn't care. If the word was delicious then I felt it deserved a chance to be written in my school book and I was quite affronted when my teacher would scratch it out and provide a more suitable alternative.

My class was made even more delightful with the added inclusion of Lily. She sat three rows in front of me with her twin sister Carla. Her silky long blonde hair seemed to sparkle in the sunlight streaming through the school window and my eye was caught lingering on her more often than not. If I stared long enough I was certain that she even glowed a fuzzy halo that shimmered when she moved. Though I had never been in close proximity I was convinced she would smell like ginger biscuits and lemonade. I adored her. Her unfortunate sister was destined to remain in her shadow and be invisible to me. There could be only one true Lily. Lily of the valley. Lily of the meadow. Glittery tinkly fairy Lily. Dancing and skipping, holding my hand and beaming. And she had absolutely no idea I existed.

Coming from a home that worshipped the ground I stepped on meant that I was perplexed at her indifference. It bewildered me that she didn't come rushing towards me whenever I entered the classroom. So I determined to make her my friend and show her how wonderful I was.

One Wednesday morning at midday break I summoned the courage to go and say hello. She was alone, her sister having engaged herself in a game of hopscotch. She was holding a little box in her hands and chuckling to herself. I neared her, smiling and tentative, sitting quietly beside her until she noticed my presence.

'What are you doing, Lily?' I opened the conversation, somewhat curious about the contents of the box that held her captivated.

Lily looked at me blankly before pasting a secret smile on her face.

'Nothing.'

'What's in the box?'

Lily looked up and scanned the playground before responding. 'Nothing.'

'Come on, Lily. Tell me what's in the box. I won't tell anyone.'

Lily frowned and looked at me again. She placed the box on her lap, covering it with her tiny white hands. 'It's just a box,' she declared resolutely, her back straightening.

This was starting to bother me. I knew she was lying, I was sure I could hear scuffling coming from inside the mysterious container and I wanted to see it.

'If you don't tell me I will tell Mrs Pompour.'

She stared at me aghast. She studied the playground again and searched for her sister. Carla was deeply engrossed in her game and unaware of her sister's dilemma. She patted the box and glared at me before returning her gaze back to the box. She wriggled her toes in anguish.

'You wouldn't dare! It's none of your business. Go away!'

But I was not so easily dispensed of. 'Show me what's in the box or I WILL tell Mrs Pompour. I will!' I made to stand and find the teacher.

She bit her lip and glowered, considering her options. At that point Mrs Pompour chose to enter the playground and clang the bell for everyone to return to class. She looked at me again and brought the box quickly up towards my face. I held my breath and waited. She carefully lifted the lid a little and I peered eagerly into the darkness. In the corner staring back at me was a little field mouse bristling his whiskers. I gasped and smiled wanting to hold the tiny furry creature but Lily had already slammed the lid shut and placed the box into her satchel. What a surprise. As she trounced towards the classroom I marvelled at her daring. All the other girls in the class would scream and squeal at the sight of such a rodent and here she was cuddling and cooing at her pet as if she were the mother. This made her all the more magical to me and I followed with a more sanguine step close behind her.

I wanted to be her friend. I wanted to share my sandwiches. I wanted her to play in the field with me and for us to catch frogs and mice together. But I didn't know how to achieve this fine goal. She remained wary of me every time I approached her at lunch. I knew my presence was unwanted but showing great tenacity I continued to sit next to her and talk.

'What's his name?'

'Albert.'

'Where did you catch him?'

'Behind my house.'

'Can I hold him?'

'No.'

I tried again. 'Can I PLEASE hold him? I'll be very careful.'

She pouted. 'He's mine, not yours.'

'I'll give him straight back. I swear.'

She gently held the mouse in her hands making sure he had a little hole to breathe. Her thumb patted down the mouse's back and she murmured sweetly to him. She rubbed her cheek against his fur, closing her eyes and smiling beatifically. 'No.'

Inwardly I fumed. The fact that I could have easily caught any number of mice on my own did not matter. I had to have hers. If I had her mouse then she would belong to me and do as I say. This was my master plan. I plotted during class, trying to think of ways to snatch the box. She kept the satchel close to her at all times, even hanging it on the hook closest to her desk. She would glance occasionally at her bag throughout the lesson with a slight smile on her lips. Her sister Carla appeared uninterested in the furry pet and I wasn't even sure she knew it existed. I had to think of a way to distract Lily from Albert so I could make the clean getaway.

Finally I had my chance. I decided the best way to get closer was to keep my distance. I pretended to be more interested in playing with my friends. I made sure we kept relatively close to where she always sat so I could keep watch without her realising. I would joke and shout and swagger around just like the other boys but always keep a second eye on her. Occasionally she would leave her satchel for a few moments when Carla insisted she come over and play with her. I had to wait for just the right time as sometimes she lost interest quickly and raced back to her beloved mouse. Carla would stamp and fuss but she knew her sister well enough to realise it was a lost cause. How could twins be so unalike?

Showing a patience I never thought I possessed, I bided my time. I waited and plotted. Finally she stepped away from the satchel and headed over to her sister in a distracted air. Carla had insisted she play a full game of hopscotch with her as her other friends had grown tired. I scuffled up with the stealth of a cat and swooped upon her bag. Quickly rustling through, I grabbed her mouse to hide under my jacket. I raced back to my friends smirking at my temerity. She hadn't even seen me. So when the bell pealed out the end of play I jostled in with the other boys and snuck the mouse into my bag. Thankfully Lily didn't check her bag before she hung it up and my first stage was completed.

After school I raced home and fed my acquisition little pieces of bread. I hid him in my room and bounced down the stairs to talk to my mother about my day, withholding my secret mission. We loved our chats; she was fascinated with everything I did, making her my most favourite person in the world. My heart swelled with love for my mother and I would do anything for her, bringing her special posies of wild daisies and when the gardener wasn't looking, the odd flower from his plot. I'm sure he knew it was me. I wasn't very gentle when I snapped the stems, but he knew better than to complain to the mistress. She seemed to cherish each gift, clutching it to her bosom with tears welling in her eyes, before calling Meg to fetch her special crystal vase to place them in. They would stay there, with my father praising the wild array as if it were the finest arrangement from London. Only when the petals had dropped and the stems had darkened was the maid allowed to dispose of it.

The following day I ran to school, holding the mouse carefully. I tucked him into my jacket pocket, feeding little crumbs to keep him mollified. I had the upper hand at last.

Lily

Lily and Carla were already sitting at their desks. Lily looked forlorn and Carla was absorbing her mood by looking glum too. A pair of sad beautiful twins on a crisp spring day. I couldn't wait to be the big swashbuckling hero for Lily. The time heaved its way ponderously to noon before I could approach my future best friend. She sat dolefully under the tree in her usual spot and barely looked up when I approached.

'Hello.'

'Hello.'

'What's the matter, Lily?'

'Albert's missing. Have you seen him?' she asked me.

At that moment, Albert wriggled in my pocket causing me to hastily place my hand on him, preventing his escape.

'I may have.'

'What do you mean by that?' Lily looked at me suspiciously. 'Where is he?'

I smirked and pulled Albert out by the tail. He struggled against his abductor but I was very experienced at rodent control. My time at the estate had been well spent. I regarded Lily with a triumphant expression as her mouth dropped and tears welled in her eyes.

'Let him go. You're hurting him!' She made to grab the mouse but I pulled away just in time. I bobbed Albert around in front of her, tormenting her just as she had tormented me. The tears trickled down her cheeks as she tried again to get her treasured pet back.

'Give him back!'

Carla heard her sister call out and raced over to help. She saw the wriggling mouse between my fingers and guessed it was Lily's pet Albert. She pushed me on the shoulder and growled indignantly at me.

'You give Lily back her mouse right now or I'll tell on you!'

This was not how I imagined it would go. I stuffed the mouse back into my pocket and looked with some consternation at the growing circle of children surrounding us. The noise from the twins had drawn their attention and with the added bonus of a furry creature it was too wonderful by half. Mrs Pompour's attention was alerted as the crowd grew. Things were going from bad to worse and any control I had, vanished. The children had started chanting, 'Give it back. Give it back.'

'Give what back?' enquired Mrs Pompour entering the melee. 'What exactly have you got, Charles?'

I shifted uneasily and was met with a sea of angry faces. Where were my mother and father when I needed them? It was at that moment that Albert chose to make his escape. He scurried out of my pocket, along my sleeve and down my jacket. This caused sheer pande-monium. The girls screamed and the boys yelled with excitement. They rushed to try and grab Albert, who took a despairing leap onto the ground and into the bush. The thundering sound of feet chasing after him gave him the added drive to dash straight into a plant, franti-cally looking for sanctuary. But the boys were made of hardier stuff. They dived in after him, scrambling and digging their little hands in the dirt and ignoring Mrs Pompour's commands to stop. With a roar of success, one boy pulled the mouse out by the tail and raised him up jubilantly. It was all too much for the little creature and he expired right in front of them. Lily saw every-thing and ran away sobbing, with Carla close behind.

'Throw that dirty little thing away immediately!' ordered Mrs Pompour.

The boy shrugged and tossed the body into the bush, uncertain at what all the fuss was about. I tried to join the group returning back to class but Mrs Pompour collared me.

'What is the meaning of this?'

I stared bleakly after the boys as they left me to it.

'Come on. Speak up!'

I shuffled my feet and looked at the ground.

'Right! If that is how you wish to play it, Master Fenton, then you can go and see the headmaster, Mr Brown. I'm sure he would like to know what your excuse is for bringing wild life into my classroom.' She grabbed my ear and marched me to Mr Brown's office.

The walk to the headmaster's office was painful. Every step I took was as if I were stepping through a muddy quagmire. I dragged my feet slowly, which aggravated Mrs Pompour into pinching harder on my ear to speed me up. It had the desired effect and I lifted the pace slightly. We reached the door and she knocked.

'Mr Brown. Young Charles here feels it's appropriate to bring a rat into my school. I caught him playing with it in the playground and teasing the girls.' She pulled me in, as I started to snivel.

Mr Brown glared over his spectacles at me, frowning.

'Indeed, Mrs Pompour, indeed. That's simply not good enough. We have rules for a reason, young lad, and they are not to be taken lightly. Perhaps it is time to be taught how to remember that for the future. I shall see to it, Mrs Pompour. Thank you.' He nodded at Mrs Pompour, who nodded back and released me. She left the room, closing the door behind her.

'So what exactly inspired you to bring a rat into my school, Master Fenton?' he asked, coming out from behind the desk and leaning against it.

'It wasn't a rat. It was a mouse.' I stared back at him.

Mr Brown blustered at my response.

'You insolent little rascal! How dare you correct ME!'

I swallowed and dropped my gaze quickly to the floor,

kicking myself for speaking out. It was quite the tactical error and I knew I was in for it.

He stood up and strode towards the cane propped against the wall. My eyes widened as I watched him pick up the dreaded thing and swish it in the air. I had heard stories of this punishment but had never been a victim to its sting. Mr Brown had the reputation of a tyrant who believed in the saying, 'Spare the rod; spoil the child.' Considering I had never even been smacked at home before, I could only imagine the agony I was about to experience. My imagination was superlative and gave me no comfort. He swished the cane again, ensuring I could see him and then turned to face me with a smirk.

'Drop your pants, boy, and bend over.' He pointed to a stool.

I trembled as I slowly unbuttoned my drawers. They fell to lie disconsolately around my ankles. I waddled over to the stool and leaned my elbows on it. My little white bottom shivered in the cool air with both cold and dread. Tears bubbled over and trickled down my cheeks onto the stool. I bit my lip trying to hold them back but to no avail. I could hear the headmaster remove his coat and place it over his chair. He picked up the cane again and marched towards me.

'For your punishment, Master Fenton, you shall be receiving five of the best. And let this be a lesson to you, boy, never to bring RATS into the school again.'

I heard the air whistle as the cane sped down and hit my buttocks. I held my breath.

'One!'

The pain was sudden and sharp.

'Two!'

I counted silently in my head, flinching at each wallop. My tears had turned to sobs.

'Three!'

Two to go, two to go. I murmured inside.

'Four!'

Almost there, one more, one more. Ouch, ouch, ouch.

'Five!'

Mr Brown returned the cane back to the wall and put his coat back on. He was puffing slightly as he returned to his chair. My face was red and slimy with tears mingling into snot. I silently pulled my trousers carefully over my buttocks. My bottom felt as if it were on fire as I stood to attention in front of his desk. He was writing a note for my parents.

Shame

I walked home with lead in my shoes. The pain and embarrassment were almost too much to bear. I could feel the note searing in my pocket, adding to the heat coming from my nether regions. I had been instructed to go home and give the note to my father who would have to sign it so I could return it as being witnessed. There was no escape from further punishment, which was what Mr Brown was hoping for I could tell. He seemed to be particularly satisfied with himself after my caning and I hated him for it. I muttered to myself all the nasty things I craved him to endure. If the evilest goblins in the world should come to snatch him and take him away to work in their underground caves, then I would have personally cheered them on and strewn their path with flowers. I crossed both my fingers and wished with all my might that this dreadful thing would happen to him. My imagination ran with it and I began constructing different scenarios of torture that the goblins would enforce on my headmaster. This kept my mind engaged and I was somewhat flabbergasted to arrive at my front door. The enchanting images evaporated and I returned with a thump to the present and unavoidable confrontation to be.

I skulked in, not wishing to see my mother. I was her golden boy and I felt deeply ashamed at my asinine behaviour in front of Lily. It was best to face it like a man and get it over with. I knocked on my father's study door and waited for the response.

'Come in,' I heard.

I breathed in a deep breath and walked in, closing the door behind me. My father stopped writing and smiled initially at seeing me, but the smile dropped quickly on observation of my serious expression. He frowned.

'What's the matter, son? Why are you home so early?'

I reached into my pocket and handed him the note. He opened it and read carefully, ignoring my sullen presence. His face was unreadable as I watched his eyes dart left to right along the paper. The clock gonged stridently in the background. He folded the note and sat thoughtfully with one hand touching his elbow and the other stroking his chin. Finally, after an interminable amount of time, he regarded me.

'Well, well, Charles. I see you have been a naughty boy.' He spoke quietly.

I stood with my heart in my mouth and nodded.

'Mr Brown has written that he has punished you from the school's point of view but wishes me to enforce my own personal reprimand as I see fit.'

I gulped and bit my lip to stop me from crying.

'What exactly did he do?'

I lowered my trousers and turned around so that my father could see the welts. They were raised and red and the bruising was just starting to appear. I heard a sharp intake of breath and for a moment I felt a brief surge of hope that he might grab his stick and batter Mr Brown black and blue. I knew my father's strong conviction on physical discipline and my spirits rose. The goblins would have nothing on my father's ire. I re-buttoned the trousers and looked at him with hopeful anticipation. However, I was wrong. He stared at me with a myriad of emotions fleeting over his face, then sighed.

'That looks painful, son, but the shame you bring to the Fenton name cuts me deeper still. You represent this family whenever you engage with other members of our community. It is your responsibility to maintain that good name at all times. It saddens me to think you could break the school rules so blatantly and not only that, but also talk back to the headmaster. Whatever were you thinking?'

I stood silently, sombre in mood.

'I stand by Mr Brown's punishment and will endorse his recommendation of my own personal punishment.'

He pulled a box down from the bookcase shelf and placed it in front of me on his desk.

'In this box is a brand-new edition of *The Boys Own* book by William Clark that I had purchased in London with the specific intent of giving it to you for your birthday. I know how much you have been wanting it and your mother and I felt you were old enough to get one this year. But now, after your little debacle, it is with the greatest of regret that I will have to return it.'

I cringed. I had been bothering them about the book for some weeks now. It had everything a boy would want to know about combustion in and under the water, how to change a card into a bird, plus my personal favourite, the art of hideous metamorphosis. I could use all of these skills to my greatest advantage. I salivated at the thought that the book was within arm's reach of me and was now going to be taken away. Life was very, very unfair.

'I will tell your mother that the book was unavailable. We shall not inform her about your poor behaviour. It would break her heart to know her boy was a heathen.'

The shame washed over me in a flood. If I could do anything to make things right with my father again, I swore to myself I would do it. He was a magnificent and wise man and I had let him down. My gratitude at his discretion was immense and I solemnly apologised and promised to never be naughty ever again. I watched sadly as he put the book back on the shelf. He hugged me briefly and dismissed me.

I plodded up the stairs to my room. Thankfully my mother seemed to be visiting her friend Magda and this enabled me to have a good wallow without her finding out.

I had to lie on my stomach as my behind was throbbing and hot. Rivers of self-pity let loose and the dams broke as I cursed Mr Brown for his malevolence. I punched my pillow, visualising his face lying on top of it and in my fervour I accidentally caught the edge of the brass bedstead, making me bellow in agony. Meg came running in.

'What's happened, Charlie? What did you do to yourself?' she asked, scanning me for injury.

'Mr Brown is a horrible old toad and I hate him!' I exclaimed, rubbing my hand angrily.

'Your headmaster? Why would you ever hate him?' She drew my hand to her mouth and blew on it.

'He hit me, Meg! He hit me over and over with a gigantic cane.'

Meg gasped. She had never heard of anyone being allowed to hurt me in that way. I could tell her heart ached at the thought of her little Charlie being punished. We had a secret friendship that had grown. I was called Master Charles in front of my parents and she was Nanny, but it would quickly revert back to Meg and Charlie in the privacy of my room. She was like my second mother and I loved her as dearly as my parents. The feeling seemed warmly reciprocated.

'Why did he do that, Charlie? That's awful.'

'All I did was show a little mouse to Lily. It was hers and I was going to give it back but she cried and the teacher caught me with it.' The truth as I saw it.

Meg was indignant.

'That horrible little girl. I told you to be careful with her. She has something not right in her head.'

I nodded sagely. In hindsight, my Meg was obviously right.

'I'll go get my balm and put it on your wounds. It will make it feel much better.' She dashed back to her room and returned with a pot of ointment in her hands. 'Right. Show me where it hurts.'

I hesitated. Even though Meg had changed my diapers and bathed me most of my life, I had required her help no longer and had not shown my nudity for some time. I reddened.

'Master Charles. Drop your drawers. You have nothing to be ashamed of with me,' she remonstrated. 'Come and lie on the bed.'

She sat on the bed and patted her knee impatiently. I crawled over and whilst lying on my stomach, inched my trousers down. The cool air soothed my pink cheeks. She sucked in her cheeks sharply upon looking at the stripes and then set to work gingerly applying the soothing balm. She had a delicate touch and her soft sympathetic murmurings as she continued were music to my ears. She was so earnest in her desire not to cause me any more pain that I relaxed and enjoyed the whole sensation more than I realised. It was only when I felt something in my groin that I came to the horrid conclusion of what was happening to me. Meg noticed my body stiffen straight away and I hurriedly pulled my pants up whilst she watched bemused. She was an earthy girl and thought nothing of it, but, demurring to my embarrassment, she excused herself and left the room.

Burning at both ends, I was left to consider how wretched the day had been with the dawning realisation I had to face my classmates tomorrow.

Meg and Jack

The sun blazed merrily above me whilst I took the arboreous walk towards school. The peaceful leaves danced gracefully around me, almost begging me to climb their trunks. But I walked the mile to school determined not to be distracted. I was a soldier who had experienced pain like no other, and, with my chin jutted out and my chest puffed, I was prepared to become a man. My father would be proud to call me his son. I had erred, this was true. But I had taken my punishment and now it was time to move on and put it all behind me. The sooner this day passed the better.

Meg had offered me an old nappy to pad my bottom for sitting on the class chair. But, being the man that I was, I declined. Pain was what I deserved and it would be good for me, I thought stoically, imagining myself in full army regalia standing proudly on a mountain with the wind sweeping through my hair. No Fenton would EVER lower themselves to returning to a nappy when times were tough. I sniffed. We were made of sterner stuff.

So I strutted to school and proudly ignored the whispering of the girls as they glanced over at me. I showed the boys the red marks as they oohed and aahed at my seemingly cavalier attitude. I regaled my friends with the thrashing I had received, whipping them into a frenzy about the monster that was Mr Brown and how I had barely flinched when he had beaten me. Mr Brown transformed into a spitting horned demon with rotting foul breath, who, try as he might, could not break my spirit.

They swallowed it. And I had transformed to hero status. I was in full swing when regretfully Mrs Pompour rang the bell to start class. They patted me on the back with admiration and we walked to our seats.

I eyed the rigid seat with some concern. Now that Master Charles Braggart Fenton had spun his piece, there was no turning back. If I hadn't been such a blabbermouth, I could have sat on the seat and let people know how much it hurt. But now, I was considered impervious to pain, and a rock. The slightest sound would lower my standings that I had built up to so covetously. Clenching my teeth together I dropped cautiously down onto the seat and held my breath. I dared not utter a word, knowing my friends were watching with bated breath and praying that before long the lesson would start so their attention would be placed elsewhere. My prayers were answered and Mrs Pompour tapped the blackboard to begin.

I quietly breathed out and surreptitiously wriggled my buttocks from side to side throughout the lesson.

Leaning forward onto the desk helped but it needed to be discreet or I would be caught out. I looked at Lily and her sister from time to time and re-considered my thoughts of the fairer sex. They were far more trouble than I had originally thought and it might be best to steer clear of them for the time being.

Walking home after school, I considered the fastest way I could redeem myself in my father's eyes. Though I had a lot to do with Mr Walton our farm manager, I felt more at home with Jack the stable hand and instinctive-ly drew myself towards the stable to discuss with him – man to man – some potential ideas. He always made me feel welcome and let me currycomb the milder horses when my father wasn't looking. I didn't usually bother him straight after school but I was anxious for his wise counsel. Nearing the building I heard a feminine voice and moved to stealth mode to investigate inside.

I sneaked behind a hay bale and peered down to see Jack speaking to Meg and was about to halloo when I realised they seemed closer together than would seem proper. I watched interestedly. Jack was shifting a strand of Meg's hair back behind her ear.

'Meg, you look as handsome as ever. I didn't think I'd see you today and it made me so wild. I can't seem to keep my hands off you.'

'I can't be long, Jack. Charlie will be home soon and the mistress grows suspicious.'

My ears pricked up at the sound of my name.

Jack look deflated. 'So we'll just have a chat then?' he asked.

Meg hesitated. Jack noticed the indecision and pressed his advantage by kissing her lingeringly on the cheek and then her lips. I screwed my nose up at this disgusting display but kept watching.

'Well…I shouldn't really, Jack. We don't have much time,' she offered.

He nuzzled her neck and whispered in her ear. 'We best get moving then, love.' And he picked her up and placed her on a bed of hay. She giggled and quickly unbuttoned her pinafore to expose a milky white breast. Jack chortled with glee and began sucking her pink nipple making her moan. I sat dumbfounded wondering what to do. I thought only small infants needed breastfeeding and Jack was far too old to be doing that now. What a baby!

'Ohhh, Jack. You are my lovely man.'

'Aye. And you are my woman.'

'I am. I am your woman. I love you so much, so much.'

'Me too, pet.'

I watched the fumblings of the couple, feeling a growing sense of disquiet. Their lascivious fondling should not be witnessed by my sweet innocent soul but to tear myself away was impossible.

She grinned at Jack and proudly raised her mouth to

his to kiss him passionately. He returned the kiss and started dismantling his own trousers, scrabbling around before shoving them down past his buttocks. The dual white mounds of flesh winked at me as if they knew I was complicit with their actions. I felt a sudden shot of guilt and knew I had to leave. I wiggled backward, feeling with my toes for the exit and unable to tear my eyes away. In my haste to depart I managed to upset a tin of molasses sitting sneakily in the corner. The noise was calamitous.

'What the heck was that?' said Jack, standing up and searching in the direction of the noise. His standing had immediately exposed not only his excitement but the nakedness of my Meg. She clambered to reattach her clothing, smoothing down her petticoats and tying up her drawers. She hurriedly covered her breast and tidied her hair, pulling pieces of hay out anxiously. She stood next to Jack and spotted me immediately. Her face darkened.

'Get out here now, Charlie,' she ordered. Distractedly she glanced at Jack. 'Jack! Your trousers!'

Jack sighed and quickly pulled them up whilst giving his groin a sympathetic squeeze and cuddle.

I trounced out, with a smattering of molasses over my shoe. I was in trouble. Again. Only this time it was with my beloved Meg. I stared at the ground.

Jack and Meg looked at each other and then together

at me. They seemed at a loss as to what to say. Meg took control.

'What were you doing back there, Charlie? Were you spying on us?'

'No?'

'Well, it certainly seemed that way. What sort of nice young gentleman spies on other people?'

'I was just coming to visit Jack and talk with him.'

'You know you are supposed to go directly home after school. That was very naughty of you, Charlie. What would your father think?'

Oh no. Surely I wasn't to disillusion him twice in one week. I sighed.

'I was coming here because of Father. I wanted Jack to help me think of something nice to do for him. But when I came to him I saw you here and I didn't want to disturb you both.' I glanced up at them, noting Meg turn red. Interesting. Meg and Jack exchanged a speculative glance. Jack shrugged his shoulders and let Meg carry on.

Meg cleared her throat. 'What exactly did you see?'

'I saw Jack's naked bottom and your tit.'

Meg flustered while Jack stifled back a laugh. Meg's tits were lovely, there's no doubting that.

'Well, you shouldn't have! That was private stuff between me and Jack, Charlie. I am very annoyed with you and have a good mind to smack your bottom.'

We both knew this was a meaningless threat as she had never laid a hand on me before and she was well aware of how sore my bottom already was. I smirked.

'Don't you dare smirk at me, Charles Fenton! Don't think I won't do it. Or maybe I'll just go straight to your father and tell him not only were you spying but you wasted a whole tin of molasses and ruined your school shoes. What do you say now?' She looked triumphant.

My face soured. She had me right where she wanted me. Score one to Meg and zero to Charles. Jack watched on at the browbeating I was receiving. His admiration for Meg went up another step and he sat down on a bale of hay impressed at the show. Meg moved in for the kill.

'Well?'

'Well what?' I asked.

'Well, where's our apology? And while you're at it, wipe that surly look off your face. It is unbecoming for a young gentleman.'

My face darkened further and I scuffed the dirt floor with my sticky shoes. I was beaten. The only way to escape further castigation was to wave the white flag and surrender humbly. She crossed her arms and waited.

'Sorry,' I muttered.

'Pardon me? I didn't quite hear that.'

'Sorry.'

'Well now, Charlie. That's much more like it.' She

glanced at Jack and winked. 'I hope you have learnt your lesson for today and will keep your business to yourself and mind others theirs.' She drew close and ruffled my hair. 'Go on with you back in the house. I'll fix you a slice of the cook's apple pie and some juice.'

My countenance brightened and the mouth instantly filled with drool. Cook's apple pie was the most delicious thing I had ever tasted and one of my personal favourites to come out of her larder. I turned and ran towards the house.

'Mind you clean your shoes up before you go inside,' Meg shouted at my departing figure. Jack cuddled her from behind.

'I'm impressed, love. Remind me never to get into a fight with you, I'd surely lose every time.'

Meg reached up and touched his cheek tenderly. 'Aye. Well, I think you and me might have to cool it for a while. That was a close one.'

Jack threw his head back and laughed. Meg turned and frowned at him and then started to laugh too. Who was she kidding? He gave her a gentle smack on the bottom as she sashayed back to the house, with Jack admiring the view. He whistled to himself and returned back to work smiling.

I sat impatiently waiting at the kitchen table for my promised piece of pie. But I was vexed. Though the appearance of the pie was agonisingly slow it was a question mulling in my head that bothered me more and I had to speak it regardless of the danger.

'Meg.'

'Yes, Master Charles,' she responded, cutting deep into the apple pie and placing it on a plate in front of me.

'Can I ask you a question?' I probed.

'Depends what the question is.' She smiled at me.

I stuffed some pie in my mouth and chewed thoughtfully. 'Why aren't you and Jack married?'

Her shoulders sagged and the smile vanished. 'None of your business, Master Charles. Now eat your pie.'

But I was made of sterner stuff and didn't know when to give in. 'But there must be a reason. You seem to really love each other and Mother always says that people that love each other get married.'

'Your mother is right. People do get married when they are in love. But that is out of the question for Jack and me and I don't want to talk about it anymore.' She wiped her hands on her apron and then turned angrily back to me. 'And I don't want you pestering Jack about it either. You must promise me that you won't, Charles. Promise me!'

I stopped drinking my milk and solemnly nodded. This appeased her and she kissed the top of my head and pasted a smile on her face. 'Come on then, Master Charles, it's time for us to go through your homework.'

I grimaced and left the table, grabbing her hand and

squeezing it. She looked down at me with glistening eyes and smiled bravely before squeezing me back. It was all very confusing and sad at the same time, which I didn't like and I determined in my mind that I would make Meg happy again. I knew just the person to see when I could grab the chance to get away from prying eyes. She could fix anything.

The Visit

It was some days before I was able to make my escape without detection. Meg had accompanied my mother to town for some supplies and though they tried to include me in their journey I was able to masterfully dodge the bullet by appealing to their feminine nature. Screwing my face up in a monstrous manner at the idea of shopping with two women on such a fine sunny day caused them both to peal with laughter. They gathered their baskets and with a cheery wave in my direction, they got into the buggy and bade Jack to ride on.

I was free at last. I breathed a deep breath of fresh air and was king of the world. I plucked an apple from the kitchen and set off jauntily in the direction of my mother's good friend Magda.

My feelings were mixed towards her. She had shown nothing but goodwill and kindness to me but I shared my father's uneasiness at something that I couldn't explain. She was nothing at all like my Meg or any other lady I ever had occasion to speak with. She exuded a mystical power and secretiveness I wasn't privy to. I had vague recollections of her making me feel better when I was desperately unwell and my mother reminded me often how I owed my existence to her. In fact she called her my white mistress. It was a secret name that only she and I used in private whenever she spoke of her dear friend. She was my protector and adviser, an ally in need and enemy to my enemies. I was to show her nothing but respect and gratitude and heed her words, my mother commanded.

As I neared her cottage, my joviality evaporated. I had never visited her alone before and if it wasn't for my beloved Meg, I may have turned tail and headed back instead. But a Fenton is not a coward, so I drew breath and knocked resoundingly on her door.

'Master Charles! How delightful to see you on this glorious spring day. Do come in, my boy.'

I smiled weakly and walked past her into the passageway.

'I must have sensed you were coming as I have just pulled out a fresh loaf of bread and would love to share a piece with you.' She led me through to the kitchen where delicious smells wafted into my nose. I was instantly ravenous and drooling and watched impatiently as she carved a thick slice of warm bread and smothered it with butter and honey. She placed it on a plate in front of me and I attacked.

'Thank you, Mistress Williams,' I managed to spit out between bites of this most delicious ambrosia.

'Magda please, Master Charles. I'm sure your mother

won't mind a relaxing of the rules in etiquette. I do find it so…dreary at times.' She smiled at me secretly and poured me a large glass of milk.

I smiled back at her and drank heavily from the glass. The milk was sweet and cool. It was the perfect accompaniment for my bread and honey. She really was quite the cook. She sat quietly watching me as I gulped down my drink.

'How can I help you, Charlie? she asked, progressing to the pet name my Meg and I shared. I barely noticed and realised I had nearly forgotten what my initial goal had been. I regrouped my thoughts.

'Excuse me, please…Magda.' She nodded at the use of her name. 'But I just wanted to help my Meg with something, but it's strictly between you and me though. She wouldn't like me meddling.'

She waited patiently as I shuffled in the seat. 'And what may that be, Charlie?' she asked fondly.

'Well…I may have seen Meg and Jack kissing last week.' I reddened at the memory and stole a glance at Magda. She raised an eyebrow and looked straight back at me, causing me to drop my look to the table and mumble on. 'And Meg caught me looking. I thought I was in big trouble but thankfully Meg said she wouldn't tell about me spying.' Magda snorted but held her peace. 'But then she got upset when I asked her about them getting married and told me to mind my own business.'

'That was wise counsel from Meg.'

'But I want to know why she didn't want to talk about it. They would be a great husband and wife and they look so happy with each other. Why is she being so mean?'

Magda leaned forward and stared at me. I flinched under the attention but held my gaze.

'What makes you think you are entitled to such knowledge? And why should I tell you?' she asked.

I sat and thought for a minute.

'Because she has raised me from when I was a little baby and I don't like seeing her cry. I made her sad when I asked her and I want to make it better. If I don't know why she won't marry Jack, then I can't help make her happy again.'

'Sometimes, little man, there are some things that you can't help people with.'

'Even you?'

'Yes, even me. If I told you why they can't marry, it won't help Meg at all. There is nothing you can do about it.'

My curiosity surged. What deep secret could be stopping their true happiness? I had to know.

'Magda, please. I PROMISE I will never tell another soul, not even Mother. I just want to help her'

Magda studied me and saw my genuineness. She sighed and reached for one of my sticky hands. 'Meg and Jack can't marry, Charlie… Jack is already married.' I was thunderstruck. Jack had a wife?

'But before you get all high and mighty, Master Charles, listen to the rest of the story.' She settled back in her chair. 'Many years ago before you were born, Jack was married to a local girl called Rebecca. They were both very young when they married, but deeply in love and wanting to start a family together. Rebecca was blessed soon after and they had a tiny boy called George. They loved him and Jack would regale your mother with stories about how strong his boy was going to be. They had visions of George helping his father at the Fenton Estate and becoming a wealthy farmer one day. Rebecca was a most devoted mother and barely let the little baby go unless it was straight into Jack's arms. They made wonderful parents, just like yours are. But it wasn't meant to be.

One morning, Rebecca woke up and discovered that during the night whilst breastfeeding little George, she had accidentally fallen asleep and smothered the infant, killing him. It drove her mad; she stopped eating, bathing, showing any interest in the outside world. Jack tried to manage, refusing any suggestion from do-gooders wanting to take her away. But he had to in the end, when he came home and found her putting her wrists onto hot coals and burning herself badly. She was packed up and sent to Northampton General the very next day and she hasn't been seen since. Jack used to visit her regularly but it only made her worse so they recommended he stay away. The doctors there have tried every therapy known to mankind, but without success. She's an old woman in a young woman's body who has lost her soul to a world you and I daren't care to enter.'

I sat transfixed at the story. Visions of the crazy people filled my head immediately. Poor Jack was tied forever to a mad woman. I felt a deep despair at their tragic tale. No wonder Meg didn't want me to talk to Jack! It would have saddened him greatly. How awful.

'What can be done about it? This is so sad,' I asked Magda.

'Nothing can be done. The vows of marriage are sacred. He will just have to wait and pray the madness ends. So now you see why he can never marry Meg. It would be only the death of his wife that would allow it, and no man could ever ask for that on their conscience, no matter how unwell Rebecca is.'

I nodded and started to cry. Magda watched me for a while before walking around the table to stand behind me and put her arms around me. She uttered soothing words I couldn't hear but I realised their gentle intent. After some time I ceased crying and blew my nose on her handkerchief.

'Fear not, Master Charles. These things have a way of working out in the end.'

She showed me to her door and I walked glumly home, not noticing the thoughtful look in her eye as she turned back into the kitchen. Jack had suffered for far too long she mused.

Northampton General Lunatic Asylum

The night seeped around the building standing stark-ly on the field. It was slightly foggy and damp with a mossy hint in the air. The stars and the moon seemed apathetic on this cool, dank night. The hospital alone was imperious to it all and held its ground as chief probationer of mad souls. It gave hope and despair to all that drew towards it. Staff and residents on first sight of this building would shudder uncontrollably at what scenes might lie inside. But onwards towards the rather antediluvian door they walked, for inside lay a slight chance for redemption and a better future. However slender and tenuous it may be, it was still another opening in a narrowing world. With a rising fortification of shadowy despair, they gritted their teeth and got on with it.

Magda considered the asylum in front of her. The structure had no evil forebodings to her. She had visit-ed on a number of occasions and could only look upon the patients as unwell and afraid. Not too uncommon in the outside world either really. Some of them she had assisted to a full recovery and some of them she had put into the institution by her own hand. But the latter deserved every torment that lay with them now and regret for their actions had become their own bitter pill. She wasted no sympathy on them. Magda slowly drifted past each room peering in the small porthole of the doors. She had full access to all rooms thanks to a spell performed on the guard earlier to relieve him of his keys. When he woke, he had no recollection of her and spent hours hunting for his lost keys. It was only after he had searched everywhere twice that he surrendered and went to confess to the head matron. He stood in front in her in pusillanimous shame as the caustic vitriol fell out in staccato sentences advising him of his responsibilities to the security of the establishment. After she had finished, she handed him the spare set and dismissed him from the office.

The visiting hours were over. All the residents were tucked into their chambers blissfully loaded up with antimony tartrate and calomel. Some had gloves carefully secured at the wrists in an attempt to reduce self-harm. Some wore them because it made them feel secure. Others were wide awake as no chemical could nullify their mania. Magda slowed at the sight of one man enthusiastically drawing on his wall. She could just make out one line. 'Like shades in love and death's oblivion lost.' It stirred her and she repeated it to herself so it would be remembered and revisited later. She noted the man's body shape but was frustrated at not seeing his face. She consoled herself that she would visit him next time and learn more.

Dragging herself away from his room, she carried on searching for Rebecca. The hospital staff at Northampton were oblivious to her presence. They walked down the corridors routinely checking on their patients. During the night shift the sounds they heard were familiar in their own evocative way but no longer disturbing, and Magda was mere shadows and whispers in their minds.

Rebecca's room was near the end by the communal lounge. Magda looked in and could see she was sitting cross-legged on the floor swaying and chanting. She quietly opened the locked door with her brass key from her pocket and walked in. Rebecca was gaunt. The hospital gown she wore hung desultory on her shoulders. Her hair was neatly plaited down her back and had been shampooed by one of the nurses. Her fingernails were trimmed short and clean and she attended the shower bath therapy twice weekly. Yet, with such care and devotion, she maintained an air of abandonment. Her arms were heavily scarred and Magda noticed bruising around her neck. She had recently attempted to strangle herself but fell unconscious before finishing the deed. They had begun to force feed her in a last-ditch effort to keep her alive. Her collarbone jutted out and the leathery skin sank between each rib. Her eyes were dead and her hands flew like spiders in the air. She was a dreadful sight to behold and Magda wept a tear looking at her. She sat down on the floor in front of her.

'Rebecca,' she whispered softly, touching her on the knee.

Rebecca looked at her knee and continued swaying. She went quiet.

'Rebecca. Look at me. I am the white mistress.'

Rebecca looked up at Magda and stopped swaying. She stared curiously at her face, which seemed vaguely familiar. Her hand jerked upwards and twitched towards Magda. Magda held her hand and brought it to her heart.

'Look at me, Rebecca. I am here. Feel my heartbeat. I am alive. I am your white mistress and I have come to help you.'

Rebecca placed her hand flat on Magda's chest and closed her eyes. She focussed on the thump-thump of Magda's heart and became soothed. She smiled and opened her eyes again.

'Good, good. You hear me now. I am in front of you. I know you, what you were and what you have become.'

Rebecca stopped smiling. She looked deeply into Magda's eyes.

'You have suffered, my love. You have suffered more than any woman should bear. The loss of a child has taken you to the darkest Hell and bound you to it.'

A small tear welled in Rebecca's eye and tipped down her cheek. She remained mute.

'I am here to free you. To take away the pain you have submitted yourself to. You have punished yourself enough and have earned your liberty. George is waiting for you. He wants you to join him in the spirit world. He knows you have been trying for so very long now. Trying and failing. But you have never given up. Never. You are strong in your love for him. He knows that. He has always known that. He is your blood.'

The tears streamed down her face as she listened attentively. She nodded.

'I, the white mistress, release you. I can give you the power to be with him. If you wish to end this misery, you may have it now. Tonight and forever… Is this what you wish?'

Her face shone with hope and she nodded again with surety. Magda nodded slowly back at Rebecca and squeezed her hand. She reached into her pocket and produced a small glass vial with a purple-coloured liquid inside. She handed it to Rebecca.

'Mind carefully. Once you drink this, there is no turning back. Think of what you are doing.'

Rebecca took the vial and smiled. 'Thank you, white mistress.' She emptied the vial and handed it back to Magda.

Magda smiled sadly back and helped her to her bed. She kissed her forehead and whispered to her.

'Go to him, little sparrow. He waits no longer.' Then she left the room and locked the door. She muttered, 'Like shades in love and death's oblivion lost,' and then disappeared into the night.

Jack's Loss

I heard Jack's anguished yell the next day. Being fleet of foot I arrived before the household staff and came across Jack clutching a white piece of paper given to him from the hospital orderly. Tears were streaming down his face and he collapsed to his knees moaning. I hesitated, then ran to him and tried to hug him. He shuddered, then seeing me, grabbed me with a wild strength, holding me so tightly I could barely breathe.

I was so upset at his outburst that I began crying too without really knowing why. Meg came running in, followed closely by the cook and my mother.

'Jack. What has happened?' my mother asked softly.

Jack stared mournfully at her, his eyes bloodshot and puffy. The suffering in his face caused her to step back. He raised his right hand holding the sodden letter out to her. She stiffened and came towards him to take the letter and read it. We all stared at her wondering what had caused him so much misery. She sighed handing the letter to Meg.

'I'm so sorry, Jack,' she said, touching his back gently. 'She was a good woman. May her troubled soul rest in peace.'

My eyes widened and I frowned, guessing at the contents with horror. Was my visit to Magda in any way connected to the sudden demise of his wife? Had I unintentionally provoked some ancient curse and wished her dead without realising? The timing was surely more than coincidental and I shivered, feeling cold to the core. I wanted my mother and managed to wrestle out of Jack's arms to race into hers. She hugged me sweetly, mystified at my abject dismay. How darling her son was to be so sad for his friend Jack. She kissed my head and cuddled me more. She loved my sensitive spirit.

The guilt sat thickly inside my gut. I had a hairy, black spider crawling inside me, reaching into my limbs and weaving threads of darkness around my organs. Why did I have to be so nosy? If only I could leave well enough alone for once instead of sticking my fat beak into it. I would have given anything to have the power to undo what was done but it was too late now. I glumly stared over at Meg as she read the letter. She padded over to Jack and cuddled him, oblivious of the eyes watching.

'My poor Jack. My poor Jack. I'm sorry, my love,' she cooed into his ear, nestling his head deep into her bosom. He burrowed in seeking sanctuary whilst sobbing. I peeked at my mother with interest to see how she would react to this open display of affection. She seemed unperturbed. I guessed she had known all along about their relationship but had remained discreet about their privacy. I hugged her again with love.

My father had been in the office and was unaware of the drama unfolding in the courtyard. It was only when my mother sent the cook to inform him that he arrived and stared in confusion at Jack and Meg embracing with tears.

'What's happened, Elizabeth?' he asked quietly in her ear. She whispered to him with me still entangled around her legs. He nodded occasionally and rubbed his chin with his fingers. He looked to the couple and back at her in askance. She nodded sadly as it dawned on his face. He stood thinking before approaching the couple awkwardly.

'I'm sorry to hear the bad news, Jack. Dreadful business, dreadful. Rebecca was unwell for an interminable amount of time and we all know how much you cared for her.' He watched Jack unfurl from Meg to stand and shake Charles' hand.

'Thank you, Master Charles. I appreciate your kind words.' He rummaged in his pocket for a handkerchief to wipe his eyes and blow his nose.

'I understand that you would like some time off to attend to the funeral arrangements. We would be honoured to assist in returning her back to the estate and burying her next to your son George.'

Jack's eyes filled again and he jutted his chin out and

nodded. Then he turned and walked back to his cottage. Meg made to go after him but a sober glance from Jack stopped her in her tracks. He stared right through her with soulless eyes and shook his head. A sob caught in her throat and she falteringly turned back towards the house with my mother. I was at a loss as to what to do next so I clasped my mother's hand and followed her. My father beckoned to the hospital orderly to come inside and wait whilst he wrote a note arranging the return of Rebecca's body to Jack's cottage. Silence filled the courtyard.

Rebecca's return

Rebecca's body arrived the next day on a hearse pulled by two black horses. The funeral had been arranged in three days to allow Rebecca's family to arrive. The coffin was cautiously unloaded and carried into Jack's cottage where the table lay bare waiting. I watched from my window, peering at the black drape covering his windows. He was dressed in black and bowed his head as the coffin passed him.

I had never seen a dead person before and I was concerned that Mother wished for us to pay our respects to Jack and his departed wife Rebecca. Her matter of fact tone with regards to viewing the body stunned me into mute submission and I had nodded dumbly when she advised we would visit after supper. And now that time had come.

'Meg?'

'Yes, Charlie.'

'Meg, what do dead people look like?' I asked timidly.

She thought for a while, aware I was studying her like an eagle. I was shrewd about any dishonesties she was hoping to expel from her mouth. I wanted the clear bare truth to prepare me for what lay ahead.

'Well, Charlie, they look the same as when they were alive, just not moving or breathing.'

I needed more information. It was too simple. I waited.

'In fact, some relations have been known to take photographs of their loved ones as if they were still alive as a memorial of their passing.'

Now really, she had gone too far with that one. I was sure that was a falsehood. She noticed my doubting face and straightened defensively.

'It's true! I have seen the photographs myself. They sit them in chairs and paint their eyelids to make them appear alive. Ask your mother if you don't believe me. It is quite the going thing to do.' She sniffed.

I narrowed my eyes. 'Don't mind if I do, Meg.' And I trotted out of the room to search for my beloved mother, leaving Meg biting her lip. I found her in the kitchen, preparing some tea cakes to take to Jack.

'Mother? Is it true that people sit their dead loved ones in chairs and take photographs of them?' I asked her. She frowned at me.

'Who told you that?'

'Meg.'

'Well, she shouldn't be filling your head with such things. But strange as it sounds, my son, it is true. It is a sign of respect and love to have them forever captured in their last portrait.'

Meg was right again. I should have known better by now.

'Is Jack going to do that?' I asked.

'No. Jack has chosen to leave her in the coffin. That is where we are going now.'

No escape. She carried her basket of cakes over her left arm and held my hand tightly in her right. She had correctly identified my unwillingness to visit and was not tolerating any mutiny. I was going to do my duty whether I liked it or not. And I liked it not one bit.

The smell assailed my nostrils as soon as we entered the cottage. The cloying sweetness from the wave of flowers that nearly buried Rebecca, could not quite camouflage the rotten meat smell emanating from her body. I was queasy immediately and had to fight the rising gorge of bile coming up my throat. The windows held no relief as they were blackened and shut tight. There was a very real tangible presence of death in the air and I hated it. My mother pretended there was nothing wrong and made sympathetic chat with Jack whilst presenting her cakes. We both secretly dreaded that he might insist we stay for tea and were relieved when he seemed content just to listen and nod quietly. I needed a distraction.

I looked at Jack's clock and was puzzled. I had recently learnt how to tell the time and something was definitely not right with his. This was his Nanny's clock, passed down through the family with the greatest of pride to the eldest son. He had let me, on the times I was being very good, turn the lever for winding the clock up. I had developed a possessive interest therefore in its maintenance and felt almost offended to see it stuck on quarter past nine. Clearly it needed attention. I cleared my throat.

'Excuse me, Jack. You haven't wound your nanny's clock today.'

Jack looked uncomfortable and glanced at my mother. She gave me her stern look.

'Hush, Charles. Mind your manners.'

'But… It's not the correct time,' I protested.

'What did I just say to you?' she growled. I scowled but kept my peace looking at something else that perturbed me. Jack had also covered his mirror with a sheet. Now what was that all about? I stared at it with confusion written all over my face. This wasn't right either. Why would you cover a mirror? The whole purpose of a mirror is to be able to see yourself in it and he had made that very hard to do indeed. It really wouldn't do in my mind at all. I turned to my mother and opened my mouth to form the question. My mother is the dearest, gentlest and most softly spoken woman, but the glare she gave me at that precise point in time was strong enough to block the words from coming out of my mouth. I literally was not able to let them out, even if I wanted to, due to the force of her glower. She had seen me studying the mirror and had correctly guessed what I was thinking. I realised then that self-preservation was more important and anyway, I could always ask Meg later. She knew everything. I closed my mouth and remained silent.

It would not have been seemly to leave as soon as we had entered, so my mother politely sat and battled on as a mark of respect to her dear stable hand. I was soon in no fit state to speak anymore, fearing if I opened my mouth the vomit would gush out onto his floor. I stared morbidly at Rebecca instead and was aghast to see a fly walking over her face, exploring her eyelid with its long black tongue. It buzzed quietly, sometimes hovering over her before returning to inspect her corpse again. I remained mesmerised as the fly circled to and fro on her lifeless cheek before defecating a little black spot on her cheek bone. What a foul and depraved thing to see. I was torn by the fact that Rebecca's dignity duly owed in death was demeaned by the dirtiest insect on the planet. The same insect that flew merrily and fed from piles of dung and rotting food scraps had just tainted the sad and lonely face of Jack's wife. I should have indignantly swept the nasty little beast away and cleaned the soiled spot but I remained bolted to the chair. There was no honour in my cowardice but I soothed my sickly guilt by mentally cursing and threatening the fly with all manner of things. As usual, my imaginings were vivid and bloodthirsty and soon I was sidetracked towards fighting a duel with the fly monster that had developed into a six-foot beast. We had moved onto a pirate ship with silver-sparked cutlasses and thick snake-like ropes hanging from the sea-battled masts. I had the black winged monster at my mercy, little pieces of wings breaking into dust with every touch of my weapon. That fly monster was a fool and a cad for soiling Rebecca and he shall never be able to do it again. As I brought the cutlass down for the final death my reverie was shattered.

'Charles! Charles. We are going now. Give your respects to Jack.' My mother was looking at me strangely and I guessed correctly the battle had played out on my expression. I quickly glanced at Rebecca's face and was warmed to see the fly had gone. I was the victor.

'Charles!' Jack had even woken from his gloom and was looking at me in askance whilst mother reprimanded. I reddened and hurriedly walked to Jack and shook his hand, muttering my condolences. He accepted the handshake and returned back to his darkness. We left the cottage and stepped back into the fresh, sweet sunshine with mutual relief. I hurried up to find Meg. She was busying herself with the mourning clothes for both me and her to wear at the funeral. I had been so excited about this shadowy ceremony that I had badgered my parents to let Meg take me until they'd relented. It was not the done thing for the master and mistress to attend the funeral ceremony, but they had kindly allowed Jack use of our coach to travel to the cemetery behind the funeral hearse. Since I was the master's son, I had the privilege of riding in the coach with him, as long as Meg would be responsible for my welfare. My mother had warned me that it would be a sombre and sad event but I refused to listen and could only see the coach ride into town with my sweet Meg and the food that would be provided after. The downside was wearing the suit that now lay, freshly ironed, on a hanger. I groaned at my sacrifice to comfort before remembering why I had come to see Meg. I had questions to ask.

'Meg, why is Jack's clock not wound up?'

Meg sat on my bed and sighed.

'Jack has stopped the clock at the time it was felt his Rebecca passed away. It is a sign of respect to her death.'

This didn't really make sense to me, but I let it slide.

'And Jack covered his mirror. Why did he do that?'

Meg paused, not really sure if she should tell me. I crossed my arms.

'It is believed that if a dearly departed is by an uncovered mirror, their soul can become trapped within it. The sheet is a protection against that happening.'

My jaw dropped. This concept filled my head with images of her soul swirling around the mirror, pushing at the surface to try and escape. I wasn't sure if Jack had covered his in time and on reflection, I was CERTAIN I remembered a slight tapping behind the sheet when we were visiting. I was horrified and quickly hid my head under the pillow on my bed, scared that the soul was locked in forever. Meg heaved the pillow away exposing my terrified face.

'Charlie! Get out from under there. You'll smother yourself in that cushion.' She stroked my face and kissed my cheeks.

'Oh Meg, it's awful. When we were visiting Jack I swear I heard Rebecca's soul tapping on the mirror. She's caught in there and she can't get out. She'll be trapped forever!' I groaned.

Meg squeezed me into a warm cuddle. 'It's all right, Charlie. She wanted to leave this world, so I just know she wouldn't try looking into any mirrors. She was a clever lady.' She smiled wretchedly and kissed me again. 'She's at peace now, Charlie. Her soul has departed.'

I calmed down, listening to Meg's wise counsel. Her words made sense to me but nevertheless I would be giving that mirror a wide berth from now on. My mind stewed on this information, while Meg spoke again.

'Probably best you don't tell your parents what I just told you. They might not like me telling you this sort of thing. All right then, Charlie?'

I nodded and considered the strange day I had experienced. Now only the funeral remained.

The funeral

The morning of the funeral was cold and drizzly. My mother had ordered mine and Meg's mourning clothes from Jay's in London. I was obliged to wear my best dark suit with black trim and to keep clean and quiet. A small task but odious as my suit scratched and irked me but I didn't complain as I knew the day would be fascinating and end with a pile of delicious food baked by our cook.

Rebecca's family had all arrived and had seen both her and Jack at the cottage prior to the coffin lid being closed. I was grateful not to see her face again and struggled daily with deliberately sweeping her flyblown image from my memory. Jack had been putting money aside for Rebecca's funeral long before I knew of her existence and he proudly refused any offer of help from my parents. They insisted, however, that he take a month paid sabbatical before returning to work and arranged a temporary man to take care of the horses.

As the family squeezed into the cottage, they dutifully admired the richness of the coffin, whispering later how much Jack must have loved Rebecca by the obvious expense involved in her final dwelling. The brass knobs alone would have cost three months' wages each they calculated avidly. There were nods of admiration as they ran their hands down the deeply burnished oak that had been presented so superbly.

The voices dropped further as they speculated about the possible cause of Rebecca's demise. Many knew where she had been residing for the last nine years and were keen to impart that information to the few who didn't. The gossiper was usually rewarded with a delicious expression of horror that Jack's wife had died in the asylum. She was only skin and bone according to a cousin who had witnessed the body before the coffin was sealed. They further fed the scandal by whispering titbits about possible suicidal involvement causing many to piously pray for her damned soul to be redeemed. The official cause of death was dysentery which explained her emaciated body, though many raised an eyebrow at that. It was only respect for the dead that swallowed further words being aired.

Jack was oblivious to the clucking behind him as he sat awkwardly next to Rebecca's mother and father. They were strangers to me, but since they were sitting right in front I knew they must be significant. I sat next to Meg and pulled her for information.

'Who are those people next to Jack?' I whispered in her ear.

Meg sniffed. 'That's Mr and Mrs Done, Rebecca's parents. Not that they were very good at it. When

Rebecca became unwell they never attempted to visit her.'

'What was wrong with her?' I continued with my façade of ignorance. 'Why didn't they visit her? Was she contagious?'

Meg collected herself and fixed me with a no-nonsense stare. 'You always like to know everything, don't you, Charlie? But you can't always get what you want. It's enough for you to know that she was sick and now she is dead. Leave it at that.'

I quailed at the telling-off and sat docilely in my chair for the remainder of the service. For the most part I dutifully joined in singing the psalms and reading the prayer book. On the rare occasion that I wandered into my dreamland, I was quickly returned with a pinch on the arm by Meg. At the end of the service we trailed out behind the pallbearers loading the coffin carefully into the hearse.

The hearse was the first I had ever seen. It was jet black and protected from the elements with polished glass, which also allowed clear view of the dearly departed. The horse was brushed to a fanatical extent, gleaming black with a festoon of feathers adorning its head. It was a modest hearse but the horse put our own stable horses to shame. I admired its blackened polished hooves and handsome black head that reared and whinnied with the sudden influx of people.

Flowers were surrounding the coffin, freshly cut and fragrant, to accompany Rebecca to her grave. The mutes had been standing guard outside during the service draped in black sashes and holding long sticks covered in black crepe. They were hired to be the protectors of the dead and held this contract with great dignity, accompanying the coffin with the most solemn of expressions. Unbeknownst to Jack, however, they had secretly warded off the cold with intermittent nips of brandy and, as the service was particularly long, they were the epitome of concentrated melancholy.

Our coach followed behind the hearse. Rebecca's parents accompanied us and were in awe of my family's ordinary coach. I was introduced to Mr and Mrs Done, who expressed a servile gratitude at letting them use the master's coach and for gracing them with my presence. I puffed up a bit and sat slightly more regally on my seat. We all piled in and enjoyed a brief interval of warmth and comfort until we reached the outskirts of town. As this point, the coach emptied and we walked behind the near-staggering mutes through the streets, noting the respectful lowering of bared heads as we passed. Any exchanges of goods and services ceased as we were observed and only recommenced once there was a considerable distance between us and the merchants. It was only when we had cleared the town that we could again embark and travel on to the cemetery.

The mutes regathered themselves for the final obligation they held. They sucked in the cool air and shook their heads to clear the mind and put all their energy into making their most despondent faces. Any future employment would be riding on the last impression they gave. A basset hound could have delivered no better. Their final ponderous steps to the gravesite were humble and sober, and one could nearly believe it was one of their own darling wives that was now lowered into the ground.

Jack plucked a long-stemmed flower and whispered lightly into the bloom. He then kissed it softly and threw it on the coffin. He turned to avoid the inquisitive eyes and looked down at the tombstone of his son George. He stood in bowed silence staring at the inscription whilst we watched deferentially. It was only the noise of someone coughing that broke his contemplation and saw him briskly return to his carriage leaving us to follow.

It was my first funeral and as we filed back I took one last look at the grave-diggers piling the dirt onto Rebecca's coffin. A slight movement on my left shifted my attention and I was alarmed to be held in the full stare of Magda, who had privately joined the ceremony. She looked deep into my soul still battling with the secret guilt and smiled sadly. She blew me a kiss and disappeared, and I wondered if I had even seen her in the first place. Wisely, I kept my own counsel but shuddered as I mused, running to grab Meg's hand for security. She squeezed my hand and promised me a big wedge of bacon and egg pie with apple cider once we got back to the house. It was my reward for being such a good boy. How little she knew.

New beginnings

My education continued and I had ripened and outgrown my little country school. My father decided it was time to cease and desist the mollycoddling of his heir. I saw immediately through his terse babble-jabber that he was really heartbroken at my forthcoming farewell, but I displayed a suitably stoic face and united front when he broke the news to my mother.

Because the most suitable school was Rugby just east of Warwickshire, the only most practical solution was to be a boarder there. With railway lines rapidly winding their way through the countryside, the traverse to London would be simple with regards to expanding my horizon and future edification. I had promised that I would be coming home for holidays without exception to ease the anguish of my mother. Secretly I welcomed the development especially with the added comfort that my good friend Henry would accompany me. At times, though I would never admit it to the open air, the dedicated affection and love slathered onto me caused me to scarper with false gaiety to the fields. I loved my parents dearly yet my wings wanted to stretch and fly and I had barely been allowed to peek over the nest. My mother was beside herself.

'What if he should become poorly, Charles? What of that? We nearly lost him and it was only the grace of God and Magda's contribution that kept him on this green Earth.'

'That was eight years ago, Elizabeth. He has been the most hale and robust creature to walk on this land since. You worry far too much.'

'And you worry too little. I can't risk losing him. He means so much to me.'

'And me also, my dear.' Charles tenderly touched her face and kissed her. 'But we have to let him live and see the world. It's precisely because we love him that we must let him go. Surely you can see that.'

Elizabeth considered this and grudgingly realised it to be true. Her heart ached at the thought and she had tried repeatedly and most unsuccessfully to change young Charles' thinking that a private governess would be much more fun than school. He had a bar of pure stubbornness in him, which she conceded probably came from her. The discussions became more and more desperate with her son, with both sides fiercely nego- tiating and pushing their agenda. Secretly she knew he was right and if she was really being honest, there was a small spark of admiration and pride for her son at his determination. But she ached at the thought of him leaving and so turned her maternal attack onto her husband, who proved to be of equal calibre. Now that she was resigned to the fact, she determined that she would get Magda to concoct another herbal tonic to settle her nerves. She hadn't forgotten Magda's repeated predictions that Charles was to be famous and a name to live forever. She had never been wrong before and Elizabeth trusted Magda unreservedly. This decided, she sighed and kissed her husband back.

'Yes. I do see. I just find it so hard to let go. Of course you are right as usual, Charles, and I must learn to listen more to your wise counsel.' She sniffed. 'Will you be going with him to Rugby?'

'No. I don't have to catch the train back to London until the following week. Henry will travel with him and Jack will take them both directly to the school. They will be expecting the boys late evening and have arranged supper on their arrival.' Charles kissed Elizabeth's furrowed brow. 'He's a Fenton, my darling. He will not only survive Rugby, he will flourish and become a man of worth. I was a pupil there and it did me no injury.'

Elizabeth snorted. 'Yes, Charles darling, but don't forget how close to danger you like to dangle.'

Charles laughed, remembering wistfully the escapades he'd enjoyed whilst at school. If only Elizabeth knew half of the stories; though perhaps not, she would never let their son go. He patted himself on the back at the foresight of self-censorship. Lizzie, free spirit that she was, would be shocked at the 'teachings' that went on. Ah, the mystery of womanhood he mused, looking at his wife.

'The only injury I receive in my life is when I cross you and that is a danger I enjoy and cherish every day.' He gazed fondly at Elizabeth, who responded by tweaking his ear. 'Ow! How succinctly you prove my point.'

While my parents were discussing my leaving home, I was busy helping Meg pack my luggage to head to Rugby. I say that I was helping, but she appeared not to appreciate the essential items I felt needed to come on the trip.

'Charlie! You are not taking that tattered old slingshot or Mr Dumples. I have already told you that, and don't think I can't see what's happening now. I have eyes in the back of my head, Charles Augustus Fenton, and you'd better mind that or there will be trouble!'

I cuddled Mr Dumples affectionately, hoping he hadn't heard the evil things Meg had said. He was my secret friend that had grown up with me and had been bought for me when I had recovered from my illness. His fur was ratty and one of his ears had been chewed off by Mr Walton's working dog when I'd inadvertently left him in the field one day, but to me he was a warrior. I had told him all of my secrets late at night when we snuggled in together at bedtime and it was impossible to think my time had come to say goodbye once and for all. Meg could sense my outrage.

'I'm telling you right now that if you take Mr Dumples

to school with you, all the other big boys will laugh and call you a big sissy. Is that what you want? None of them will be bringing a soft toy with them, I can promise you that. Only little poopy babies do,' she taunted me mercilessly, snatching Mr Dumples and firmly placing him on my bed.

'He stays here. And I'll make sure to give him a good washing so when you come back he'll be all clean for you.'

I grimaced for poor Mr Dumples. I remembered the bath nights when I had to succumb to Meg's determined scrubbing. His other ear will be off before she's done with him.

'I don't like it,' I grumbled.

'Tough. It's the way it is and will be. Now pass me those brown socks.'

I sullenly passed the socks, pocketing my slingshot with the plan to pack it later once eagle-eyes had gone. I trounced out of the room to show I wasn't going to 'help' anymore, a fact she seemed to accept quite happily. I headed outside to climb the oak tree one more time and practised with my slingshot.

My thoughts were all directed to tomorrow. Henry and I would leave at first light and my excitement was boundless at the thought of meeting new people and making lifelong friends. And so, while Meg was packing my trunk, I was already half a world away and dreaming of my adventures to be.

The trip

'I've heard that their cricket team is one of the finest in our country's schools,' Henry excitedly said as he bundled into the coach. I had already bid my parents a tearful farewell and watched Henry do likewise with his. He shared my exhilaration and after waving madly at his parents as they faded into the distance, his mind was instantly removed to our destination.

'Tom Pathurst came from Rugby. He played for Warwickshire right up until he lost his eye in last season's match. Gory stuff it was. Had his eye socket shattered with Langdon's speed ball in the first innings. My father told me all about it. He said they carried him off on a stretcher, with his face covered in blood. Apparently the doctors had to remove his eyeball completely because it was all speckled with bits of bone. He looks like a pirate now with his eye patch. He's just missing the parrot and the wooden peg.'

I laughed. Trust Henry to turn a horrible situation into a comedy with his puerile slant on the situation. I remembered the story. My father had read the article out to me from the newspaper after breakfast one morning. At the time, my stomach had turned when I heard of the horrific injury, envisioning Pathurst cradling his eye in his hand and thinking how I would have reacted if it had been me. Even my delusions of grandeur wouldn't allow me to be that courageous and the dread of losing part of my sight had turned me cold. Langdon visited him in the hospital every day and was now considering leaving the sport altogether. He probably would have been dropped anyway considering the loss of pace in his bowling attack.

'I guess that would mean that there is now an opening for you, Henry.'

Henry's face lit up at the potential before spotting my grinning face. A more avid and skilled cricketer could not be found, though his academia was somewhat dusty. Between us, we made the perfect lad and I knew with my intelligence and his striking physical athleticism that we would be a formidable match to any challenge laid down. Not that my own cricketing skills were too shabby, especially after the hours spent bowling and batting each summer on the greens. I just wasn't in the same league as Henry.

After a while our stomachs began growling, especially as the basket Henry's parents had provided for the trip was jostling gently next to us and whispers of delicious scents were sneaking through the wicker. We implored Jack to stop for lunch and tempted his sense of duty by listing the food luxuriating inside the hamper. It would have been an injustice to the cook to let such delicacies sit unloved and ignored in the dark. Besides we were growing lads and were constantly in a state of insatiability. Jack complied and we settled down happily to a fine lunch of pigeon pie filled with juicy pieces of meat and spiced with nutmeg and coarse black pepper. We quenched our thirst with cool lemonade and finished with buttery shortbread and ginger gems. The hamper still beckoned with unwrapped parcels of food but our stomachs were fit to burst and we ruefully closed the lid with the promise of a revisit later. It was with a more ponderous step that we returned to the coach and continued on our journey. The swaying and jostling of the carriage caused us both to regret our gluttony and we sat quietly holding our bellies.

It felt like forever before we reached our destination and with our digestion restored by then, we held a more energetic interest in our new residence. Passing through the school gates we were both gratified to see the expansive playing fields littered with exuberant schoolboys playing football. Henry was fair twitching to race out and join our new chums, but first we had to see the matron, who showed us where to put our trunks to be unpacked.

Each room had twelve beds, which held boys of all ages, from the juniors such as us and the praepostor. The praepostor was the senior boy in each room who was given the responsibility of ensuring we maintained a gentleman's behaviour and discipline suitable of a Rugby man. His experience as a leader for young boys would teach him to lead in the adult world and we benefitted from having a fellow student to call upon for guidance. For this security we repaid his beneficence by taking turns to fag. A fag would be asked to do menial tasks like cleaning or collecting supplies or even sending messages to fellow praepostors. These tasks were done with the knowledge that one day we too would be able to call out in a querulous manner at whim and we all harboured a dark desire to wield a strong arm on that auspicious day.

Our praepostor was there to welcome us on our first day. He was a thin, slight, young man with wavy hair and intelligent eyes. He walked up and introduced himself.

'Charles Dodgson is the name. You will c-call me Dodgson.'

'I'm called Charles too. Charles Fenton. May I present you with my friend Henry Felldon?' We shook hands with him and wondered quietly at our new senior.

'Fenton. Felldon. A p-pleasure to make your acquaintance. How smashing to have another Charles in our midst. Which area are you both from?'

'Wellesbourne. Our families have adjourning estates just out of the township.'

'Ah yes. I have a cousin who lives there. Lovely place. My mother has visited the Leamington Spa nearby and rates it quite highly. Have you p-partaken in the waters?'

We both shook our heads. Our days were better filled with more exciting activities then bathing yet again.

'Fair enough – fascinating place though.' We nodded politely. 'Oh well, I'd best be showing you around. Would you care for a tour b-before supper?'

We excitedly agreed and after donning our coats, he led us first outside whilst it was still light. We marvelled at the immensity of the school and the solid bricks holding the genius and vim of Rugby's best within. Everywhere we looked we could see rolling fields, classrooms, trees; all of them unexplored and therefore strange and foreign to us. As the night settled in, he drew us inside through the library and then through School House hall. We had become frozen in that short sojourn and moved hastily towards one of the blazing fires crackling on each end of the room. My hands were numb and blue and it took fierce rubbing and flirting dangerously close to the flame before I could feel warmth creeping back into them. At this point Dodgson left us to return to his study and we made our acquaintance with several of the boys standing around the fire.

Feeling cultured and civilised, we worked our way through the throng of lads, shaking their hands and introducing ourselves. In a manner not dissimilar to dogs lifting tails and sniffing, we established who was what and where we fitted in with them. Henry had already chummed up with a boy called Benjamin Roberts, who turned out to be a fanatic of spin bowling in the summer and a dogged flanker in the winter. We were deep in discussion regarding the rules of rugby when I got a tap on the shoulder.

'Hello.'

I turned around to come face to face with a dark, thinly built student sporting the most prominent set of ears I had ever encountered. They seemed to balance on each side like a teacup, poised to be picked up and held between the fingers. To make up for his pendulous ears he seemed to have been apologetically given eyes that sparkled with intelligence and wit and a friendly smile of pearly straight teeth. I liked him immediately.

'Hello to you, too, sir. My name is Charles Fenton and this is my friend Henry Felldon, and this is Benjamin Roberts.'

'Arthur Mannings.' Henry and Benjamin shook hands and returned immediately back to their conversation. I had already bored of that subject and beckoned Arthur towards the fire to learn more of my new friend.

'Do you play sport at all, Mannings?' I quickly adopted the terms of address used at Rugby.

'Not at all. I have two left feet and asthma. Not a winning combination.'

I had to agree.

'So what do you do in your spare time then?'

'I am an astronomer.'

'You look at stars?'

'Much more than that, Fenton. I hope to one day become an astronomical photographer and take images of another planet.'

Perhaps I was hasty with my first impression. Clearly, the boy in front of me was quite mad.

'But that's impossible!'

'Not so. John Draper has already taken a photograph of the moon and with time and advancement of the refracting telescope we shall be able to take photographs of solar systems just like we would of our dear mothers.'

I laughed. I remembered the studio daguerreotype my mother had insisted we sit for prior to my leaving home. The tweaking and twiddling involved before we were even poised to stand absolutely still in our suffocatingly tight best dress was agony. I had fidgeted so much that even my mother had lost her patience at me and she threatened to send me to bed without my supper. She knew my Achilles heel and I had promptly frozen in aching fear. Cook had venison stew with dumplings bubbling away on the stove. This was a gastronomic delicacy not to be missed. My mother's face was black as thunder and the resulting image set forever of our family was stern and forbidding, with only the flowers looking cheery and bright.

'You may laugh, but there will be a clear picture of our moon showing at the Crystal Palace Exhibition in Hyde Park this very year.'

'Really? My father has promised to take me there during the holidays in May.'

'How exciting. I shall see you there then. My father is of like mind and sees this as an opportunity to broaden my knowledge and inspire my creativity.'

I withdrew my earlier doubts of Mannings. He was a friend of great potential.

'Did you bring your telescope?'

'Yes. Would you like to see it?'

'Absolutely. I'll bring the supper.'

I prised Henry away from Benjamin and negotiated for him to have mine and Arthur's share of kitchen's supper in return for the leftovers in his mother's wicker basket. He agreed after determining what was on offer for tonight's menu. To my great delight, Arthur was in the same room as mine, which was a fantastic stroke of luck. I hauled the basket from Henry's room through to ours and emptied its contents out onto my bed whilst Arthur fossicked through his trunk to find his telescope.

'It was my father's but he has given it to me on the proviso I pass all my exams.'

He opened the small rectangular box and carefully removed the telescope from its velvet bed. It was the first telescope I had ever seen and I stared at it greedily.

'Can I hold it?'

Arthur hesitated. 'You may, but be very careful. It had to be ordered in from France and cost quite a bit.'

I sat down on the bed and cradled the telescope like a newborn baby. It was hard and cylindrical with a potent aura of mystical powers. We simultaneously looked at the window but luck was against us with rain teasingly tapping against the pane. The viewing would have to wait.

'It's fantastic.'

'I know.'

'Could I go with you next time the sky is clear?'

'Of course. It would be a pleasure.'

I sat staring at the thing, marvelling at the technology that existed in my world. The magnifying glass I had used back at home seemed pathetic and trivial against this mighty machine. I speedily forgot how thrilling it had been with my father pointing out Orion's Belt with its three main stars: Alnitak, Alnilam and Mintaka. With Arthur's telescope I would be able to see so much more and it was with some unwillingness that I handed it cautiously back to him to put away.

Once he restored it to his trunk, we turned our thoughts to the food lying forgotten on my bed. We made short work of it and before too long all that was left of the feast was crumbs and brown paper. During that time we talked about our families, our friends back home and what we wanted to be once we were older. It was an auspicious start to a firm potentially lifelong friendship. As night settled and candles were snuffed, I settled down in my bed and wondered what my first day at school would bring.

Beaks

I woke from a troubled sleep disturbed by strange noises and creaky bed springs. The sadness I had felt from missing my mother's bedtime kiss was soon overrun by the quiet sobbing of other boys and I furiously wiped away an errant tear running down my cheek before it could hit the pillow. Where was Mr Dumples now? I hoped Meg was being gentle with him. My bottom lip trembled and I bit it as punishment for my weakness. I was a Fenton, not a namby-pamby sookie boy. All the same, the enormous amount of food I had eaten the night before did nothing to fill the aching loneliness I felt inside for my mother, father and Meg. The grey dawning sky matched my sombre mood and the faces of those around me as we clambered out of bed drearily meeting the day.

We moved in zombie-like fashion through the morning ablutions to present ourselves as best we could. My shoes were buffed to a gleeful sheen and my collar as white as new snow. Only my face was dark and gloomy and it took some doing to wrench my features to a more normal countenance. We filed out to the dining hall and spooned thick hearty porridge silently into our mouths coupled with a mug of hot tea, which warmed frozen hands. Spirits lifted gradually and we tried to portray a mutual nonchalance towards the impending first lesson. The seniors snorted but kept their peace and continued eating.

My first teacher was with Mr Wiseman, who was cursed with the task of teaching us Latin. Perhaps this explained the rather waspish expression on his face as he spoke.

'Beatus homo qui invenit sapientiam,' he enunciated whilst etching our faces into his memory for future digestion. 'What does it mean?'

The silence was only intermittently broken by shuffling on seats. No one had a clue and if this was our expectation then we were seriously underdone and under-prepared.

'Not one of you can tell me this simple phrase from our own blessed book of God?' He turned and scribbled on the blackboard behind him.

'Beatus homo qui invenit sapientiam. Blessed is the man who finds wisdom. And this will be your class motto, gentlemen. You will learn this by the end of the lesson with the simple act of repetition. I want each of you starting at the front here, to stand, give me your name and then recite our class motto.' He tapped his cane on the desk in front of the first boy. 'Off you go.'

A pale little lad two rows in front of me slowly stood

and in a Scottish brogue introduced himself and recited the Latin phrase. The words dribbled out of his mouth in a despairing attempt to escape and fell down into a mumbled heap on his desk. Mr Wiseman sighed before indicating the boy next to him. As each boy called his name and spoke the phrase it became more familiar and easier to speak. Some had even managed to say it entirely without looking at the blackboard, a point that made Mr Wiseman smile thinly and nod. When it came to my turn I spoke clearly and thoughtfully but didn't dare to risk not looking. He barely registered my first effort and I sat somewhat belligerently, knowing my mother and father would have shown greater enthusiasm at their golden boy. Reality sat with me as I thumped down and crossed my arms in consternation. This was going to be tough.

Mr Wiseman handed us each a Latin dictionary and book. We stared at them in concern. The books were immense and would no doubt kill a man if fired accurately. We looked at him in trepidation.

'Gentlemen. This is your Latin grammar book. You will be required to write four lines from a Latin poet or a phrase and translate them to English. These lines will then be recited to me CLEARLY in our following class at the start of the morning. Failure to do so will result in a doubling of lines to be handed to me during your lunchbreak. Is this clear?'

We nodded glumly. I still had the 'beatus homo qui invenit sapientiam' ringing through my head. I glanced around and noted many faces reflecting my own. Unfortunately this did not console me at all and my shoulders dropped in surrender.

We got to work immediately, flicking through the pages, searching for the tiniest phrase or line we could see. My eyes caught on 'cogito ergo sum'. I think therefore I am. Perfect. I scribbled it down and continued my hunt. 'Tarde venientibus ossa.' To the late are left the bones. Gruesome. Fantastic. Brilliant. Now my mind began wandering back to the goblin underground cave where I could almost smell the cadaverous beings thrown into dark corners awaiting their doom. I studied the gaunt faces sunken in a macabre mask of misery all around me. I hadn't forgotten Mr Brown and there he sat in my fantasy wailing and begging my mercy for his evil Draconian ways. His flabby jowls wobbled and I watched him with contempt whilst the goblins heated their branding irons on the fire to sear onto his arms and belly. His squeals would challenge a milk-starved piglet torn from its mother and the goblins cackled at the sound. I donned my shield of invincibility and strode towards my grateful headmaster, brushing the goblins aside with a flick of my silver sword. They couldn't touch me and any attempt met with a stream of putrid sludge that hardened immediately and set them like stone. They stood in bewilderment whilst I casually lifted the blubbering headmaster and threw him over my shoulder to march out of the cavernous hole and back into the sunlight. Tumbling him onto the grass he would then crawl, weeping inconsolably, to clasp my ankle and kiss my boot in gratitude.

A clip around the ears drew me back to the real world and scurrying through the pages again.

It seemed to be barely minutes before the school bell rang and we charged out of the classroom and raced to the dining hall for some fresh crusty bread smeared with butter and slabs of cheese plus crisp apples and another mug of hot tea. We were not able to play outside as the weather had turned sour, so we contented ourselves with board games by the fire to fill in the lunchbreak. Before long the bell rang again and we less than eagerly moved to the next class, studying arithmetic and working on our penmanship. It was with great relief that we finally made it to the end of the school day and could relax in our study. Arthur Mannings, Benjamin Roberts and my friend Henry joined me by the fire and we compared the day.

'I never thought it would be so tough,' said Henry saddened. 'I hate Latin! It's all mumbo-jumbo to me. Give me a sound page of multiplication any day of the week. It's much more practical and holds no trickery.'

We nodded grimly.

'Mr Petersworth caught me writing with my left hand and snapped the cane down right on the fingertips. Look at the bruising.' Arthur showed us his hand and we flinched at the sight. The index finger had discoloured and the fingernail had partly dislodged from the nail bed. I felt my stomach turn and hurriedly looked away. Arthur studied it with curiosity, pressing the nail to see if it would reattach itself.

'Strange. I thought it would hurt more. If you look closer you can see the matrix unguis, which is normally protected by the nail bed, is partly exposed right down to the lunula. Once the swelling has gone the nail should fall back to the rightful place and I'll be back to new.'

We didn't share his enthusiasm.

'Put it away, Mannings.'

'Yes, Mannings, put it away before you make us vomit.'

Arthur raised his eyebrows but lowered his hand. This caused it to throb a little but he covered the discomfort easily. At this point Charles Dodgson, our praeposter, entered the study.

'Mannings, I need you to clear my study d-desk and replace the c-candles.'

'Sorry, Dodgson, I seemed to have injured my hand.'

Charles Dodgson looked at the proffered hand and recoiled. He turned his attention to me.

'Fenton it is then. Hop to it.' I followed him and set to my duties obediently, thinking of the not-so-distant times where staff would do what I wanted them to do. Conforming to my new role stung my ego a little but it was overdue. In the spirit of newly found humility I decided to completely expunge all arrogance, and pray in the church after supper. Little did I realise what I encountered there would burn in my memory for years to come.

The church

My shoes clacked down the aisle as I piously chose a pew to kneel at. My religious renewal started with a firm clasping of hands and bowed head.

'Our father who art in Heaven, hallowed be your name. Your kingdom come, your will be done on earth as it is in Heaven. Give us this day our daily bread and forgive us our debts, as we also have forgiven our debtors. And lead us not into temptation but deliver us from evil. For thine is the kingdom and the power and the glory, forever and ever Amen.' I mumbled my favourite prayer under my breath imagining God riding down on his white cloud delivering bread and saving us from the evil monsters. I allowed myself a few minutes visualising the scene before refocussing back to the task at hand.

'Dear God, make me a good boy and teach me to mind my teachers and praeposters. If you can help me learn Latin I promise to pray to you every night before bed and twice on Sundays. Keep my parents under your loving care and look after Meg and Jack for me so that maybe they can get married once he's feeling better. I'm sorry for what happened to his wife and I hope she can forgive me. I didn't mean for anything bad to happen to her. I didn't. If you can watch after my family and Meg I will always be your most humble servant. I promise. Amen.'

I considered the prayer books in front of me and whether I was pushing the whole saintliness thing a bit far. Too much prattle might make the Lord above suspicious. Probably best to finish on a genuine note. I closed my eyes and counted slowly to ten to seal the deal and think about supper. The sounds of footsteps tapping down the aisle turned my head to encounter the priest, who stopped by me waiting until I stood to shake his hand.

'How lovely to see the new students begin the year in religious reflection. I hope this activity continues throughout your schooling and you can encourage others to join you.'

'Yes, Father.'

'And what is your name, young man?'

'Charles Fenton, Father.'

The priest offered his hand to shake. 'Charles Fenton. Welcome to my church. I am Reverend William Fleet.'

I shook hands and took note of his appearance. He was slight in build and short in stature. His eyes twinkled and his smile broadened to show a gleaming row of pearly white teeth. His cheeks were flushed a rosy red and he was sporting a clean shaven boyish face topped with a mop of blond hair. He seemed too jolly to be the serious voice of God, but I had always been taught to not judge a book by its cover. At least he appeared sincere in his wish of making my acquaintance.

'Nice to meet you, Father.'

'The pleasure is all mine, Fenton. Tell me, how are you finding Rugby School?'

I hesitated. 'Very nice, Father. A lovely place.'

'I detect you aren't completely convinced?'

'Oh no, Father! I do like it here very much.'

'And yet?'

Was I really so transparent? I realised God was helping him to see right through me. It was best to come clean.

'And yet… Well, to tell you the whole truth, Father, I miss my parents and my nanny Meg something terrible and I'm finding the whole Latin thing a real trouble to understand. I don't think I'm clever enough to learn and that worries me as I've loved words and writing all my life. What if I'm not cut out to be what I thought I could be?'

'And what is that?'

I had told Arthur Mannings and anyone else who inquired that I wished to follow in my father's footsteps and become a lawyer but secretly I wanted to be something else. I had never told another soul what that was because I feared they would laugh at me. Reverend Fleet studied me battling my inner demons deciding whether my soul would burn in Hell if I lied to a man of the cloth. I considered the misdemeanours I had tallied up so far in my short life and decided not to risk it. Taking a deep breath I gave existence and voice to my true aspiration.

'I want to be a writer.' I stared at him fretfully, waiting for a bellyful of laughter to erupt from his mouth.

He nodded seriously. 'Good for you, Fenton. This world could use one less lawyer.' And with that, he smiled, patted my shoulder and walked away, leaving me looking after him dumbfounded. I may have stayed in that pose if it wasn't for a small sob interrupting my meditation.

'Who's there?' I called out, walking towards the sound. It appeared to be coming from behind a curtain in the adjoining room. The sob stopped and was over-ridden by a hasty shuffling and banging. I reached the room to find James McDonnell, the Scottish boy from my Latin class, buckling his belt and wiping his eyes. He glared at me.

'Go away!'

'McDonnell? Are you okay? What's happened?'

'I said tae go away! Mind yer own business!'

He was hunched over and looked terrified. I looked around fearfully wondering if whoever it was that had scared him so deeply was still in the room. It was empty apart from him and me. He was clutching his stomach and seemed in pain. I felt cold inside and very,

very afraid. Something had happened to him that was wicked and wrong, but what was it? My mouth went dry and my limbs turned to stone. I stared aghast at the ball of terror in front of me.

'Did… Did someone hurt you?'

He turned on me and latched his fists around my shirt collar, pinning me hard against the wall. I looked right into eyes that had witnessed Hades and burned with anger. His spittle flew onto my face and mouth as he furiously pushed my head back with his clenched knuckles.

'You listen here, Fenton. You leave me tae Hell alone and forget what ye saw.' He banged my head hard in unparalleled hate. 'Did ye hear me? You saw nothing. You…saw…nothing at all. Or so help me God, I will kill ye. I will kill ye and I swear it on yer mother's life.'

I had never before looked so deeply into the eyes of such a tormented soul. My bowels turned to water and I could feel tears trickling down my cheeks. Never ever did I have a doubt in his sincerity of intent and I nodded and promised to keep my mouth shut. He stared at me, turning from fury to anguish and back to fury. I wanted my mother so much I ached. He shook me a few more times, then dropped me like a stone and stormed away. I crumpled in a heap and sobbed and sobbed, shoulders heaving and my head sporting a small egg-sized lump where he had slammed me so hard. I decided to hold our covenant as if we had written it in blood and I knew I would rather die than break my word to McDonnell even if it meant that it would torture me for the rest of my life. The threat to both me and my mother was too much to consider risking. The other thought to consider was that I didn't truly know what had happened anyway and could only suspect the worst, which I hoped most sincerely to be wrong about. It took some time before I could regather and clean myself up enough to quietly retire to my room with all thoughts of supper vanished. I crawled into bed and closed my eyes tightly to shut out any conversation with the arriving boys. I wasn't ready to face them yet; it would have to wait until tomorrow.

Cloudy days

The night had been cold, dark and lengthy. There were dreams that had swirled inside my head, scary nightmares, but to pin one down to remember it gave only a sketchy result at best. I didn't want to recall anyway. I sought the comfort and cheer of my fellow friends after a morning spent learning grammar.

'Fenton! Where did you skive off to last night?'

'Yes, Fenton, you missed a fine draught of ale that Dodgson snuck in. Quite fruity it was.'

I curled a smile onto my face and pushed the McDonnell incident firmly into a box.

'Sorry, chaps, I was busy working on my lines for the Latin class after lunch. I lost all sense of the time and nodded off. Curse that Mr Wiseman.' I pretended to scowl, watching with relief the acceptance of my story.

'Wiseman is a twat,' the others agreed.

We spent our lunchbreak eating corned beef sandwiches and swapping horror stories about the teachers. Either their body stank, they had raging halitosis or a suspicious hair piece. No one was immune to our observations and we felt quite superior and marvellous until the bell rang for the next class. Away we slunk with Arthur Mannings and I heading to Latin, where I shared the class with James McDonnell.

He sat a few rows in front of me and to the left, so he was unable to know that I was studying his face and manner through most of the lesson. If I had not come across him last night, I would never have guessed of any wrongdoing. He was quiet, but so were we all. I was so lost in my contemplation that he turned around and caught me staring right at him. He stared vacantly through me though I felt my blood turn to ice and my hands begin to tremble. I quickly moved my attention to the page in front and muttered my lines in my head in preparation for my turn to speak. I dared not look his way again for the rest of the lesson.

And so my days passed, and with time I was able to move the incident to the recess of my mind. I would occasionally catch myself glancing his way and just as quickly would train my attention somewhere else before he noticed. He kept to himself and was considered a bit of a recluse, which was put down to him being Scottish and therefore dour in temperament. Only I knew the reason for his self-banishment and even then, it was only a hazardous guess. I kept up my evening prayer and Reverend Fleet would always stop to have a friendly chat and had even offered to assist me with my Latin homework. I grabbed this with both hands. To have words and language become my nemesis was quite intolerable and I battled nightly to overcome this learning block and ease my growing concern that I was not cut out to be an author. We arranged to meet Tuesday night after supper and I collected my books, determined to win the battle in my mind. He greeted me into his study with a smile and a pot of tea in his hand.

'Fancy a wee drop of my herbal tea to help your concentration, Fenton? It clears your mind and opens your eyes to knowledge.'

'Yes please, Father.' I watched him pour a generous mug of the strangely smelling tea and hand it to me. It smelled like summer hay and I screwed up my nose before taking a tentative sip. He chuckled at my expression.

'Yes, it is an acquired taste but you'll get used to it by the end. It's very good for you, Fenton, so drink every last drop.'

He sat beatifically watching me labour my way through the foul-tasting brew. If this was going to help me, then I was going to drink it. We were both very satisfied when I finally drained the cup and placed it on the side dresser. He didn't offer another as he could see how challenging the first had been but was grateful of my attempt. We opened the Latin grammar books on the table and began to study.

Reverend Fleet was a patient man who would have made a fine teacher if he hadn't chosen the path of God.

He got me to sound out each word clearly and equate the sound to what was written on the paper. Taking the last two letters from the end of each word could sometimes make the word appear more familiar and I found that as we worked through a particularly long phrase I could translate most of it without trouble. I grinned at him stupidly and he tousled my hair in response, his hand resting companionably on my shoulder. I turned the page to begin a new phrase and stared at the words before me. They seemed a bit blurry so I blinked a few times to try and refocus. This didn't work, which was quite perplexing as now the lines were starting to weave and wobble making the paper look covered in tiny wriggly ants. I shook my head and frowned.

'Are you all right, Fenton?' Reverend Fleet asked.

'I…I think so. I'm just a bit dizzy.'

'Oh, that's too bad. We were getting along so well.' He touched my forehead. 'Though you do feel a shade hot; perhaps it might be best you lie down for a while on my settee. You could have a little nap and will feel much refreshed. Here, come here, Fenton, I'll fetch a cushion.'

He helped me to stand and I was overcome with a spinning sensation. The room was dancing around me and I gratefully grasped his proffered arm to assist me to lie down on his settee. He judiciously puffed a cushion under my head and kindly dabbed a cool wet cloth on my forehead, advising me to breathe deeply and slowly to calm the giddiness. I closed my eyes and drifted off into a deep slumber, my head filled with strange colours and patterns. This was most unusual and I wondered how I had become so fevered in such a short time. Thank God for the kindly Reverend Fleet, who watched over me with such dedication.

I woke in a dark room, feeling cotton-mouthed and disorientated. The dizziness was still there but much improved and I sat up cautiously to look for Reverend Fleet. I was alone and I presumed he had gone to prayer, leaving me to rest. My clothing was dishevelled probably from me tossing around on the small settee, so I tidied myself and stood up. My head thumped a little and the dizziness increased, but I managed to breathe deeply and it slowly abated. Strange, very strange, and I had a vague notion that something wasn't right. I gathered my books and groggily headed to my room to sleep.

The train ride

It was with great relief and delight that I found Reverend Fleet's teachings to have a most positive effect on my ability to learn Latin. The language no longer held me prisoner and I bloomed to the point of being one of the better pupils. I attended further lessons with the Reverend but politely declined any more tea, which he accepted with some sadness. I had no further bouts of fever and it wasn't long before he proclaimed me learned in Latin and the lessons complete. Mr Wiseman began to pay more attention to me and had even smiled occasionally much to my immense pride and satisfaction. I passed what I knew to my fellow comrades and though they weren't as proficient as me they all noted a huge improvement and repaid my tutoring with many delightful snacks.

Life was good and I became a sponge for all the tutors could throw at me. I devoured Wordsworth, Shakespeare and Dickens. I breezed through Algebra, Geometry and long equation, and Biology, Geography and Chemistry enthralled me. My confidence grew and I strutted down the corridors as if I owned the entire world. The only sting that presented itself was the occasional glimpse of McDonnell shadowing the school corridors. His encounter with me was firmly pushed into obliviousness.

Spring was upon us and I was delighted to read from my mother's frequent correspondence that both my mother and father would be taking me to London to see the Great Exhibition at Hyde Park in May. I counted down the days impatiently and was pleased to hear that Henry and Benjamin Roberts would be joining Mannings and me in seeing the exhibition. All of the country was hungry for any titbits of what might be presented there and all parents felt they were duty bound to expose their children to such an educational experience.

'My father writes me that there is over 1,000,000 square feet of glass incorporated into building the framework. Prince Albert himself has been personally overseeing the erection of the Crystal Palace and was at the opening with the Queen,' Henry Felldon said.

'God bless Queen Victoria.' We all patriotically hurrahed and cheered our beloved monarch.

'I can't wait to travel there by train. My father arrives in London in this manner every time he is required to work at his law office. It flies along the track at 60 miles per hour!' I said.

'Has he booked it with Thomas Cook?' enquired Mannings.

'I think so. We are going in the morning. Mother and Father are staying at the Innkeepers' Lodge tonight and collecting me after breakfast.'

'I believe we share the same train, which means our plans are not dissimilar. We will have to introduce them to one another.'

Benjamin Roberts and Henry excitedly responded affirmatively to joining in and we wrestled with our pillows that night as our thoughts whirled around the mystical palace and train ride. As first light arrived, we bounced delightedly out of beds and shovelled breakfast in at the pace of the locomotive's wheels. Our parents found us lined up spruce and shining in front of the school gates awaiting collection for the train station. We took great pleasure introducing them to each other and observing their mutual satisfaction and congeniality at their new acquaintances. My parents made a handsome couple and I swelled with adoration to be associated on such intimate terms of our relations. I wore my Fenton pride honourably emblazoned on my chest and would have fiercely battled a bloody death defending it.

Mr and Mrs Mannings carried a bookish air and I privately acknowledged the auricle inheritance came from his father. His mother stood awkwardly thin, her eyes overcoming the face in their googly dominance. I was reminded of the praying mantis poised to collect an errant bug that should come walking aimlessly by. Her lips were virtually non-existent and I pitied Mannings in his childhood, when they were obliged to kiss him good night. It would have given me to recoil seeing her nearing my cheek to embrace. Her distracted smile on introduction made me suspicious that she was unaware of my name seconds after hearing it and the vagueness swirled around her as she clung to her husband like an anchor to a boat tossed at sea. I feared if she let go that she might fly away into the sky and merge with the clouds staring down at us in confusion. Mr Mannings must have been aware of this too because his clasp on her arm enfolded with his was quite protectively possessive. Why he should consider anyone would be even margin-ally enamoured with google eyes I have no idea, but love was still a mystery to me. I knew Henry's parents well and held no discord with them and was delighted to see that Mr and Mrs Roberts were of a friendly disposition and matched Benjamin's good looks accordingly. So it was a merry little bunch clasping their timetables that traversed towards the train station bearing onwards to Hyde Park, London.

The train was hot, dusty and the strong wall of body odour assailed my delicate nostrils with vengeance. The ladies fluttered their fans to quell the domineering stench and scathing heat. Because of the popularity of The Great Exhibition, the trains were packed to over-flowing and my long-awaited ride became a wretched torture. The initial polite and carefree conversation was now limited to the barest monosyllabic response, a telling sign where etiquette usually reigned supreme. The eyes drifted and the heads nodded, perpetually checking pocket watches willing the time to summon the end was near. The sweat trickled down my neck and brow pooling into wet patches that stuck my shirt to my skin determinedly. I glanced out the window at times to try and ascertain my whereabouts and if landmarks of London were pending. It helped to know that outside was freedom and fresh air, just a window pane away.

My peripheral vision captured a corpulent gentleman tucking into a pork pie with great gusto, flicking flaky crumbs of pastry in careless fashion over unlucky neighbours. His hat leaned rakishly, threatening to fall off with any bump but the greasy hair stuck it to his head with aplomb. The buttons pulled tight, holding the shirt together with little wisps of hairy belly poking through. His pocket held a laundered white handkerchief, snowy and bright with little embroidered initials in one corner which looked like 'AH'. This held my attention for a few minutes as I considered what his name might be. He was duly named Archibald Hogstown. My scrutiny then continued southwards to his trousers. This particular garment appeared to groan under the pressure and I was sure it wasn't my imagination that showed stitches fraying and unwinding in front of my incredulous eyes.

Any moment the trousers were going to pop and his mass of flesh would spill out and smother us all. Each mouthful of that pork pie was a mouthful closer to death by suffocation and I willed him to stop by sending strong telepathic messages. He must have sensed one as he raised his head and caught me staring at him. I quickly looked away until his attention returned to the ever-decreasing pie and then began watching him more covertly. I couldn't believe, when the last shred of pastry had been plucked and nibbled from his trousers and the last fleck of gravy licked from his mouth, that we were all still here and the trousers had stood firm. He shuffled and flicked smaller crumbs onto the floor, catching me yet again by the eye and handing me a firm wink. I withdrew my attention smartly and avoided eye contact for the remainder of the journey.

The relief was palpable to everyone when we finally and painstakingly arrived at our destination. Lassitude was replaced with fervour as we eagerly exited the carriage. Sucking in the slightly fetid summer London air was still a huge improvement on what my lungs had previously endured. I caught the tail end of Archibald Hogstown waddling towards a tavern to replenish his unquenchable thirst. A small part of me was sad that the seams had endured and that I would never know the alternative outcome. However, it was time to fill my mind with wondrous things from all over the globe and I had a real hankering to look at the astronomical photographs Mannings had described earlier. We walked invigorated towards the Crystal Palace, taking in the many sights, sounds and smells.

'Pies, get your meat pies here...'

'Muffffins. Muffffins. Freshly baked, nice and sweet.'

'Buy a flower for your lady, sir? Only a penny.'

'Shine your shoes, laddie? Make 'em like extra nice for the ladies.'

We stopped at a particularly well-stocked street vendor to choose a quick meal before entering the mighty palace. I studied the arrangement of pickled eels, sheep trotters, penny pies and baked potatoes with slight alarm, remembering cook's fastidiousness with hygiene after my childhood illness. Flies were sleepily landing on the food, loading their excrement on the warm, juicy surfaces whilst enjoying a rancid sup of their own. My loathing of flies had not deteriorated since their defilement of Jack's beloved and I tugged at Father's coat arm to pull him away. The jelly-like goo the eels slid around in made a slurping sound, moving their black serpentine corpses backward and forward. My mother had turned slightly pale and fanned herself vigorously as she purveyed the trolley with me. Father had one last look at the baked potatoes before demurring to our more delicate senses and moving on to the muffin man. Here we were able to purchase a more agreeable cinnamon muffin accompanied by currant cake and coffee.

The badgering of the vendors continued throughout our meandering towards the exhibit. My ears were assaulted with the cacophonous banter thrown stridently out across the air. They were the parasites leaching onto the wealthy and sucking them dry of any loose change clanging in their pocket and we fell for their vociferous peddling by spending a small fortune on things of vital importance that I absolutely had to have to survive another day though I had never previously given them a fleeting thought. My arms were laden with windmills, flags, marbles and sweets, so much so that my father was obliged to purchase a carrier bag for my pile of treasured goodies. I may have been content to wander endlessly, dragging my parents from one desired necessity to the next, if we hadn't all felt the presence of the Crystal Palace drawing us in. It stood like a grand lady shimmering in the rare London sun and now that our stomachs were full and my father's coins weakened, it was time to appreciate the magnitude and brilliance of the architect Mr Joseph Paxton.

The Great Exhibition

I had never felt so proud to be an Englishman as I did that day. We walked in with wonder and awe at the immensity and ingeniousness of The Great Exhibition. It just couldn't be possible to imagine how such a structure could be made in our lifetime. The building was over 1800 feet long and 128 feet high. There was a vast gallery down the middle of the two-storey structure with a left and right wing branching from it. Everywhere we looked we were greeted with glass, fountains, trees, flags from every country and masses of bodies. Rich and poor alike mingled and dallied between each exhibit with their mouths open wide in amazement, though the rich endeavoured to be more circumspect in their manner. How could you not be bedazzled by the riches and engineering virtuosity on show?

I dashed off, ignoring my mother's cries to stay close, and ran from display to display. I had read the brochure listing the various objects that would be available to view. The country that held the most mystery and allurement was India with its wonderful exhibits. I had never seen an elephant and they boasted a fully sized stuffed elephant draped in a coat laden with rubies, pearls and diamonds. They also complemented this ostentatious spectacle with an intricately carved ivory throne fit enough for an eastern king. I ran, side-stepping people swishing around decorously, with my eyes lit up at any gap that opened between the crowds to speed towards my final destination. The mystical allure of the Arabian guests called my name through silken dresses and veiled eyes. I half-expected a camel to appear and kneel before me in submissiveness. I was so caught up in my ecstatic state that I started scanning over the heads of people for the donkey of the desert. Strangely it did not appear and I had to journey onwards by foot.

The beast did not disappoint. Its noble head and enormous white tusks carried the opulence with grace and dignity. I stood by its feet and stared up at its monumental ears thrusting out between the reds and gold and that covered its body. I would have given up all my trinkets and a year of candy just to be able to clamber up and ride behind its ears through the Sahara. But even in this I was torn. What was better? To be the fearless mahout in charge of the elephant or the powerful and respected maharajah travelling in comfort and luxury on the howdah strapped on its back. On reflection I decided upon the maharajah as I could always order the mahout to show me how to control the animal AND when I wished to retire after a long journey, I could be settled into the rich lush tent, fanned by my boy slaves and fed sweet dates and spiced cakes. No more fagging for stuttering praeposters who could be doing it themselves. My eastern beauty would be lying at my feet admiring my courage and tenacity, though in this daydream her face took on the features of Lily clasping her latest rodent friend. I sighed. Luxuriating in my daydream, I conveniently forgot my drive to be a more humble and hard-working student, who, devoted in prayer, was a mentor to all. Now all I could imagine was wearing richly embroidered coats with diamonds sewn in by gold thread making me catch the sun's rays and dazzle my surrounding admirers. It was a dangerously egotistical time and it took my mother tugging on my ear to drop me back to earth.

'There you are, Charles! We have been searching for you everywhere. What is the meaning of running off like that?'

I blushed at the public humiliation I was enduring, but kept my tongue, knowing how protective and loving my mother was to me. She was flustered and wide-eyed trying to keep her concerns under control. Her tight grip made my ear smart but she didn't want to lose me twice.

'Elizabeth. My pet. We can't control the excitement of the boy in a place such as this. Let's just relax and let the lad take a free rein within the exhibition,' my father cajoled. 'He won't be interested in the things we wish to see and neither will we be in his. So why don't we agree to meet him at closing time by the tree where we had our muffins? I know some beautiful stained glass that is calling for your undivided attention and we could move at a leisurely pace more becoming of your gender.'

I loved my father.

My ear was restored to its master and my mother demurred gracefully to my father, but not before listing the do's and don'ts in avoiding dangerous accidents at the exhibition. She missed my grateful grin at my father as I dashed away into the crowd before she could prepare a list of what else I must be aware of. He smiled watching my disappearing form and gave his wife a conciliatory peck on her hand before placing her arm in his and strolling off towards the glass artworks.

Now that my Indian fantasy had been ruined by maternal powers, I headed to the American display telling myself I was interested in the American Eagle. However, I knew my real ambition was to ogle Hiram Power's statue of a Greek slave. She was modestly housed in her own velvet tent of red and was completely naked bar the chains around her wrists. She was not hard to find with the crowds humming, some making scintillating remarks, in a ring around her form. Some attempted a face of disgust for such lewdness and made clucking noises as such but stayed lingering around her beautiful form. This concupiscent sculpture lured us in and I stared and stared at her in captivation. The story attached to her was a story of sadness and slavery. She had been stolen by the Turks who'd murdered her family and was to be sold to the highest bidder. Her dedication to Christianity was shown by the inclusion of a cross and her purity shone through in the face of adversity and debauched sexuality.

Apart from the momentary glimpse of Meg's buxom breast, this was the first time I had seen a woman in naked form. A small part of me fell in love with her on the spot and I resented the other people drinking in her beauty so much that it was with difficulty I restrained myself from challenging them all. When I first arrived at her pedestal I was too shy to gaze directly but that quickly changed to plain fascination and I was caught practically drooling by my fellow classmates, who had found their way there too.

'Oh ho! It's Fenton! We should have guessed you'd be the first man here,' said Benjamin Roberts, who was followed closely by Henry and Arthur Mannings.

'Cor blimey. She's gorgeous!' exclaimed Henry, admiring her curves with blatant ogling.

'Ah yes. The Greek slave. Carved in 1844 by the American Hiram Powers. He was a son of a farmer who dallied as a rather inventive mechanic before turning to sculpting in Florence. This lady is his most famous piece of art.'

'Trust you, Mannings, to make this a school trip.'

'Yes Mannings, do shut up.'

Arthur Mannings looked at his friends, surprised at their outburst, but held his peace. He proceeded to read his brochure to ferret any more information about the statue. We continued to admire her feminine curves and would have stayed all day if it hadn't been for a group of stern elderly ladies heading our way preparing to do war against obscenity.

Mannings pointed us towards the astronomical photo of the moon and I had to admit once we had arrived at the target that he was once again correct. There was the moon in its full glory, photographed. Though he was as riveted by the picture as we had been by the Greek slave, we were less inspired and were fidgeting around him to move to the next display. His intelligence was thankfully married with an easy-going nature and he bore us no resentment at moving away from his most anticipated spectacle.

The Koh-i-Noor diamond beckoned us next. We had all been taught the history of this precious stone at school, and were anxious to see it. The allure of the diamond was heightened by the addition of a dreaded curse. 'He who owns this diamond will own the world, but will also know all its misfortunes. Only God or a woman could wear it with impunity.' No one could doubt the authenticity of the curse; of all the male rulers who'd had the ambition to own it, very few had escaped its power. Wars had been lost, men tortured and illnesses rained down on the possessors of the Koh-i-Noor diamond. It was rumoured to have graced the conquered Mohammed Shah's peacock throne, which he handed over in defeat to Nadir Shah after over 20,000 of his men were killed on the battlefield. This rumour proved false as the clever Nadir Shah was informed by one of the defeated emperor's harem, that he had hidden the diamond in his turban. During a grand feast he proposed that the emperor and he exchange turbans in a show of newly fought for peace and brotherhood. The emperor had no choice but to oblige and the diamond became Nadir Shah's. It was at this stage, when he opened the turban and exclaimed 'Koh-i-Noor' or 'Mountain of light', that the diamond was finally named. Not long after his successful takeover, the curse rose and he was brutally murdered in his sleep. And it didn't stop there. The next ruler Ali Kuli was quickly dethroned and blinded by his own brother, who was himself to suffer the same fate before being killed by his own troops. This was a recurring theme as the following king, Shah Rukh, was also blinded. But unfortunately he was left alive and then tortured with boiling water poured over his head to confess to the hiding place of the Koh-i-Noor diamond, after which he painfully died of his injuries. With this bloodthirsty history it may have been met with some surprise that on March 29th 1849, when our beloved England claimed India in her British Empire, that part of the treaty ordered the surrender of the Koh-i-Noor diamond to Her Majesty the Queen. And now it was ours.

We waited in line for what seemed to be hours, though any temptation to jump the queue was quickly quelled by the presence of two formidable policemen. Their no-nonsense expression and pugnacity muffled any potential uprising from the crowds. We meekly stood and shuffled towards the enormous birdcage holding the sacred Koh-i-Noor. Whilst we waited, we compared trinkets and goodies we had all cajoled our parents to buy for us. Arthur Mannings had convinced his father to purchase a Cuban cigar to give to our headmaster after the holidays. I noted it with some jealousy. He admired my large cache of lollies and soon I was able to swap a piece of coltsfoot rock for some treacle toffee. We were all happily chomping on the sweet treats when we finally approached the diamond.

'Well, it's jolly big, isn't it?' stated Felldon.

We agreed politely. We studied it further.

'Not quite what I imagined though,' he continued.

The head nodding endorsed his point of view. We recalled our history lesson and the blood spilled on the diamond's behalf and looked again.

'Probably just needs a bit of a polish,' he concluded sagely.

'Quite.'

And with that, we walked away vaguely disappointed. The cigar was preying on my mind and similarly on the others'.

'Mannings. That cigar of yours. Let's have another look at it,' Henry asked.

Mannings brought it out for us to admire. We each took turns at holding the cigar and smelling the earthy fragrance. It was a very great temptation.

'It's a fine specimen.'

'Looks as if it could get broken in amongst your other things.'

'Can't be having that.'

'No. Absolutely not.'

'They are supposed to be smoked while they are still fresh.'

'The heat it's been exposed to on the train and in the sun could well have damaged the flavour and soured it. You can't give that to the headmaster.'

We all agreed, bar Mannings, who clasped in anguish the soon-to-be-ruined cigar. This cigar was not good enough for our headmaster, Mr Goulburn. He deserved nothing but the best and we were in fact, SAVING him from tampered goods. He should be grateful for our thoughtfulness.

'But my father…'

'Don't worry about that. He'll never ask Mr Goulburn.'

He stared at us beaten. We quickly decided to head out into Hyde Park and find a shady tree. The wrapper was soon dispensed with and the lucifers presented. The only bump in our plan was the lack of a cutter. We deliberated as a group and were elated to spot a young gentleman enjoying his cigar resting on a park bench. In our best wheedling tone we managed to convince him we were to cut the cigar for our father as he had inadvertently dropped his cutter on the train. We pointed vaguely at a group of men by a fountain, which he scanned to seek a paternal figure. One appeared nebulously to fit this description so he cut the cigar and we raced back to our leafy headquarters to light it before he caught on to our chicanery. With a magnanimous gesture towards Mannings, we voted and determined it only honourable that he should be first to enjoy.

He held the cigar in his mouth and sucked deeply as Henry eagerly lit a match and held it to the tip. We watched in fascination as he inhaled sharply, firing the embers to a golden yellow and perfuming the air with the whirling smoke. He coughed soon after and bent over hacking and gasping for air. His eyes were watering and red and we laughed scornfully at him as he surrendered the cigar to me.

I had seen my father smoke them many times and he always struck me as having an air of contentedness in the way he drew the cigar in. I found it hard to believe that same cigar could produce so incongruous a reaction from Arthur Mannings. Undoubtedly he had used an incorrect technique and was handicapped with having a non-smoking father. It was my privilege to show him how a man was supposed to handle his cigar. I may have even bowed slightly in deference to my enlightening entertainment. I leaned nonchalantly against the trunk of the tree and adopted a handsome and cavalier representation. This sort of thing was not to be rushed but more to be appreciated as part of an elaborate ritual of manhood. Wafting the cigar around in the air, I breathed deeply the fine aroma that whispered around me. Then smiling sardonically, rolled it between my thumb and two fingers to observe the quality and thickness of the tobacco nestled inside. I sniffed the cigar smoke and demonstrated an air of meditative assessment before judging the cigar was worthy of my inhalation. When the time felt right I placed the cigar to my lips and inhaled, posing in what I felt was a sage and mature manner. As I exhaled, the plume of smoke billowed over my appreciative fraternity and though it stung my eyes and my throat burned I determined to maintain my poise.

'You didn't inhale!'

'Yes, I did!'

'No, you didn't! It hardly entered your mouth.'

I frowned at the realisation I would have to suck in the foul smoke again.

'Watch and learn, gentlemen. Watch and learn.' I plastered a smile onto my face and placed the cigar to my lips, praying that I could dupe them again. The boys came closer and studied the placement carefully. I felt a slight trickle of cold sweat emerge from my forehead and I braced myself.

'So this is what you are up to!' A strong masculine voice boomed directly behind me. I jumped in fright and turned to see the young cigar-smoking man we had so foolishly conned earlier.

'You lying little buggers.'

He glared at each of us, annoyed at being tricked so easily. He shook his fist at me. I dropped the cigar in fright and my mouth fell open. He spotted the fallen cigar and smirked in a manner I was not comfortable with.

'And you all wish to smoke?'

We shook our heads with fear and kept silent.

'It was just you then?' He pointed at me. I could feel the other boys urging me not to be a blabbermouth. It would never do to be a snitch. I shivered and hesitated, despondent about my dubious honour. I sighed and cursed my stupidity silently.

'Yes, sir... It was just me.' I prepared myself for a clip around the ear but it was much, much worse.

'Pick up the cigar and smoke it. Every little bit of it. Now.'

I paled. I could hear the boys behind me softly groan.

This was not going to be good. I slowly picked up the smouldering cigar and sucked in the now-putrid smoke. He stood over me with his arms crossed and pressed me onwards to keep smoking. No sooner had I exhaled than he would order me to inhale. The cigar seemed to be fighting with me and refused to burn any quicker no matter how much I desired it to be gone. I was coughing and spluttering with each breath and my stomach was heaving. Sweat dripped off my pale face and my eyes watered to complete my saturation of Hell. My friends watched in helpless wonder as I sucked and sucked at the heinous stick growing more and more waxen. Any minute now I was going to empty my stomach and fall in a sodden heap. I was hot and cold at the same time and I swore on the Virgin Mary I would never touch another cigar so long as I should live if she could just let me survive right now. Have mercy on this poor little sod of a boy. I am a stupid raving idiot. Whose bright idea was this in the first place? I couldn't even make eye contact with my friends. I wasn't able to stand and felt as sick as a dog. Dropping to my knees I gathered the last reserves of strength and inhaled the final bit of the cigar, giving the butt numbly to the man. He took it between two fingers and nodded grimly.

'I hope you have learnt your lesson, lad?'

I nodded woefully. He walked away, flicking the cigar end onto the grass. I fell to my hands and knees and vomited. My stomach heaved and emptied itself and I was a sad excuse for what had been earlier such a dapper young man. Henry, Benjamin and Arthur grimaced, looking at me draw my insides out to the world. It was not a pretty sight at all. Benjamin took pity and after I had regurgitated and spat, he offered me his handkerchief to mop myself up. I sat back, wearily resting against the trunk and sucking in cool draughts of air with my eyes closed. There must be something wrong with men who think cigars are gratifying. They are not.

Henry ran and fetched me a glass of water from inside the Crystal Palace, which I sipped gratefully. They all offered me lollies to sweeten the acid taste in my mouth and I gingerly accepted a peppermint cane. With mumbled words of gratitude drifting into my ears, I waved them all away to leave me alone and return back to the exhibition. I had had enough for the day and was still in the exact position when my parents found me. I explained my pallor and squeamish stomach away by blaming an over consumption of candies. They accepted this, knowing my fondness for sweet things and my mother clucked over me all the way back on the train home. We finally arrived back at the Fenton Estate late that night and I plodded to bed in a miserable state, not moving until the sun had risen many hours later.

Summer break

I loved Fenton Estate as a man would love a favourite winter coat. It was comforting, reassuring and familiar to me and I wrapped myself up in it happily. My charming Meg was so excited to see me again that I feared I may be smothered in her embrace. She covered my face in kisses and cuddled me dry, patting down my hair and lifting my hands outward like wings to get a clear assessment that I was sound and healthy. Satisfied, she imprisoned my hand and marched me to the cook for jam tarts and apple cider. The cook set to work immediately and with a flourish presented me with an enormous slab of bread and butter to accommodate the sweets. The look in her eye as she firmly placed the plate in front of me disallowed anything but a complete annihilation of her baking at risk of offending her. Being of sound appetite made this task a pleasant experience for both me and her, knowing how much she admired my capacity to eat.

After my plate was wiped clean, I was moved to the stables to reacquaint with Jack. He was sweeping up when I made my entrance.

'Hello Jack.'

Jack turned round and grinned at the sight of me. I still had remnants of jam on the side of my mouth.

'Well, hello Master Fenton! I see you've been to the cook already.' He gestured towards my mouth chuckling. I blushed and wiped my mouth.

'Are you a learned scholar yet?'

'Not really, Jack. But I've made some friends.'

'That's grand, Master Charles, mighty grand. You'll never go wrong with a good set of friends to back you up in your life,' Jack said.

'I know. We all went to the Great Exhibition together.'

Jack nodded in appreciation. He was hoping to go on his day off next week with Meg.

'What was it like?' he asked, throwing me a brush to start brushing one of our horses. We spent the afternoon chatting companionably about the Crystal Palace and I humoured him immensely by recounting my cigar incident. He was holding his belly and wiping his eyes by the end of the unfortunate debacle. Luckily I was not over-sensitive to his mirth and I even managed to find the funny side myself, something I would never have thought possible the day before.

He repaid the favour by telling me the story about the duck and our cook. She was about to wring its neck when it escaped. It went straight through the house to where my mother was entertaining some lady friends during a high tea. The duck took no notice of the company and headed blindly towards the tiered cake stand sending it flying. Slices, cakes and tarts went everywhere, with some of the cream sponge unfortunately landing in Mrs Spellings' lap. The duck then catapulted onto her hat before desperately flapping out an open window quacking. There it was dispatched by Jack with one quick flick of the wrist but not before Mrs Spellings discovered the duck had also relieved itself on her hat. She was not amused. My mother had hinted in her regular correspondence of the event, but neglected to report the added insult deposited by the duck. She had told me, however, that Mrs Spellings was a colonel's daughter and as such, held great fortitude and nerve. She merely insisted on being a guest once the duck had been cooked and it was reported with amusement, that she ate the fowl with great relish.

While I was wiping my eyes with laughter, Jack started to get a bit fidgety and restless. Strange, I thought, he seems to have something on his mind.

'Err, Charlie.'

'Yes, Jack?'

'I have a bit of an announcement.' He shuffled and blushed slightly.

Curious. 'What is it, Jack?' I asked, intrigued.

'Well, it seems to me…that is to say…what I'd like to let you know…is Meg and I are going to be married.' He fumbled with his hat.

'What marvellous news!' I spontaneously hugged Jack and then shook his hand. 'I always thought you two should be together. You sly old dog, you.'

Jack grinned and fiddled some more with his hat.

'We're planning the wedding in spring. Cook's already agreed to the catering. I hope you can come back for it, Charlie.'

'I wouldn't miss it for anything. I can't believe Meg didn't say a word!'

'She wanted to, but we both liked the idea of giving you a surprise for your visit home. The mistress is well pleased. She thinks my home needs a woman's touch and Meg's just the lass to do it.'

I can imagine Meg sweeping through with all her cleaning potions and embroidered cushions. Jack didn't really stand a chance against her once she got started. Jack gave me a sideways glance and lifted his eyebrows. He was thinking the same thing and I shook my head and clapped his back in sympathy. Women. I'll steer clear of them, thank you very much. I still hadn't forgotten the headmaster's cane.

My summer days were thus filled with helping Jack out, listening to Mr Walton our farm manager and accompanying Meg to the village. On fine days I collected Henry and a few other lads and went fishing on the river or playing cricket at the green. We swam when we were hot and ate when we were hungry, knowing that the cook would have the cupboards replenished the moment we left. Life was good. And yet before long I started to look forward to returning to Rugby School. Although Meg and my mother meant well, I began to feel the creeping sensation of suffocation, particularly when they insisted on taking me to visit elderly aunts and uncles that had expressed an interest in my wellbeing. I had to dress up in good clothing and sit politely answering the exact same questions I had answered the day before with yet another ancient relation that seemed to have popped out of the woodwork. Meanwhile the sun would shine in taunting me with its vivacity and liberty. I swear even the snails were jaunty in their sunny sojourn, leaving a sparkling trail of slime behind them. I crushed one once in a fit of peevishness.

I had my suitcases packed and was raring to go by the time the summer holidays ended. The dormitories were buzzing with school friends re-connecting and sharing stories and I fell in with the beehive gratified at my return. I was oblivious to the dark times ahead.

James McDonnell

I shuddered at the sight of James McDonnell. In amongst all the animation, he stood out in his torpidness. His centre of gravity seemed to have dropped and his body sagged with indifference. His entire frame had shrunk and he looked so lifeless that I was worried he might faint. I stepped towards him, remonstrating with myself for earlier cowardice.

'McDonnell.'

He appeared not to have heard me. I tried again.

'James.'

He looked at me vacantly and then looked down again. I was very worried. I gently touched his arm.

'Feck off!'

I retreated as if scalded. The fire burned in his eyes like it had all those nights ago at the church. I recognised it immediately.

'I just want to help.'

'Well ye can't. Not now. Just leave me be.' He walked away and I let him go. I just let him go on his way.

The classes continued and games of cricket turned to games of rugby, though I knew myself to be far inferior with the less familiar pigskin ball. This was Henry and Roberts' forte and though I envied their panache and ball-handling skills I was quite content to play in a lower grade suited to my cloddish ability. I still enjoyed myself tremendously and was tackling players with great enthusiasm. Mr Campbell, our sports teacher, was less enthusiastic.

'Go lower, Fenton! You will never get the man down skipping around his chest. Try again.'

I lined up my opponent and squared the shoulders. This time I went low, but failed to grab his legs fast enough so he deftly side-stepped and carried on to the line. Mr Campbell scratched his head.

'Why can't you obey a simple instruction? It's not too difficult, is it?'

I shook my head. 'No sir.'

'Hit the tackle bags, I've had enough of you. And do ten laps around the field before you head in.' He stormed away muttering to himself.

I felt slightly miffed at the deleterious report of my skills and trudged off with a similar expression. Imagining his face on the tackle bags gave an added incentive but by the time I had completed my laps I was ready to turn in. I picked up my gear bag and headed towards the dormitory.

I felt somewhat cheerier once I had bathed and eaten, though it could be said that Mr Campbell was not yet my most cherished teacher. In fact I considered him to be a twat of the highest degree regardless of the fact that both Henry and Benjamin Roberts felt he was a mastermind. There was no accounting for taste.

The school chapel beckoned me for my nightly ritual of evening prayer before bed. I liked to go when the others were studying and there was an opportunity to pray in peace. As much as I enjoyed their company, I also cherished small moments of reflection and silence. Occasionally Reverend Fleet would stop and chat for a while but generally I had the place to myself. Tonight I would try, once again, to pray for humility and patience, particularly with regards to my sporting nemesis, Mr Campbell. These were challenging times, both for me AND God. But one had to admire my tenacity.

I saw James McDonnell straight away. As I opened the door to the chapel, my eyes were immediately drawn upwards to his swinging body. His neck was squeezed tight by the noose and his tongue protruded from his mouth thick and sluggish. A faecal smell assaulted my nostrils showing that he had lost all control of his bodily functions at the moment of his lonely death. The rubbing of the rope against the beam dominated any other sound and grated my ears. This I remember most of all. An overturned chair lay apologetically in the aisle. I felt as if I were in a space void of oxygen and I couldn't breathe. My lungs were incapable of continuing, whilst my heart thumped wildly in my chest. I don't know how long I stood like this but eventually my body returned to me. I breathed again.

The door seemed a million miles away as I ran for help. Mr Campbell was the first to hear me yelling and came running at a pace belying his age.

'Sweet Jesus! Who is it?' he said, mortified at the sight.

'James McDonnell,' I murmured.

'Let's get him down, lad. Give me a hand.'

We put the chair upright and he gingerly stood, holding the body with one hand and cutting the rope with the other. I held his legs, trying to ignore the stench from his bowels emptying into his trousers. We carefully laid him down on the floor and Mr Campbell removed the noose from around his neck.

'Poor lad. Poor wee lad. He's nothing but a child.'

I sat on a pew and watched the teacher gently put his coat over James McDonnell's face. He bowed his head and did a silent prayer, with me accompanying him. After he had finished, he looked back up at me.

'Fenton. Go get Mr Goulburn and don't talk to anyone on the way. This is a private matter of a very sensitive nature that requires discretion. Go now.'

I nodded, walked straight to Mr Goulburn's office and knocked on the door.

'Enter,' he said.

I walked in pale and quiet.

'Excuse me, sir, but could you please come with me

to the chapel? Mr Campbell would like to see you there as soon as possible,' I said, noting another teacher in the room. Normally such a request might have been expected to be queried, especially due to the urgency of the request, but he seemed to realise something was amiss. He grabbed his coat and followed me over forthwith. Mr Campbell was standing guard at the door and took Mr Goulburn aside to explain the situation. Mr Goulburn covered his mouth and murmured, 'Dear God.' They both looked at the body and then at me. I sat wretchedly, wishing I were home with my mother.

'Go to your room, Fenton, there's a good lad. I'll send a messenger out immediately to the McDonnell family and get the matron to clean the boy up. The family will notify the funeral directors to come and collect the body. We'll lock the chapel doors and get him laid out here. There's less chance of anyone seeing him,' Mr Goulburn said.

Mr Campbell looked at me and put a comforting hand on my shoulder.

'It's all right, son. You couldn't have done anything to save this poor boy; he meant to do it either way and you just happened across him first.'

I cringed at his words as if they were daggers coming for me. Maybe I could have stopped this. Maybe he wanted me to find him first. He knew that I came here every night to pray.

'Get yourself cleaned up and ask the cook for a hot chocolate and something sweet before you settle in for the night. If she gives you any trouble, send her to me and I'll sort it.'

I nodded and with one last look at James McDonnell's body lying on the floor, I left.

I slunk into my room without calling in on the cook. My stomach wouldn't have tolerated any morsel entering its rolling innards. The news of James McDonnell's death seemed to spread like wildfire through the school, though it didn't originate from me. The matron was overheard talking to Mr Campbell by one of the students but mercifully no mention of the hanging was made. The classes continued but I was allowed the day off by the matron, who had visited me and declared I was too poorly. She tucked a hot water bottle in bed with me and left a plate of broth and hot chocolate on my nightstand.

Mr and Mrs McDonnell arrived mid-morning. I had wriggled out of bed and was keeping watch on the chapel. I saw them walking stoically towards the chapel, followed at a respectful distance by the funeral director. I shuddered involuntarily.

A short time later a coffin was carried out and loaded onto the funeral director's hearse. The parents were talking to the headmaster and I could just make out Mrs McDonnell wiping her eyes with her handkerchief.

Mr McDonnell put a strong arm around her and stiffened his shoulders. I expected them to follow the hearse out of the school grounds and was troubled to see them heading to my dormitory instead. They were accompanied by Mr Goulburn and it wasn't long before the door to my room opened, leaving me face to face with the grieving parents. I felt sick.

'Charles Fenton. This is Mr and Mrs McDonnell, James' parents,' said Mr Goulburn. I shook their hands numbly. 'They wish to speak with you about what happened last night.'

The anguish on their faces was painful to look at. I swallowed a lump in my throat.

'I understand ye saw our laddie first?' Mr McDonnell enquired.

'Yes, sir.'

'And he's in a few of yer classes?'

'Yes, sir.'

'Did he ever talk tae you at all?'

'Occasionally. But I didn't know him very well.'

'You're looking a bit peely-wally. Are ye all right?' I had gone white.

'The boy has been a bit off-colour since the event. It had been upsetting for everyone,' said Mr Goulburn.

'Fair enough so. I'll leave it at that. But just one more question. Is there anything ye can think of that might have made him do it?' said Mr McDonnell.

I shrunk within myself. What did I know? I knew something but nothing I could substantiate. Mr and Mrs McDonnell watched me and waited. I couldn't look either of them in the eye or even trust my own voice. I shook my head. They appeared accepting of my response and indeed, would have seemed shocked if I had answered in the affirmative.

'Thenk ye anyway, son. We appreciate the care and respect ye gave tae our son. God bless ye,' said Mr McDonnell and they left the room with Mr Goulburn.

I crawled back into bed and stayed there all day and night praying for James and wishing I had done more. My soul was troubled and though with time it got easier, I never forgot the sound of the rope rasping against the beam. That was the last time I went to the chapel on my own and my nightly prayers whispered in my bed from then on, always included James McDonnell in a hope that he rested in Heaven now. I could only hazard a guess as to whether God would allow me to enter the hallowed gates but I was even more determined to give him no more cause to doubt my inclusion.

Mr and Mrs Sloane

Another year passed at Rugby School and my education was progressing despite myself. I was neither the top of the class nor the bottom. The only exception was surprisingly Latin, which had troubled me so much in my first year. It rolled off my tongue now with ease, much to Henry's chagrin as he toiled onwards.

'Come on, Henry. Palma non sine pulvere,' I quipped, watching him with amusement.

'And what does that mean exactly, smarty-pants?' he grumbled.

'No reward without effort.'

'Well, we can't all be clever clogs, can we?' He sighed. 'I just need one more phrase to learn and then I'm done.'

I thought for a minute.

'How about this one? Scire quod sciendum. It means I wait for no man in the quest for truth,' I suggested, keeping my face neutral.

'Brilliant! Thanks, Fenton. You are a brick,' he said and settled down to writing the phrase.

It wasn't till the following evening that he realised he had been tricked.

'You little rotter! What a load of bollocks you gave me!' He was not so grateful now.

I laughed. 'What happened?'

'I got up all confident and said to Mr Wiseman, 'Scire quod sciendum,' to which he responded, "Good for you, Felldon, at least you got that one right," and then everyone laughed. I couldn't figure out why until I looked it up.' He pointed at me. 'You are a little shite, Fenton.'

'Scire quod sciendum. I know that I know nothing. Under the circumstances Felldon, probably not a bad quote to present to the class,' said Arthur Mannings smiling. 'You are not exactly renowned for your Latin skills.'

'I'd beat you in a one-mile dash any day of the week, Mannings,' he retorted.

'No doubt you would and thus we share our strengths and our weaknesses,' he acceded.

'And I've noticed you haven't touched a cigar since we were at Hyde Park Fenton.' Henry turned on me. I blushed.

'Not exactly my finest hour, I must admit.' I grimaced. 'And I must say the likelihood of my touching a cigar again is less than infinitesimal; it is a disgusting habit.'

Arthur Manning and Henry laughed.

'I must be off. I'm heading home this weekend for Meg and Jack's wedding,' I said.

They wished me a safe journey and I settled into the

coach back to Fenton Estate. I must have nodded off on the way, as it seemed only a short while before my luggage was being unpacked and I was welcomed back by my doting parents. It was very late at night and my mother look fatigued, so I excused myself as soon as I politely could and went to bed.

The next morning I went straight to Meg's room. The wedding was planned for 10am that morning. It was a simple affair with a small group of us meeting at the church and my parents being the witnesses. Jack wanted it kept as low key as possible in deference to his departed first wife, Rebecca. They were going to announce their marriage by calling cards, requesting close family and friends to visit them at home. Meg had already printed the cards ready to be distributed. She was busy fixing her hair.

'Hello Charlie.' She hugged me and kissed my head.

'Oh Meg. You look beautiful.'

Meg smiled and continued to fiddle with her hair. She had her best dress on with some added white lace adorning the neckline and across the bust. In her hair were little flowers of orange blossom entwined and held securely with a comb.

'Did you know your mother has kindly organised a photographer to take a photo?'

I cringed, remembering the last sitting. She laughed at my expression.

'Don't worry, Charlie. The photograph is of Jack and me only.'

The relief passed over my face, quickly followed by shame for showing it so openly.

'You know I would pose for it if you really wanted me to, don't you?' I shuffled my feet.

'Of course, Charlie. You have a good heart inside you. I have never doubted that in all the years I've looked after you.'

I smiled shyly at the praise.

'Now be off with you and leave a lady in peace. I'll see you at the church later,' she said. I impulsively gave her a peck on the cheek and left.

We were all dressed in our Sunday best and as I watched Jack pulling at his neck collar and squirming, I felt I was a kindred spirit. I couldn't wait to get out of these threads and tuck into the feast our cook was busily humming over when we departed. I spied a heavily frosted fruit cake and some delicate little cupcakes but the cook was well aware of my presence and kept an eagle eye on the laden table. It wasn't until I had completely left the kitchen that she released her vigilance and breathed again. My disappointment was lightened by the fact that I knew beyond any doubt I would be tucking into the goodies later that day. My stomach growled in dismay but I chose to ignore it valiantly.

The wedding service, therefore, seemed unreasonably

long. I suffered through the solemn vows of eternal devotion and dedication to each other in ill grace. Surely the whole process could have been slightly more efficient. The prayers in particular seemed punishing in their length and the signing of the wedding certificate was dragged out in a painfully hesitant manner by both the bride and the groom. I urged them mentally to consider all hesitation at this stage was ill-advised and to think of their enduring guests. Perhaps they heard me as the rituals were finally complete and they walked out of the church to receive our congratulations outside.

I hugged them both in relief and pleasure that this day had finally come for them. A small part of my mind weighed briefly on the circumstances allowing this joyous reunion, but I quickly flicked it aside. It was time to celebrate and feast, looking forward rather than reflecting on a sad memory. We returned to the estate and the happy couple were set upon by the staff hugging them and praising their union. This all delayed my getting to the wedding breakfast but eventually we were seated and with speeches made, we began their first joyous meal as a husband and wife. My father was particularly jubilant as one of his reviled Chartist activists, Feargus O'Connor, had been recently installed into the Chiswick asylum. He reminded my mother several times, to her growing impatience, that he had predicted Mr O'Connor was crazy and would end up there before too long. This newsworthy update was whispered into her ear so as not to fall upon Jack's and ruin his happy day. Feargus O'Connor and his mob, he muttered on, were the reason behind the sharp drop in corn prices and a loss of profit for the Fenton Estate. A point made darkly even though it bore us no frugality owing to Mr Walton's fine nose for farming business. It took a wintry reminder from his beloved regarding the festivity at hand before he withdrew his murmured ranting and refocussed. I watched the exchange with interest having never before seen my father chastised. Mercifully I was the sole witness and the highly regarded respect and veneration for my father was maintained. The head of the Fenton family was still viewed as proud and honourable. I stopped studying Mr and Mrs Charles Fenton and regarded the happy newlyweds. It was then I realised Meg was my nanny no longer, but had now become the respectable wife of Mr Jack Sloane.

My first official rugby game

Mr Campbell had whipped us into shape as much as any man could have been capable of with such feeble fodder. I felt fit and manly and held a secret belief that the team would soon be lifting me onto their shoulders in a fit of post-match reverential adulation. The tackling had improved and I wasn't the slowest man on the field. My ball-handling skills still needed a bit of work, but I was far superior to Billy Sedgwick. Billy Sedgwick had the rotundity of a melon with legs that appeared to sprout from underneath even though they lived in a fleshy shade. His arms wobbled in windmill rotations in a mad dash to catch the flying ball when it came his way, but inevitably the ball would hit his middle and bounce off before his hands could even touch it. His only ability was his strength in the forward pack. He merely had to lean on the opposing scrum with the forward push of his fellow men behind him and the opponents would drop like skittles.

On the other scale was Harold Schuman. He was our fly-half responsible for clearing the ball from the scrum and passing it out to the backs so they could run for the try-line. He was a weed possibly from the dandelion family. With the large pale blue eyes forever darting around and the bony body crouching, jumping and hurling itself around, I was reminded of a small summer gecko. He couldn't tackle a baby, nor did he have any power to be mentioned but he was able to read the game with chess-like ability and free the ball into spaces you would never have predicted to open. He ran our team with his own sharp-eyed decisions, marrying the forwards and the backs seamlessly. Mr Campbell judiciously made him captain. A point I resented quietly.

We would be playing our first game against Mitchell House and had decided that we would make it one hour each way as the wind gave unfair advantage to one team. We eyed each other up like strangers though we were all from the same school. I couldn't help noticing one of theirs had the build of a gorilla and made a mental note to give him wide berth. I adopted my angry menacing face to try and frighten them into submission, unfortunately they were equally fierce and I quavered just a little bit. The whistle blew and the game began.

I was on the wing, selected for my obvious speed and great tackling ability. We started with a hiss and a roar, driving hard in the forwards and making great yards down towards the try-line. Billy Sedgwick ploughed through with our forwards following behind. Harold cleared the ball to our centre, who then cleanly kicked it over between the posts to score first points. It was the backs' turn next with some breaking through the defensive line of Mitchell House and fending one poor sod into the mud; the second five-eight dashed straight ahead and landed with ball in hand over the try-line. Mitchell House fought back and managed to kick successive goals and then a sneaky push-over try from the forwards. I had run with the ball a few times but had been tackled, though not before passing the ball back into another player. My friends yelled encouraging advice from the sideline, which I promptly ignored and was punished for it.

At halftime, we guzzled down water and tried to suck in some breaths. I was fit but now I was feeling the pain. A ruck mark I had received earlier had resulted in a score down my calf and I was grateful my mother wasn't there or she may have ordered the school nurse to run onto the field and clean and dress it. I admired it proudly and hoped it would scar.

The second half was brutal. I had been able to score a try after a brilliant pass from Harold through to our centre. He drew and passed to me leaving a clear run to the try-line and with an accelerating speed egged on by the heavy thump of boots behind me, I placed the ball over the line and was promptly whacked on the back and had my hair tousled by my grateful team.

Billy was exhausted by the second half and a slightly less obese replacement was selected. Harold and the rest carried on and we were nearing the end, with Mitchell House only a few points behind us. The final play was upon us and we drew from the depths of our soul to finish the game bravely. I was facing the gorilla that I had managed to keep clear of for most of the game. He had the ball tucked under his arm and was barrelling down towards me at a great rate of knots determined to score the final points. He had already fended two players off and they lay on the field moaning. It was me and him. And I was the only thing stopping him. I had to tackle him. I could feel Mr Campbell's eyes on me and I swear I saw his lips moving in a muttered prayer. He had drilled me and drilled me and I knew this would be my moment of glory unsurpassed by any other. I took a deep breath and squared my shoulders, bracing for the impact and lining the gorilla's legs up to break into two. He thundered on and seemed to have a glint in his eyes suspecting I would be soon eating dirt. I was going to prove him wrong.

I ran towards him and drove my shoulder towards his legs. He lifted his knee and got me cleanly between the eyes. I saw stars but grimly held on, being dragged behind him but not releasing my death grip. I was soon down to his right ankle and now in the deepest of dire straits. I lifted his ankle up and flicked it. I landed heavily to the ground wrenching my shoulder but realised I had done all that I could. I looked up in hope and was supremely staggered to see him falling like a great oak tree and crumpling to the ground. The ball trickled out and the whistle blew. We had won. The school nurse had to bind my shoulder in a sling for two weeks and I sported two black eyes but it was worth it. I would have done it again in a heartbeat, as there's no higher place than on the shoulders of your comrades.

Puberty

The school had moulded me into a strapping lad of fifteen years. Hairs were sprouting in unseemly places and I forced to begin shaving my silken down peeping from my chin. This fact was tutted about amongst all of us MEN, bearing this tedious chore with secretive glee. Rubbing one's hand thoughtfully along one's shaven bristles lent a more sophisticated air than ever thought possible when we were just sissy milksops. We watched the juniors arrive from our lofty perches and hatched lists of meaningless tasks for them to perform to remind them, if they hadn't already realised, that we were their superiors.

1855 saw the bread riots in Liverpool with starving people raiding the shops for food and the Crimean War leading our British soldiers into bloodthirsty battle. These were desperate times for many people and lives were squandered with Government ineptitude but we flitted along oblivious to the skeletal-rich and bloodied fields.

Last year a distant relative of Jack Sloane had been embroiled in a sordid scandal. Both he and Meg refused to talk about it but we had read the daily rag sent from

London with the court report printed with all its salacious gore. His second cousin Willie Sloane and his wife Agatha had been found guilty for their mistreatment of the housemaid Jane Williams. She had turned up at a charity hospital a mere skeleton covered in bruises and filth and riddled with flea bites. She had been hired by Mr and Mrs Sloane to clean the house but was kept as a slave. She was locked in a closet at night with no food or water and only allowed to use the chamber pot once a day. Mrs Sloane would punish her if she dared to use it more by pushing the excrement into her mouth and then making her mop the floor clean of her vomit with her ragged dress. She forced raw liver down her throat and beat her with a table leg over the head and shoulders until she bled. Mr Sloane kicked her in the stomach when she dared to ask for some rags to staunch her menstrual cycle and the blood would trickle down and dry on top of the filth crusted over her skinny legs. Her only sustenance was the vegetable peelings and meat scraps gnawed off bones. Her teeth were broken in several places and the gums so swollen and infected that her entire mouth had to be emptied of all dental commodities. She had lost sight in one eye when it had become infected and the suppurating orb had to be operated on as soon as she got to the hospital. The doctors had never before seen such a pitiful creature of woe. It took several weeks of dedicated medical treatment and nursing to bring her back from the brink of death. The outrage that ensued after the court hearing was fanatical. It could be offered that the Sloanes got off lightly with three years' hard labour in preference to a mob confrontation. My mother wrote that Jack had taken it very poorly and denounced any relationship with his second cousin whenever asked. It was a subject unspoken of at the Fenton Estate, quickly boxed and secreted away into the inky darkness of the past. This was something we were very efficient with.

None of this human degradation or suffering touched our world at all. Henry, Benjamin, Arthur and I fished in the river, swam, played cricket on the green, rugby in the winter and traipsed around the surrounding farmlands and villages without a care in the world. Benjamin Roberts had acquired a small goldmine of French postcards through sources he would not reveal. They contained photos of nude and near-nude French women lounging on chairs, draped in chiffon and even legs open wide studying themselves in handheld mirrors. He soon had us in fierce bidding wars for the honour of leasing his cards for one week each. Arthur Mannings was the soundest of savers with his accounts and therefore maintained top bid for the first week. Benjamin Roberts pocketed his coin and handed the postcards over with strict instructions to take care of them and keep them well hidden. Henry and I had faces of jealous thunder as Mannings bowed and disappeared with the winning bid.

After a week had passed he returned them observing that the quality of the photographs was slightly grainy but passable for the intent of the picture. His scientific analysis fooled no one as we had hardly seen him the entire time he'd had the postcards in this possession. His sudden desire of long walks in the fields to sketch landscapes must have been very stimulating as he always came back flushed and animated. Not many sketches though.

I was the second highest bidder and I elatedly snatched the postcards and hunted for an area of private reflection. Every room was against me. When I eagerly turned a door knob to look inside, invariably there would be mountains of lads staring back at me. The study, the library, the gymnasium were all populated with students. These were restless times for a chap like me on such a clandestine mission. Finally my prayers were answered and I found a broom closet so rich with cobwebs that it was surely never to be frequented by mankind on any but the rarest of occasions. The only downside was the poor light, but with the door opened a chink, I was able to see the pictures without much difficulty.

I settled down into a corner and opened the envelope to reveal the first postcard. She was a raven beauty with bold curls framing her expressive eyes. Covering her was wispy gauze in toga fashion that flaunted a dark areolar nipple winking at me saucily. Her index finger lingered partly in her mouth and was partly cushioned on rouged lips with the merest sense of a tongue coming out to greet it.

I was in lust immediately and stared, hypnotised by her eyes. The air in the cupboard became very constricting and without me realising, my trousers seemed to fall down to my ankles and I tentatively touched myself, keeping a wide eye on the gap in the door. She egged me on, urging me to stroke faster, and to please her I obeyed immediately. My head flicked constantly between her passionate looks and the door, but soon she won over and I was captured and entranced. I forgot the door and focussed on the job at hand, wanting to close my eyes in pleasure but wanting to watch her too. I groaned deeply imagining her there with me, kissing me and touching me, biting my earlobe and giggling naughty words, telling me what she would like me to do to her. I could almost feel her soft hands caressing me and urging me on, and see her tweaking her nipples and bouncing them in front of me teasingly. The cobwebs quivered around me as I indulged in the throes of self-passion and the spiders hid in their corners, too afraid to snare the large beast caught in their trap. She carried on taunting me, touching her pointed breasts, licking her finger and whirling it seductively around the darkened circle and then moistening her finger again to touch the other nipple. I was wild with hunger and brutally pulled at myself in pleasurable pain.

'Ah. Ah. Ah. Oh yes. Yes. Yes. Urgggghhhhhh!'

Sticky smutty cum spurted out all over the cobwebs, soaking them. This drove the spiders to anarchy and they crawled out in numbers, confused about why their peace had been so rudely destroyed. The webs stuck to the goo on my hands and my hair was matted in dead flies and angry arachnids. The disturbed dust settled over me and was sucked into my heavily worked lungs and promptly huffed out. I tenderly placed the pile of postcards to my left and slowly straightened my legs as much as one can in a broom closet. Looking wearily around for something to wipe with, I came across a dirty piece of sacking and with a shrug, started the clean-up. Swishing my hair to clear the cobwebs offset another thick cloud of dust and a bout of coughing followed. I finally figured it was best to leave and fix myself up at a washbasin. The brooms clattered angrily, supporting the spiders in the affront to their neighbourhood. Apologetically I dusted down and sneaking a peek, crept out of the closet with postcards in pocket. A caretaker coming down the corridor stared after me in confusion as my cobwebbed covered being sneaked off for a more thorough toilet.

Ah, those French ladies. I should have dehydrated away with the body fluids lost in that week. They were all so magical and wondrous but my favourite was the first lady of the broom closet – not that they all did not receive a similar amount of love and affection. I was deeply saddened when the week was over and I had to surrender my ladies to my best friend Henry. I only hoped he would love them all like I did.

Arthur Mannings

Now that Mannings and I had experienced and exhausted ourselves on the luscious ladies, we had to move on to other entertainment. We had taken to star gazing with his telescope on any clear night. Henry Felldon and Benjamin Roberts came with us on the first night but quickly grew bored at seeing the night sky, especially on the colder nights.

The best place to see them all clearly was on top of the hill behind the hall. Mannings had diagrams to allow us to star hop and search for each constellation. Ursa Major, Ursa Minor and the Orion kept us fascinated but we also hunted Andromeda, Canis Major and my personal favourite, Centaurus. Each time a shooting star appeared I secretly made a wish just like my mother had told me to. I was sure that Mannings, Mr Scientific Know-it-all, made one as well, but neither of us would dare confess such a nonsensical habit.

The climb up was steep and because of Manning's asthma, we took it slowly, giving him a chance to catch his breath. I daren't show any sympathy as he despised that sort of behaviour but secretly I watched his gasping for breath with morbid fear, hoping that he wouldn't drop dead on me. I had seen enough dead bodies to last me a lifetime. To pass the time while I waited to climb again, I would prattle on and admire the sweeping view we had of the neighbouring farmlands. I had a hankering to give them a closer inspection but the farmers had made it quite clear that students were not welcome. Intriguing though what might lie within. My mind was wandering lately onto the subject of women. Occasionally I would wonder what Lily was up to back home and whether she would talk to me ever again. I had already shared the story of my first futile attempt of courtship with Mannings and it so delighted him that he requested it to be told repeatedly. Each time, I swear the story became more farcical and I had to admit I used a certain amount of leniency when exercising the truth.

'I would love to meet your Lily one day, Fenton,' he wheezed whilst listening to me tell yet another version of the story.

'Our paths may never cross again I fear. She is someone destined for greater things than me.' I studied Mannings and noted his breathing had eased so I took the opportunity to ask a question preying on my mind.

'Have you ever kissed a girl?'

Mannings smiled quietly and blew his nose. 'Well, it might surprise you to know, Fenton, that I actually have a young lady friend back home. Her name is Sara.'

I was surprised, and more than a little envious.

'Why have you kept that so darned close to your chest?' I asked.

'Because you've never asked. We plan to marry one day, you know.' He looked at me.

I was gobsmacked.

'Does your mother know?' I asked him as if I were his father catching him in the middle of snatching a cookie.

'She arranged the meeting. Sara's mother is one of her very dear friends. We have known each other since childhood.'

Well, I never. Fancy him being practically already married and I hadn't even kissed a girl. This was most unpalatable, especially with the ears he sported. I was far better looking than Mannings. Life was so bloody unfair sometimes.

'How fantastic, Mannings! I would love to meet her one day.'

'You shall. I'm sure of it.' We continued on up the hill and spent the next couple of hours admiring the galaxy.

Exploring the outside world

My talk with Arthur Mannings on the hilltop that night had made me realise that my childhood years were fast disappearing behind me. The future had been set and my father was making noises about my working during the holidays at his London apartment doing light clerical work. In his mind, this would be a great opportunity for me to learn the ropes and stimulate my appetite for a lawyer's degree, but to me it was the beginning of the end. My vision of writing to the adoring masses was still strong but reality had a way of kicking me awake and shaking me resoundingly. I was considering how to broach my father for an allowance when a small stone cut me on the head.

'Who did that?'

I glared angrily around to find the little reprobate whose ears were about to be boxed. I heard a giggle from behind the hedge and swung hastily to see the hint of a small figure dashing away.

'Come back here!' With the trickle of blood dribbling down the side of my face I took off at top speed to chase down my attacker. It was a girl much to my shocked dismay. Even more shocking was the fact she was vanishing before my very eyes. She was skipping over the broken fields barely missing daunting clumps of earth that I suspected were laid purposely to trip schoolboys up. This had to be true because I considered myself nimble and still I fell repeatedly nearly twisting my ankle on more than one occasion.

'Come back here, you little brat!' I yelled indignantly after her fleeing frame.

She chortled and appeared to find another speed, challenging the hummingbird by flitting from clump to clump. She looked over her shoulder to see me fall yet again but this time into a cowpat. By the moist tenacity and grassy freshness I could judge it to be recently produced. I had chosen well, particularly when a brief scan of the field showed nothing but clean green grass and clumps. If only I had known then what would befall me because of this girl, I would have run all the way back to school without a backward glance.

Instead, I yelled after her. 'You won't get away with this! I'll find you and give you what for!' I shook my fist at her disappearing figure, touching the sore spot on my face where the blood was still trickling down. Regrettably I had not realised that the cowpat had found its way onto my hand and was now mixing in with the blood dirtying my face. The smell reminded me.

'Shit!' I whacked the dirt with my fist and swore at her. I refused to give up now my blood was boiling. With a second wind I unstuck myself and started to chase again. I could just see her nearing the Montgomery's farm and was intrigued to see her enter their doorway. We all knew the Montgomerys had no children, losing both of their sons to the fever. They had managed their farm on their own, though they had recently cut back to just one cow and some chickens. They kept to themselves and had a particular distaste for our neighbouring school probably due to the fact we harassed them the most, fishing from their river and stealing their apples and fresh hen eggs. We learned to be very wary so as I neared the cottage I slowed down and approached with great caution.

The cow regarded me, thoughtfully chewing her cud. I used her broad frame as a cover to sneak ever nearer to the Montgomery's kitchen. I wondered briefly if this very same cow was the maker of my sticky landing and this stopped me from automatically giving her a comforting scratch. Usually I loved cows and gave them the highest regard especially as I knew they were the producers of some very fine food. On second thoughts it would be best to remember my manners and so I contritely scratched behind her ears which she appeared to appreciate. She bore me no ill feeling for my previous hesitation.

I could smell small snippets of delicious food gliding towards my nostrils from the open window. My stomach rumbled to remind me of impending starvation. Could it be there was a hint of ginger apple cake? This was one of my favourite cakes and Cook made it every time I came back to Fenton Estate. My mouth watered in response and I stole closer up to the window of the kitchen. Slowly, slowly I went from crouch position to standing to peek over the windowsill and see within. On the table lay the aforementioned cake, steaming and golden. It was not alone as Mrs Montgomery had also baked a large fresh white loaf of bread and was busying herself with laying the table. I couldn't see my assailant but presumed she was washing up before the meal and would be out presently. The tablecloth had been laid with intricate pictures of flowers in each corner, which Mrs Montgomery would have embroidered when she was a young girl. The kitchen was coarse but tidy with a roaring pot stove in the corner and shelves laden with pots, plates and jars of all shapes and sizes. As I watched, Mr Montgomery entered and headed straight for the brewed coffee pot bubbling on the stove, pouring a large mug from which to sip cautiously. He turned and surveyed the meal with muted satisfaction preparing to sit when he caught a glimpse of my head as I quickly ducked down.

'Who's that spying at my window?! Get out and show yourself!' he roared.

I stood up and turned to make a clean getaway but he

was much faster than I would have considered a man of his age to be. He threw the boiling contents of his mug right over me, burning my shoulders and chest.

'Argggggghhhhh!' I screamed in pain, ripping my shirt off. He was after me and managed to grab my arm. He twisted my arm up behind my back and almost had me done but after a few cursing yards and frantic to escape, I kicked blindly backwards catching his left knee. He dropped me like a stone and I was off darting away as fast as my legs could carry me. I was much too nippy for his aging limbs.

He rubbed his knee furiously and yelled, 'Don't you ever come back here if you know what's best for you! I'll lay my switch on you next time.'

His words trailed into my ears as I dashed for the river and dived in to ease the searing pain. My skin was pink and scalding and I was stuck between the icy cold chilling my limbs and also soothing the burnt torso. It was agony. My teeth were chattering by the time I felt I could leave the stony river and I studied with sullen interest the little blisters forming from the coffee. The skin was still reddened but not as angry, the pain had subsided a little and with my drenched shirt put back over the top I was kept relatively comfortable. On the plus side, I thought acidly, the blood and cow muck had been cleaned from my face leaving just a small bump from the pebble. My shoulder throbbed from the near dislocation from its socket and I felt very sorry for myself. The long trip back home was now spent reflecting not on my impending clerical career but how I was going to get my own back on that spiteful imp of a girl. She would regret ever crossing my path.

Cross Country

School House and Mitchell House were very close regarding points for academic and sporting achievement. We had managed to beat them at the rugby and we felt we had the edge with our cross country due to my good friends Henry Felldon and Benjamin Roberts. I was part of the cross country team but only on their insistence. They weren't so forthcoming towards Arthur Mannings, however, who took the exclusion with aplomb.

'You know how it is, Mannings. We don't want to risk your asthma flaring up in the race. You are much too valuable on our chess team.' Benjamin patted Mannings shoulder, discomfited for his friend.

'Roberts, I completely endorse your selection process. I have always known my athletic ability to be the most middling of mediocrity. I shall wave the banner instead for our house and cheer as loudly as my broken-down lungs will allow.'

'You're a champion, Mannings. I always knew it. Thanks for being so generous about the whole thing,' I said.

'My pleasure. But enough of this ego massaging; it's

time to head to the start line. It would be ironic if I were to be the reason we lost anyway from dilly-dallying.'

We snorted at the old-fashioned phrase and hurried to put our sports gear on. The event ran over fields that some of the farmers had previously agreed we could use on this one special day. They had arranged for their stock to be safely fenced away from the riotous boys and even the Montgomery farm was allowing a small corner of their land to be used.

There was already a hefty horde of boys cheering on their different houses. We arrived to a hoot of cheers from the School House juniors and I waved, a little abashed at the adoring accolades mainly being directed at my two friends. Mannings made a point of including me in his whooping praise, which I acknowledged with a mortified nod. His big-heartedness always managed to make me realise how much worthier he was than me. Henry Felldon and Benjamin Roberts began stretching and warming up, so I followed suit, looking over at Mitchell House's runners, who were our main adversaries. They looked confident and unperturbed about the imminent race. I personally regretted the second helping of porridge I'd had earlier; it now sat like a tombstone in my gut.

'Ready, steady, GO!'

We were off. The pushing and shoving in the beginning soon dwindled as the faster boys raced on ahead. I was in the middle of the pack and I watched Benjamin Roberts and Henry Felldon take off with an easy stride into the distance. They ran together, pacing and cajoling one another to push a little faster. Neither of them looked back to see where I was; it was already supposed that I would not keep up and it would have been awkward for us all. I jogged onwards, going a bit faster than I wanted to but not wanting to be left right at the back of the pack. This went well for about thirty minutes but soon I began to lag and little by little I found myself watching the true runners carry on. My shoulders slumped and I cursed again at my stupidity of agreeing to join the team. As they drew away I became slower and slower and soon I gave up altogether and began to walk. With a bit of luck they would forget I'd started and I could just sneak in the school later with ego intact.

The sun was sweltering and since I wasn't continuing the race, I changed direction and headed to the river with the thought of a cooling swim. I was in such a good mood I started to whistle and it took me some time before I heard the splashing and cries for help. Someone was in the river and in trouble I could see, even though I was a fair distance away. Instantly I sped over, watching in dismay as the head went under the water. I quickly dived in and pulled hard on the clothing, heaving the person up towards the surface. It wasn't till I had reached the side of the river that I recognised who it was. The hair was straggled over her face and she was coughing and retching up water but I knew it was the girl that had hit me with the stone. For a brief second I considered throwing her back in.

'Are you all right?' I asked her in quite a stern voice. She wasn't going to get away with it easily.

She continued to splutter and started taking in large gasps of air. Eventually she turned to study her rescuer and I noticed with some wretched delight, that she flinched when she remembered my face.

'Yes. You know who I am, don't you? I'm the lad you hit with a stone the other day.' I stared at her waiting for a response. Her eyes flitted around and I half-wondered if she was looking for an escape route. Surely she wouldn't be so rude, especially after I had saved her life. She wiped her face and tried to tidy up her hair. Then she looked at me in her pitiful woebegone state.

'What exactly were you doing in the river if you can't swim? That's a bit daft, isn't it?'

Her big green eyes looked straight into mine and her black hair hung in dribbling ropes and knots. She was a mess and looked a bit feral. My hoity-toity manner dropped a scale.

'I dropped my mam's brooch in there. The clasp broke and it fell in and caught the current. It's all I have of her and I've lost it.'

I waited for the gushes of tears that would usually

follow after such a comment but she remained mute and still. She watched me looking at her and a silence ensued. I could hear the birds twittering and tweeting in the background. Still, she refused to say anything else and just sat there staring at me. It all felt a bit as if she was waiting for something and I had no idea what it was. Perhaps I should have consoled on the loss of her mother but she looked as if she would bite my hand if I tried. So I sat there and listened to the birds.

She had almost been lost to my reverie until she began unbuttoning her dress. She continued to undress until she was only in her chemise and bloomers. Then she draped her outer garments over a branch to dry before lying back on the bank with a satisfied look.

The birds were forgotten immediately and I was transfixed. Though the gentleman within me admonished my behaviour I simply could not lower my eyes during the whole process. She was oblivious to my discomfiture and stared at the clouds, singing softly to herself. I couldn't trust myself to speak so I just sat there ogling her.

'You'll catch your death,' she said.

'What?' I croaked in a stupor.

'You'll catch your death.' She gestured towards my wet clothing. 'Your choice, I guess.'

'What?' I repeated stupidly.

She laughed and propped herself up onto her elbow.

I could clearly see the outline of her breast with the soaked linen covering nothing. My throat dried up and my mouth dropped open so wide the flies could have flown in and made a home. She was a pocketful of wildness, a wild gypsy with green eyes and jet black hair. She caught me staring at her bosom and smirked.

'You can touch them if you like.'

'What?' I had lost the ability to speak coherently.

'I said…you…can…touch…them.' Now I was being spoken to as if I were an imbecile.

I sat there in numbed shock. Did she really just say what I thought she said? She waited. I stared. She waited some more. One of us had to move.

'I know you want to.' She pointed to my breeches, which were annoyingly stuck to my groin. I moved backwards covering myself, feeling as if she had shot a bullet out of the end of her finger and got me right between the legs. She laughed and lay back onto her back closing her eyes. My hands fumbled, checking that everything was still in place, and I gave a reassuring squeeze. The wind blew her nipples into hardened peaks and my resolve to escape faded whilst I watched this transformation. How magical it was, the woman's breast. The countryside was bare of any human interference, the race was sure to be halfway through and they would all be heading back home. I still scanned the horizon to check for any people but we were alone.

I shuffled over on my bottom not trusting my legs. She could hear the noise but kept still with only a slight smile skimming over her face. I was right next to her now and my hand developed its own power drawing towards her. I cupped one breast tentatively, feeling the soft bouncy weight in my hand. Half of me expected her to swipe me with a rock but when nothing happened I became more adventurous. I moved my other hand over to touch both breasts. The smoothness of her skin and firm pert bosoms was completed with a pointy tip of both nipples. My thumb gently caressed each nipple marvelling how hard they felt. I fondled both left and right in circular motion keeping my eyes on the breasts but occasionally darting a furtive glance up to her face to see her expression. To my coltish glee she appeared to be appreciating the attention she was getting. She leaned her head back making the breasts more prominent and heart-stoppingly gorgeous. I was in erotic bliss and it became absolutely necessary that I had to suck one of those glorious nipples. Her chemise was still on but stuck as a second skin and was but a wisp to me. I slowly and carefully lowered my head keeping my eyes watchfully on her. My mouth came closer and closer to her nipple and I landed my lips onto it kissing it and suckling in rapture. Oh God. I am in Heaven now. But not for long; I was soon tumbling back down to earth with a thump.

'Oi! I didn't say you could do that. Back off.'

She sideswiped my head and boxed my ears. I rubbed my ears churlishly and scowled at her for interrupting my magical moment.

'What did you do that for?' I growled.

She stood up and put her hands on her hips, her glorious orbs staring down at me at the same time her green eyes flashed.

'I'll decide what you can do to me. And I didn't say you could suck my tit,' she reprimanded me.

I flushed beet red at the direct way she spoke to me. I was not in a position of power and though my groin ached in throbbing pain I knew she was absolutely correct. I needed to retrieve some of my control even though I was crazy with lust for her. And I didn't even know her name. I dropped my head in shame.

'I'm sorry. I don't know what came over me. Forgive me.'

'I'm going back to the farm now.' She pulled her damp clothes off the branch and started dressing. I watched her in angst as my erection waned. I was an animal who needed to make amends.

'What's your name?'

She looked at me for a moment.

'Lutka.'

'My name is Charles. Charles Fenton.'

I stood up to shake her hand. She looked down at it

and laughed. I stared at my slighted hand dumbly before considering how oafish I was being. I had just sucked her breast and touched it. What an idiot. I watched her walk away from me back towards the Montgomery farm. She had a twinkle in her step and I suspected she was laughing at me quietly.

'Will I see you again?' I called after her.

She turned and blew me a kiss, then continued walking. It was some time before my limbs remembered to work and I slumped back to school. Henry Felldon, Benjamin Roberts and Arthur Mannings were all sitting waiting for me in the study.

'What happened to you? We were just about to send out a search party.'

'You wouldn't believe it if I told you.' I sat down despondently.

'Try us, old man,' said Mannings, handing me a lager.

I related the story from start to finish and once I had finished I looked at them all. I could see they thought I was half-pulling their legs but not being one hundred percent sure, they didn't refute it.

'Lutka you say her name was?' asked Henry. 'Bit of an odd name, isn't it?'

'I know. But I plan to see her again.'

'Wouldn't we all, Fenton! She sounds a right goer!' The lads all laughed and chinked mugs, drinking on and regaling me with the victory of Benjamin Roberts, who had won the cross country. It was the last day before the summer holidays so we stayed on drinking through the night, knowing we wouldn't see each other again till the new term. I was off directly to London tomorrow to begin my clerical introduction with the idea that after next year I could slide right into the career so carefully mapped out for me. My father was already there awaiting my arrival with great anticipation. I felt as if I was starting the path to nowhere and it was with solemn heart I retired late that night.

The drudgery

The train ride to London wasn't as enthusiastically anticipated as it had been when we all travelled to see the Great Exhibition. It was still bloated full of people. Fat one, thin ones, smelly unwashed bodies patting against dried up cantankerous old maids; we were all part of one big mass driving onwards to feed the beast called London. Her appetite was endless and she called us in deeper and further into her voracious belly. The conglomeration of people pupa all cushioned in together was merely an entrée on our coach. Like a queen bee sitting fat on her throne, the city demanded, chewed and spat out, grubby soul after soul. The spineless stood no chance against the beast and all the poor farmers and hard done by who strived a better life for themselves, a new beginning, a new hope, were clobbered insensible and tossed aside in an even worse state than when they'd begun. This was not a place for them.

Arriving at the station I jostled along with the rest of them to hunt down and collect my trunk. It was the same large trunk my parents had proudly bought me for my first day at Rugby School and though it was battered and scuffed, it was still a trunk to be useful, being of a size that fitted not only my clothing but also my treasured books and writing pads. I spotted it and valiantly fought my way through to grab my possession and heave it to the ground. There I might have stayed if I hadn't come across my father with his own personalised trolley in tow. The porters were descending on the masses pouring out of the carriages and were shouting and pushing to get to the richest customers. Children stood crying whilst being clutched fiercely by wide-eyed mothers dumbfounded at the clangorous reception they were enduring. Those that were lucky enough to have a male escort drew themselves away from the fray to find a safer, less volatile spot to wait patiently. They tried resolutely to block out the cacophony hammering their children's delicate ears as they kept watch over them and their purses vigilantly.

'Welcome to London, son. Let's get this trunk loaded and move to the lodgings I have prepared for you,' my father said.

We burrowed through the throng with determined air and made our way back to more peaceful surroundings. The buzzing ebbed the further we travelled from the station. My father had an office a short distance away and I was to accompany him tomorrow morning to be briefed of my responsibilities before he headed back home to his beloved Elizabeth.

My father had arranged for a meal at a nearby place called The Anchor on Park Street. As we opened the door to the pub I was struck by the masculine bonhomie radiating around us. I felt my chest expand and my height increased by at least two inches as I surveyed the clusters of men. The brick exterior drew you into rooms with low wooden ceilings staunchly supported by thick mahogany pillars. Men were peppered everywhere, good solid men of worth, with bristling whiskers and walrus moustaches. They lifted their pints of malted ale and slurped with deep satisfaction, sound in their belief that here they were imperial and the true makers of our glorious England. The cigar smoke, which made my stomach quiver, swirled convivially around their heads and wafted upwards to linger seductively on the ceiling. I watched a particularly fine-looking man who was sporting a monocle and as I admired his charismatic style I decided that I would purchase one for myself as soon as I could. The bowls of meaty shanks with lashings of potato drenched in beefy gravy were attacked with appreciative vigour and we were soon set in front of our own banquet of ale and nosh. We had progressed from father and son to two grown men enjoying one another's company in the warm surroundings of other like-minded men. It was most satisfying and the ale tasted better than any I had ever had before. We supped at The Anchor, companionably chatting over supper about my schooling and the latest news from Fenton Estate. I was pleased to hear that Meg and Jack were expecting their first child and I prayed silently that all would go well for them both. My father was delighted that I could now be a valued contributor to his London business and he extolled the sparkling future I would have when I began my career as a lawyer. I nodded meekly though inside my stomach seethed and bubbled, turning my delicious food and drink into an acidic slurry and ruining my general sense of wellbeing.

'You look ill, Charles. Did the supper disagree with you?'

'No, Father. It's been a long day... I suppose I am a little tired,' I replied.

'No. That's not it at all. Come now. Tell me what's troubling you.'

I hesitated. The inner struggle of duty versus passion emerged onto my features. I frowned and bit a finger. Could I tell my father what I really wanted?

'Whatever is the matter, lad? You've gone pale.' He placed his hand over mine in concern.

My head dropped. 'I don't know what to say... I am so very grateful for all the love and support both you and Mother have given me and yet I ask for more.'

'More? In what way do you want more? What haven't we provided you with?'

'I...I look up to you and I think you are the greatest father a son could have. I shouldn't be so selfish. Forget it. Forget I said anything at all,' I murmured, looking around.

'I certainly will not. Forget it! Forget it! What sort of father would I be, knowing my son is miserable but can't even tell me why? I demand you clear the mystery right now.' He thumped the table. 'This is outrageous.'

'I want to do this work and help you, Father, truly I do. It will be an honour and privilege to play my part for the business. Anytime you need some clerical or such tasks done, then I will be the truest and hardest working man you could ask for.'

'Indeed. Carry on.'

'It's just…it's just I don't see myself in the courtrooms at all.' I lowered my voice. 'I want to be a writer.'

I'd said it. I'd finally said the thing that had plagued me all these years and I couldn't take it back. I stopped breathing and looked at him. He looked confused.

'But you're a Fenton,' he finally said, rubbing his chin. 'When did this idea come about?'

I shrugged. 'I've always wanted to be a writer. Remember at primary school all the stories and poems I used to make up? The goblins and the monster wars I would chat to you about?'

'Yes, I do, but I never realised you were so passionate about it all. This is quite a surprise, Charles. I wish you had told me a lot sooner.'

'I'm sorry, Father. I just haven't had the courage,' I said.

He sucked in a deep breath and blew it out slowly and then he lit a cigar drawing deeply before pushing pillows of aromatic smoke into the air. I cringed and watched sadly. He didn't speak a word throughout the entire cigar, just sat there lost in thought. I dared not move a muscle and was relieved when he stubbed the cigar out and regarded me again.

'The way I see it, you are obligated to continue with the clerical work during the holidays and once you have left school. I have too much to do at home to be concerning myself with something you could do proficiently enough.'

I nodded.

'Having said that, I can appreciate your dilemma. I don't understand how you think that writing will support you and your future wife but I am willing to give you that chance. I will supply you with a small allowance once you have graduated, and passed your exams at school,' he frowned at me here, 'for a maximum of three years. If you haven't shown any promise as a writer I wish you to begin your apprenticeship in a more financially suitable trade.'

I couldn't believe my ears. My dream could come true. I was going to be a writer.

'Thank you. I won't let you down.'

'No, you won't. You are a Fenton.' He smiled and we continued the night both in a happier state. I knew my tasks and I was determined that I was going to work harder than any Fenton before me, not only in my holiday clerical chores or my school studies, but now and most importantly, in my writing.

We arose the next morning and walked to the office where my father explained my duties. I had the services of a maid named Sophie, who tended to the cleaning and cooked a hot lunch at midday. The office shared a floor with other professional firms, as an imposing menagerie of lawyers, accountants and business men worked on. My father introduced me to them and I did my level best to portray myself as an affable yet hard-working up and comer. The handshake was firm and I looked each man in the eye with a slight nod to acknowledge him as one of my own. They nodded back and I may have been mistaken, but I think I saw the odd small smile of appreciation in anticipation of my company. My office was seriously furnished with filing cabinets and shelves teeming with reports. The solid wooden desk was positioned facing the door and was in no doubt of its superiority. The ink pots, stamps and blotting paper looked almost apologetic for daring to rest on its stately cover. My father took me through the court transcripts I needed to copy and file and what had the highest priority. It seemed pretty straight forward and after sharing a light meal with him I bade him fare-well, hugging him in a fit of gratefulness. We walked to the train station where he shook my hand and I hugged him yet again. Embarrassed, he hugged me back with a firm thump on the shoulders before entering the coach to head back home.

A gentlemen's emporium caught my eye on the way back to the office and I strutted in looking suitably cultured and sophisticated. A tall, impeccably tailored man with a beak nose and sourly puckered lips looked at me and with hands behind his back, stiffly approached.

'May I help you, sir?' he sneered. My confidence faltered a little, but I was a Fenton. I carried on.

'Yes. I would like to see your range of monocles,' I replied in a slightly haughty tone. He seemed unperturbed.

'Does sir have short- or long-sighted requirements?'

I covered my confusion, cleverly rubbing my chin and tapping my nose in what would obviously seem a deep moment of brilliant contemplation.

'Long-sighted requirements.'

'Indeed.' He held my gaze a little bit longer than I felt necessary, before turning towards the cabinet to retrieve the monocle. It was really very stunning. A sterling silver chain was securely riveted to a fine-looking monocle exactly the same as the one I had seen the gentleman wearing in The Anchor. He held the monocle between finger and thumb and angled it to show the craftsmanship. It was superb.

'Would sir like to try it on for size?' he asked. I picked up the monocle and placed it carefully over my right eye, settling it under my brow and looking in the proffered mirror. My hands instinctively reached for my coat, which was parting from my puffed-out chest. A peacock could not have arrayed his feathers any more proudly than I. I looked quite spectacular and I could already picture the respectful glances I would ignore on returning to the office.

'How does it feel?' Mr Beak-nose enquired, looking on in what I understood to be a newly found respectful silence.

I studied myself for a little longer, before tearing away from the reflection.

'I'll take it,' I said, aware of the money my father had given me that was burning in my pocket. I paid quickly, and was doubly gratified to see the wonderful satin-lined box that the monocle came with. The salesman nodded slightly, exchanging my father's money for the neatly wrapped boxed monocle and bidding me good afternoon.

I dashed back to the office to try on my monocle, choosing to ignore the fact that everything I saw through it was a blurry mess. This was my new look and though it fell a couple of times during my scribing, I persevered and soon had the knack of keeping it in place. A developing headache was a small price to pay for such panache and style. I battled on through the day until it was time for home. No one had ventured into my office during that period so I was a little bothered when I didn't see anyone I knew on the way down to the street. Never mind, the public would be the first honoured with my appearance. I strode down town, contemplating how a fine ivory cane might complete the ensemble. This could not help but attract the attention of London's society and bring me to the fore of all social occasions. My mind wandered and I didn't notice an elderly gentleman coming the other way. I bowled him over so hard that he fell a full five feet away, landing awkwardly on the cobblestones. He looked so arthritic that I was convinced he would have a serious injury. I hurried over to help him back to his feet.

'I'm so sorry, sir. Are you hurt?' I asked, brushing the dirt from his trousers. Two ladies passed arm in arm and 'tsked' at me for being such a thug. I reddened and in my deepening shame, dropped my monocle which I had forgotten to attach to the button, causing it to fall onto the cobbles and crack. I picked it up swiftly and hid it into my pocket. The elderly man watched this with interest.

'I'm fine, young sir, I'm fine. I have survived far bigger lashings than this,' he responded, placing his hand on my arm in a benevolent manner. 'I see you have trouble with your eyesight too. An expected handicap when you are my age, but a travesty in one so young. It is no wonder we collided, two blind men on the pavement are one too many.' He smiled at me genially, and I blushed deeper.

'Quite,' I muttered.

'I do hope you can get it fixed easily enough. I could recommend someone for you if you like?' he offered politely. I wished the ground would swallow me up.

'Please, don't bother. I'll be fine.'

'Well. If you are sure then…' He straightened his coat and gave me a wink. 'We may have poor vision, but we have a strong constitution. You wouldn't know that I am eighty-eight years old, would you?' I had bowled over an octogenarian.

I shook my head, drowning in shame. He tapped his hat and carried on down the street, doddering merrily. I watched after him until he turned the corner, and then I walked back to my lodgings, placed the shattered mono-cle back into its box and quietly threw it in the bin.

I spent the remainder of my time learning the book-work and discovering London. Before long it turned from stranger to friend for me in the weeks during the holidays with landmarks becoming familiar and acquaintances made. Every statue, tavern and shop-front received my fullest inspection and digestion. I was paving the way for the real event when I would return a grown man soon to be a famous author, who would be read and revered for my literary genius. This was to be my destiny.

Lutka

Returning to school was always a joy. This time my usual re-acquainting was enlivened with not only my exciting new career but also the sensual delight of chasing Lutka. Like a swaggering tom cat I was determined to lay my scent on her before anyone else and the only way to do so was to seek her out. It took many a fruitless walk along the outskirts of the Montgomery farm before I finally caught a glimpse. I had her in my sight and I wasn't going to lose her now.

'Lutka!'

Lutka was heading back from the village carrying a heavy basket. I lit up knowing I could be her saviour and carry it back for her. I ran towards her cheerfully. She didn't seem quite as elated as me.

'Oh. It's you…Charles Fenton.'

She remembered my name! Oh joy!

'Yes, that's right. I'll give you a hand with that; it looks heavy.' I offered my hand in assistance.

'No, thanks. I'm fine.'

'Oh.'

I was back to being the wordless idiot. Not knowing what to do next, I meandered next to her in cretinous silence; so much for the tom cat. The weather had turned cooler and the lanes were bordered with plump juicy blackberries waiting to be plucked. This inspired me. I kept warm by running from bush to bush picking a handful at a time and chasing after Lutka, before she got too far away, to feed her some. Her hands were occupied with the basket, allowing me the delicious opportunity to feed the berries into her open mouth by hand. Each touch of her lips on my fingers sent a shiver down me and the glimpse of her tongue capturing each berry made me long to kiss and taste her sweetness. I realised I was her prey and her cool green eyes scrutinised my pathetic attempts at courtship. If she was to but say the words I would have lain down and rolled over waiting for my belly to be rubbed or ripped out according to her wishes. She nodded towards an abandoned hay barn just off the lane.

'Let's go in there. I am cold.'

I practically frolicked over in my joy of spending more time alone with her. She allowed me to carry her basket as she climbed over the fence towards the barn. I barely felt the basket in my arms though I'm sure it was full. She pointed where I was to place it and I obeyed instantly.

'I liked the berries. You may kiss me, Charles Fenton.'

'Thank you.'

I licked my lips nervously and stood in front of her.

Her teeth were ever so slightly stained from the black-berries and I found that entrancing. She studied my mouth and for a moment I worried I had something stuck in my teeth, until she moved closer and planted her lips onto mine.

Sheer bliss. I had no idea what I was doing but I was sure that my mouth should be open, so I opened it. She was thankfully a master of this and took that as an invitation to explore with her tongue. In my befuddled senses I learned from her and reciprocated the honour, tentatively poking my tongue and entwining it with hers. It was all a bit wet in my mind but deliriously exciting. I hoped she couldn't tell this was my first time and tried to be less timorous. My right hand fumbled its way up to her bosom but I was disappointed to find it safely ensconced in layers of fabric. I gave it a squeeze anyway and started exploring the dress for an opening to her skin. There was none and my tongue was beginning to tire with saliva dribbling down my chin. It was a worrying time.

She saved the situation by reaching forward and caressing my groin. I nearly fell backwards in surprise but recovered quickly, burning with shame and pleasure. She rubbed my erection as if inspecting it through the clothing and I wished I could rip at the buttons to set myself free. But she was having none of that; she smacked my hand away with every attempt to assist her man-handling. This was most frustrat-ing and I had no idea what to do next. I wanted to see her breasts again yet they seemed imprisoned and unreachable. Her dress on the other hand must have a portal somewhere.

Now I had a focus and I was determined. Still wres-tling tongues with her even with my jaw beginning to ache, I tippy-toed my fingers down to the hem of her dress. No smack so far. Emboldened I spider-fingered the dress upwards, silently cursing the multi-layered fashion of the day. How did women become so swad-dled? She continued to stroke my now throbbing pants and our arms crossed into each other's territories in deep exploration. She was more advanced than me so I redoubled my tracking. The layers! The eternal layers! They were designed by some elderly matriarch to protect all young maidens, of this I was sure. I vowed to track down this matron of the maidenheads and strike her down for her vindictiveness. I only hoped she was covered in layers of a sepulchre type to atone for her behaviour. May she rot in Hell.

As I suffered onwards I made some small progress and was even delighted to feel the soft skin of her thigh. This almost was the end of me and I had to mentally regroup and recall my first objective. A soldier must not fall down before reaching the battlefield of lust. Trying to block out her ministrations, I continued upwards,

upwards into the unknown. What was it like? The area was completely abstruse to me apart from the grainy photos on the French postcards. I only had the vague idea that that was where babies came out of and that particular fact wasn't one I wished to delve into. Onwards and upwards I continued to the final frontier. Surely soon I would discover all.

And so it was. She was wearing bloomers, the type with a gap in the middle for ease of toilet. A small edge of fabric and then I was there. I had hit utopia. It was fluffy and wet and I rushed my fingers deep within her before the moment was lost. Success! It felt so good! This is where I am meant to be. If only my friends could see me now. My pride was bountiful and I fondled her and kissed at the same time. She bit my lip which I took to be a bad sign but when I looked at her, she had her eyes closed and was leaning her head back. This must have meant I was doing all right and that she wanted me to kiss her neck so I obliged, grateful to relieve my aching jaw and discreetly wiping the drool on the shoulder of her dress.

That was a big mistake. She noticed my faux pas and stopped immediately.

'Ewwww! Get off of me now. That's disgusting, Charles Fenton.'

I tried to play the innocent but with the big wet mark displayed on her dress it was impossible. The fact that she wiped her own chin on her sleeve made no difference at all. I was in trouble again.

'Go home. I don't want to see you until you have brought me an apology present.'

'I'm sorry. I'll make it up to you. What would you like me to buy?'

She considered for a moment.

'I would like freshly cooked pig trotters which I MIGHT share with you for dinner.'

I was caught off guard yet again. That would have been the last thing I expected a young lady to ask for, but I had no leg to stand on.

'Your wish is my command, my lady. When shall I meet you for this delicious feast?'

'I will meet you here on Thursday at noon. Now off you go, Charles Fenton, before I change my mind.'

I moved hurriedly and was already counting in my head how much money I had left to spare for the trotters. It was a stretch but it could be done. Come Hell or high water I would be there on Thursday with trotters and a second chance at love.

Pig trotters

'Make sure you pick out the finest ones for her,' Benjamin advised. They had all decided to accompany me to the butcher's after I had told them what had happened with Lutka. Benjamin and Henry were the more curious of the three, wanting every explicit detail. Arthur Mannings was slightly less so and I had an unsettling impression that he didn't approve. I brushed this aside and dressed my tale up so much that as far as they were concerned, I was the swash-buckling seducer of wild women that no lady could deny. A slippery bank to stand on but I was now on top of the mountain and staying there. What could go wrong?

We reached the butcher's in high spirits and after much serious deliberation, chose four of the tastiest, meatiest trotters my meagre funds could afford. They were wrapped in brown paper with graceful decorum and we four gentlemen celebrated the purchase by partaking in a lager at The Rugby Tavern. The big event was tomorrow and I was to sneak out after the morning Latin class. We had two hours for lunch which was ample time to meet her, have lunch and hopefully continue our love making before returning to afternoon classes. It all seemed a flawless plan, especially with the boys providing helpful tips on what to do.

Another sleepless night: it was all I could do to refrain from running to the Montgomery farm in the middle of the night and ravishing her in her bed. The very idea of it kept me tossing and turning all night and it was only a trip to the beloved broom closet that helped me to relax and finally get some sleep.

Once again I thanked Reverend William Fleet for his Latin tutorials when I was but a junior. He was still teaching the young students but the grapevine had delivered information to avoid his special herbal tea. There was something quite peculiar about it and I felt so unnerved about the whole experience that I made up my mind to repress it and leave it behind. No. Life was good and going to get better come noon today.

'Amor et melle et felle est fecundissimus. Love is rich with both honey and venom,' I declared to the admiring classmates.

'Good, Fenton. Never a truer word has been said too.' Mr Wiseman chuckled. I was one of his top students and could do no wrong now. It was a hallowed place indeed.

We were nearing the end of the class and I was bristling with excitement. I had previously considered reciting some Latin love phrases to Lutka but then realised she might think I was taking the mick and the whole smarty pants thing could backfire. Play it safe was the best option on such tenuous grounds. This was not the time to be the fool. I watched the clock tick on, creeping slowly to the lunchtime bell.

If I had been in the cross country I would surely have won and broken the school record. Never had I been as fleet of foot as on this day. With pig trotters nestled in the crook of my arm, I fairly sprinted out the gate and hoofed it down the lane to the hay barn where my love, Lutka, was already waiting.

We opened the parcel together and I proudly presented her with the fleshiest trotter on show. Her eyes lit up and she made no attempt to nibble delicately but instead gnawed away in savage enjoyment. I took my cue from her and reacquainted myself with one of my father's favourite treats. He was not allowed to eat them at home as they were considered a peasant dish, so whenever we were at a tavern together we would order a plate to share in secret satisfaction. Lutka obviously shared my father's passion and was taking to the trotter with determination and culinary ecstasy. I was ambivalent at best but put on a good show for her.

When the last trotter was sucked dry of every scrap of meat and all that remained was a small pile of bones, she licked her fingers clean and wiped her greasy face on her sleeve. I was slightly more mannerly and used the discarded brown paper to dab fingers and chin. She smiled complacently and smacked her lips.

'That was lovely. I haven't had a good meal like that in years.'

'I aim to please, fair maiden.'

She snorted, then took on a more forlorn yet sly look.

'Mr Montgomery beats me and they don't feed me very much. I will leave them soon.'

I recalled the fine repast covering their kitchen table but kept silent. I knew Mr Montgomery was of foul temper after my run in with him and his hot coffee. Who's to say that he wasn't a difficult master? My poor sweet Lutka. I must find a way to keep her here.

'Perhaps I could see you each Tuesday and bring some extra food?' I suggested timidly.

'That might help. I could endure it all if I knew I was seeing you every week.'

The perfume of love floated around my ears. Yes, yes, she loves me I'm sure.

'What would you like me to bring next week?'

'Pickled eggs.'

Ugh. I'll save money and buy just enough for one this time.

'Certainly, my Lutka. Anything for you.'

'Good. Now I will do something for you.'

With a saucy smile she lay down on the ground and

lifted up her dress, revealing gaping britches. I stared at her in astonishment.

'Come on, before I get cold.'

Oh coital delight! To consummate without matrimonial responsibility…or perhaps not.

'We must not. I am too young to be married.'

'You are having a laugh, aren't you? I don't want to marry you.'

'Oh.' I was a bit peeved at the rejection but not enough to stop me from tearing off my trousers and shirt.

She laughed and lifted her arms towards me drawing me to her. I lay gingerly on top of her worried I might squash her and kissed her as I felt I should before anything else. It was a chaste kiss but the lower part of my body was decidedly more conspiratorial. I wriggled and poked until I felt that familiar wetness where so much joy lay abound. With an enquiring look at her, to which she responded with a nod, I put asunder my virginity and thrust my hips forward. I don't recollect very much apart from it being at top speed and over too soon. A million stars of pleasure exploded out of me and I was momentarily blinded. A long pumping groan emitted from my throat as I revelled in the throes of orgasm. I'd done it. I had made love. What a glorious moment to savour but, though Lutka was smiling, I couldn't help but think the moment wasn't as auspicious for her. At least she wasn't frowning, so small mercy for that. Discomforted I lifted myself off her and modestly redressed, turning my back so she couldn't see the shrivelled worm between my legs.

'Are you all right?' I enquired, politely helping her to her feet.

She brushed off the dirt and plucked off one tiny pork bone that had found its way into her hair.

'Of course I am. Are you?' she quipped, hand on her hip.

Blushing, I nodded in the affirmative. We agreed to meet every Tuesday and I became difficult to be around, mooning and sighing, prattling on about how wonderful she was to anyone that was in earshot. Over the cold winter weeks we made love over and over, with me bringing a new and more delectable treat each time much to her gratification. As far as I was concerned, we were in love, and I chose to ignore her less rapturous response in this regard. Arthur Mannings tried to talk to me but I was oblivious and regaled him with stories of her excitement each time we met. He muttered it was probably excitement for the food rather than me but I wouldn't hear of it and was mortally offended at the remark. I was Charles Augustus Fenton – who wouldn't be endeared with me? It was with saddened heart that I had to inform her of my returning back to the Fenton Estate that spring to celebrate not only my mother's birthday but also the arrival of a new baby girl for Meg and Jack. I would be back before she knew it, I comforted her, and we will see each other again. I chose to ignore her vagueness about my wretched news.

Newborn

I arrived late at night as per usual when returning back to Fenton Estate. The cook had left out some ginger apple cake and my father was waiting in the parlour.

'Welcome back, son. It's always a pleasure to see your face.'

'And yours, Father. You were happy with my efforts in London?'

'More than happy. You are a natural at paperwork. I hope to rely on you to continue with your diligence.'

'It would give me great satisfaction. I can work this summer holiday from dawn till dusk and then, with your permission, every morning once I have graduated. This will give me a few hours in the afternoon to write.'

'Ah yes, the writing.' A frown flitted across his face, which was hastily buried by a smile. 'That will work splendidly, Charles. Perhaps you might pick up the odd snippet of legal training as well?'

'I shall do my best, Father.'

'Excellent. I must retire to bed now. It is not long until your mother's birthday and I know you are anxious to see Meg's new baby.'

'I shall go see her after breakfast tomorrow.'

'Goodnight.'

'Goodnight Father.'

The cake was quickly demolished with a silent blessing towards our marvellous Cook and I fell asleep very quickly, looking forward to the new day.

I never tired of our sweet country air. It was a tonic to my nostrils so used to sweaty, male mustiness and polished wood. I sucked it in, closing my eyes and breathed out, smiling to be home again. Winter had been beaten into submission and spring laid down her wreaths of flowers in generous spirit. New life peeked outwards, timorously rising out of the rich earth in sporadic bursts of vibrant green. The sun streamed down in encouragement, urging the buds to grow and strengthen. Be strong little ones, for soon you will be big and hearty. The sparrows joined in with songs of hope and vivacity, their exuberance was infectious and if I had still been a child, I would have sprinted madly across one of our fields with arms wide open and yahooing riotously. My stomach was full of Cook's famous coddled eggs and home-cured bacon and my mother had spent the morning kissing me and telling me how handsome I had grown. Every story I told my parents held them enthralled as it had always done. I was the centre of their universe, their reason to live. What man could resist such adulation? I never wearied from it, such was my desire to be loved. With a spring in my step I happily walked to Meg and Jack's cottage to see the new baby.

'Charlie! How lovely to see you. I swear you get bigger each time!' Meg hugged me and showed me in.

'Hello Meg. You look as beautiful as ever. Motherhood agrees with you.'

She took my hand and brought me over to the crib where a tiny little baby was sleeping.

'We have called her Rebecca, after Jack's first wife.'

'What a lovely thing to do. She is a bonny baby.' I looked at the sleeping figure and smiled. Her little hand had popped out and she was suckling in her sleep with her little rosebud mouth working away.

We sat down and Meg poured a cup of tea while advising me that Jack would be home for lunch and he would love to have me share it with them. I offered to go back to the kitchen and gather a few buns from Cook. Meg gratefully accepted. She knew I had a grand appetite. We chatted about the latest Fenton news and she told me that my mother was planning a party with a few close friends for her birthday. Magda Williams would be attending, much to my father's chagrin, and she had already visited Meg herself and given her a balm to prevent nappy rash. I hadn't seen Magda since Rebecca's funeral and I squirmed a little at the thought of seeing her again. She made me a little uneasy.

Rebecca woke up whilst we were talking and I

excused myself to collect the buns, allowing Meg an opportunity to feed in private. I took my time in the kitchen, to Cook's delight, telling her how the food at Rugby was nothing compared to her ambrosia. She nodded sagely and accepted my compliments as fair due. When I felt I had given Meg ample time to feed Rebecca, I took my leave from Cook with a basket full of goodies. She insisted I take a few slices of boiled mutton as well to help nourish Meg's milk. I ambled back and knocked at the door to be absolutely certain I wouldn't see Meg breastfeeding. Jack answered it instead.

'Well, hello young master! I see you've already been introduced to our Becca.' He shook my hand and patted my shoulder in pride. Thankfully Rebecca had finished feeding and, with a clean nappy on, was ready for society. I dutifully took another look at the baby and made cooing noises to make her smile. She tried to grab my finger and suck it but I quickly pulled it away.

'Delightful, absolutely delightful. You must be very proud,' I said.

'It's the happiest time of our lives, Charles. One day you'll be a father too, God willing,' Jack smiled beatifically. I blanched at the idea but kept quiet. Meg sat with Rebecca on her knee, looking at the strange new man in her home. The home was filled with love and we sat down to a happy meal together and reminisced. We chatted animatedly about my mother's impending party and the lunch was only broken with Jack regretfully having to return to work.

'I'd best get back to it,' he said.

'I'll come with you and help if that's all right, Jack?' I offered.

'Fair enough. But those hands of yours might have softened up a bit now you are a scholar. It could cause a bit of damage.'

I snorted. I am a man. I followed him back to the stables, sneakily looking at my hands. He worked soundlessly, throwing bales of hay up effortlessly. I refused to stop even when the blisters drew up and bled. Gritting my teeth I maintained a manly air until we finally, mercifully, stopped for the day and I could withdraw, nursing my hands in private. I didn't offer to help the next day. I excused myself because I decided it was much more imperative that I help my mother with party organising. She accepted bemused as such things were normally abhorrent to me, but I shamefully think she spotted my blistered hands and surmised the real reason I hung close to her apron. Before long the party day arrived.

Party day

With even the most laborious planning there was no avoidance of the on-the-day mad panic and rush. Mother issued orders left and right and the maids cleaned and polished and shone every surface of the house. Our good china and crystal was brought out, inspected and buffed, then rigorously scrutinised once again before being gently and tactically placed on the snowy white tablecloth. The punch bowl sat ostentatiously in the middle waiting for its final flourish of liquid delight precisely timed just moments before the first guest should arrive. The cook pummelled and harassed her kitchen hands, who were whipping, peeling, dicing, and kneading with the speed of servants that had the devil's horses nipping at their back. It was debatable whom they feared the most, the cook or the very devil himself, on this special day of the Mistress. The gardener had outdone himself this year with the daffodils and crocuses bursting with colour and strategically placed around the room for maximum presentation in display. Father and I retreated to his office in a magnanimous gesture, helping Mother by keeping out of the way. She didn't seem to appreciate this sacrifice in the manner it was given so we made the exodus hastily. Father smoked his cigars and I sipped at port as we congratulated ourselves on our propensity to avoid errands. The bustle outside the door made us plunge deeper into our contented cave, relieved in the sanctum of man. It wasn't until the guests were soon to arrive that we slunk out and changed into our new suits that mother had ordered in just for this occasion. It may have been fate that made the guest I should encounter first be Magda Williams.

'Hello Charles. What a man you have become,' she said, presenting her cheek for a kiss.

I wasn't sure if she meant that as a compliment or not.

'Welcome, Mistress Williams, it's always a pleasure to have you as a guest.' I responded politely.

'Is it?' She raised an eyebrow, looking right through me. I had to struggle with the overpowering desire to squirm.

'You are looking well. How are you keeping?' I said, determined not to flee.

'I have recently given up coffee. I found it to be disagreeable to me. I think it is something we should both try to avoid, don't you agree?' She smiled sagely at me while I paled. What would she know about the Montgomery incident?

'Y…y…yes, I do. I am more of a tea drinker at present.' I bluffed my way through; it had to be a wild coincidence.

I was being paranoid and a Fenton should remain calm at all times.

'I'm sure you are.'

My mother spotted Magda talking to me and her whole face lit up; she approached gaily and kissed her on both cheeks.

'Magda, my darling, why does it always feel like forever since we last met?' she said.

'Because we are intrinsically linked to one another and will never part in this lifetime; each separation therefore seems unnatural to us,' Magda responded, holding my mother's hand and caressing it with her thumb.

My mother made a sideways glance at me before speaking. 'Come. I wish to talk to you in private before my duties as host draw me back into the fray.'

They linked arms and walked up the main staircase towards my parents' room. I stared at their retreating backs but then turned towards the party. The room was already filling with bunches of splendidly dressed ladies and gentleman. The society of Warwickshire was all invited and had preened and fussed themselves in the latest Parisian fashions. My eyes were buffeted with ribbons, feathers and pearls adorning our house like sashaying Christmas decorations. My father was there discussing the recent merits of Turkish baths soon to be opening in London. It was supposed to be beneficial to cleanse out toxins and reinvigorate the body. His companion, a Mr Roger Evenside, had already attended the Hydropathic Establishment in Ireland and he was fully endorsing my father's future attendance. The ladies looked on with muted curiosity and I resigned myself to join the conversation when some new guests arrived. I turned to welcome them in and my heart began pounding. Mr and Mrs Whittle entered and behind them, in dazzling light it would seem, were their twin daughters Lily and Carla from my primary school days.

I drank in the vision of Lily, my long lost first love. I stood rooted to the spot love-struck and stock-still. All I could see were her lovely eyes, her flaxen gold ringlets and her pert little chin. Carla was an attractive woman too – any man would have died for the honour to be in her company – but THIS man had eyes for her sister alone. Love is an enigma that cannot be explained or twisted or examined by any objective science or cause. Love cannot be bottled or preserved or dried for prosperity and presented on a wall to study or muse. Love is unfathomable and, at the moment she walked into my home, all thoughts, memories and commitments to Lutka sailed away to the horizon lost forever. This was true love. I knew that now. The scales had been ripped from my eyes, causing me pain because of her exquisite loveliness to which I was now exposed so bare. To die now would have been a release I could nearly embrace if it meant I would be in that moment forever. I was sure that my heart was going to explode, beating so hard against my ribs, as I yearned to be closer to her. I could only sympathise and dimly wonder how long it would be before I collapsed in a heap. It was my father who became the man of action.

'Welcome Mr and Mrs Whittle! Your lovely daughters grow more striking each time I see them. May I introduce my son Charles, who is in his final year at Rugby School?'

He gestured to me and I stepped numbly forward shaking hands with Mr Whittle and politely kissing his wife on the hand. They introduced their daughters to me and allowed my father to lead them to the refreshment table. I stayed behind with the sisters mentally urging Carla to follow her parents but she stubbornly did not.

'I remember you. You teased my sister once and killed her mouse.' She muttered so her parents could not overhear. Lily flinched and looked more closely at me. She held her sister's hand and squeezed it in response. They waited for my rebuttal. If Carla could read my mind right now she would have melted into an acid puddle because of the vitriolic words bubbling around in my head towards her. Leave Carla, leave.

'That was many years ago, Carla. Surely you don't mean to hold a childhood prank against me in this present day. I have changed very much for the better and can only hope that you and your sister will allow me to illustrate my amended behaviour,' I said, smiling as innocently as I could.

'Mother always taught us to forgive all those who seek redemption. It was many years ago and I was soon able to find another pet.' Lily smiled at me and I basked in her attention. Carla nodded graciously and excused herself to the punch bowl. The young men in the room magically appeared at her side to help her delicate hand in pouring a refreshing drink. They admired and wooed her in a manner becoming her cool refined beauty and she held court like a queen, gifting small smiles to those who pleased her best. They battled like gladiators for this exceptional token, the other young ladies in the room watching in lemony spite. They were no match for the Whittle twins, especially Carla. I kept Lily cornered and strove to get her out of the room as fast as possible before the others came our way.

'You are most kind in your absolving my past sins. I was a silly boy with air between my ears and scabs on my knees.'

Lily smiled. 'Your memory serves you well, Charles.'

'You see right through me, Lily. I admire your candour.'

'And I admire your courage. My sister Carla can be direct at times,' she responded.

'I barely noticed. My eyes and ears were only tuned to you.'

Lily blushed and looked over at her sister, who was encircled by admirers.

'It would seem that Carla will miss your attention greatly.'

'She will survive. It warms me greatly to see you again.'

'It is only for a short time. When do you go back to school?'

'Soon. I work at my father's firm during the summer holidays and will be residing in London once I have graduated. I hope to become a writer,' I said.

She sparkled. 'How delightful! I would love to read your stories. Have you written anything yet?'

'A few short stories, some poems...'

'I would like to read them. May I?'

I hesitated. No one had read my work. What if it was no good? But how could I resist her? I nodded and clasped her hand.

'It would be an honour.'

Her mother came and drew her away much to my dismay, but I rallied when I caught her glancing over at me during the birthday festivities. She was polite and courteous to everyone who spoke to her and I burned to fight them off with my valiant sword and sweep her away into my arms. Never had I felt so jealous before in my life and it was almost a relief when the Whittles left, knowing she would soon be safe in her family dwelling.

My mother was vibrant and energetic throughout the

night, welcoming everyone and saturating them with her joy of life. My father stayed by her side the whole night and everyone commented and remarked on the handsome couple. The candles burned low, the cake was reduced to sticky crumbs and the guests had their fill of good wine and song. It was a marvellous success. We watched the last guests stagger out to their coaches before bemusedly ascending the stairs to collapse on our beds. The dozing housemaids were woken and began the clean-up as quietly as they could, not wishing to disturb the master and mistress of the house. I fell asleep smiling, remembering my beloved Lily and every word she had said to me. Though marriage had never before been in my calculation, I was now determined that she would become Mrs Charles Augustus Fenton. My campaign would start immediately.

Courtship

'Mrs Whittle, a very good morning to you. I wonder if I may accompany you and your daughters for a small stroll on this beautiful spring day.'

I had spruced myself with a dedication of a Buddhist. Being anxious to ensure nothing but triumph, I had even employed the opinions and devotion of both my mother AND Meg. They were delighted to hear of my adoration for Lily and worked with a resolve and grit in the face of which the Iron Duke would have quailed. The Whittle family was well respected and it would be a grand coup to unite the two families. However, each race must begin with the first step and encounter the first hurdle before it is successfully won. I needed to look the part of a perfect son-in-law-to-be that any mother would titter and fuss over to gain their favour. My first hurdle would therefore be Mrs Whittle, Lily's mother.

My mother and Meg worked simultaneously. Meg ironed and brushed, folded and tweaked my daily apparel whilst the maids drew yet another warm bath and I scrubbed myself from top to toe. Mother gave no quarter, preaching the words that surely were brushed with a glimpse of Hell-fire if you were to dally from the path. The protocols were painfully draconian and monotonously specific to the very last detail. My time at Fenton Estate was brief as I was to return to school the following week. This made every attempt all the more vital to be perfect in its delivery.

Accompanied by my mother, I had already endured the necessary high teas in their front parlour. My mother was in her element and was subtle and delicate with highlighting my many admirable qualities to Mrs Whittle. They were interjected between gay banter and wistful anecdotes she had from both Lily's and my childhood. I listened in fascination to some of the stories and became immersed in the tales, forgetting that I was supposedly the main character. My memory must have been poor for I could barely hide my wonder about the brilliance I contained within. She would always withdraw before the layering became too thick and sticky to swallow. Mrs Whittle lapped it up in her decorous way, glancing often at me in admiration and I loved my mother and thanked God yet again for making her mine.

Whilst our mothers talked, I sat awkwardly with the fine bone china teacup and saucer balanced on my lap, looking at Lily and trying my best to look debonair. Both she and Carla giggled at my efforts and smirked, satisfied at having the upper hand. I had had no further discussions with Lily and was becoming increasingly frustrated at our lack of intimacy. Though my mother felt the high teas were an advantageous move I was ready to take the next step and get outside. I might at least then have the opportunity to touch her even if it was only accidental. So here I was, standing alone with a small posy mother insisted I present Mrs Whittle, asking for the pleasure of her company yet again.

'Master Fenton! What a delight that sounds. Unfortunately my Aunt Agneitha is feeling poorly and has requested my company this afternoon. The girls were going to accompany me but I'm sure they could visit their great-aunt tomorrow.'

It was hard not to punch the air and crow.

'I'm so sorry to hear of your dear aunt's poor health. Do pass on my deepest hope that she recovers quickly.' I smiled a shark's smile. 'I most certainly will and thank you for your concern. Please wait in the parlour and I will have my daughters collect you presently.' She turned and disappeared into the house.

I swaggered into the now-familiar parlour and accepted the maid's offering of lemonade. The drink tasted tart and refreshing and my eyes sparkled at the thirst-quenching drink and the anticipation of seeing Lily.

She did not disappoint. How is it possible to improve on loveliness itself? I could only marvel at her sparkling beauty and iridescent eyes. She had chosen a light rose dress with a matching bonnet accented by a pink rose and generous ribbon. In her hand was a fragile sun umbrella of lace and wire to protect her English skin. Her waist was so tiny I felt sure I could put my hands around it and encircle it entirely.

The layers I had so previously maligned, draped miraculously over her petite figure in such a becoming manner that I almost sighed with pleasure before I managed to suck it back in and behave in a more manly way. Her sister, Carla, was equally decked out in exquisite finery but it was wasted on me. She was unused to being ignored and bristled beside her idolised sister.

The stroll was magnificent. I found my voice and was able to talk freely to my lovely Lily. Only the occasional vituperative interjection from Carla marred a completely successful day. We nullified the acidic tone by completely ignoring her, making her boil even further. At length, when she threatened to return home, we fussed over her and cooed until she was mollified enough to let us continue to talk.

'When shall I get to read your stories, Charles?' Lily asked, now that Carla was happier.

'They are in my London dwelling. I will be delighted to show them to you when you are next in the great city.'

'Carla and I will be presented to society there this season. My mother has been frantic in her preparations.'

I ached with jealousy at the thought of any other man talking to my Lily. I had to ensure that my mother had also arranged for me to attend the many balls during that summer.

'I will be there. I look forward to dancing with you and showing you the wondrous energy that London has to offer.'

'Will you write to me every day while you are not here?' Her melancholy tone pulled my heart.

'On my word, I will write to you every day we are not together. I would like to hope that you will be thinking of me often.'

'You may hope and that hope shall be fulfilled.' She touched my arm and quickly kissed my cheek, blessing her sister for pretending to pick a flower she had detected some yards away. I believed I could fly at that moment and the journey back to her house was in a dream-world. I glided home and informed my mother of the twins' impending debutante season, but of course she was already aware and had begun preparations for this summer.

It was time for me to return to school.

Interruption

'I am in love,' I declared on my return to Rugby School. Henry Felldon, Benjamin Roberts and Arthur Mannings all groaned.

'What happened to Lutka?' Mannings asked somewhat acerbically.

'True. I may have been slightly off target with my feelings for Lutka. At first glance, she seemed a most wondrous girl, but in hindsight, there were some less than attractive aspects to her character.' I thought about her glutinous session with the pig trotters and shuddered.

My friends smirked at each other.

'I hope you mean to let her know of your new intentions. It would be unfair to leave her hanging.' Mannings again.

'Yes,' I muttered vaguely. I had absolutely no desire to be searching for my now recently abandoned Lutka. Her delightful promiscuous nature was scorched by a rather blazing temper. I still remembered the rocks she'd thrown. No. It was best to leave well alone and avoid the Montgomery farm altogether. Arthur Mannings studied me dourly.

'Make sure you do,' he responded.

Our final school year was filled with examinations and essays. We spent long evenings discussing our future careers and aspirations and where we would all be going in the last summer holidays. London, a place that previously had me intrigued, was now a Mecca with my beloved Lily as the esteemed guest. The filth-ridden sewers and haggard alleyways were transformed into the River Nile drawing my Lily towards me as Cleopatra, Queen of Egypt. I was naturally gifted with an innate sense of rhythm and I dreamed of sweeping her off her feet during the many dances we would share this summer. To hold her in my arms was going to be paradise and I dreamed most nights of her beauty and witty charm. Though I had forsaken Lutka, I could grudgingly acknowledge the experience she had given me carnally. This gave me much more confidence to seduce Lily and make her mine forever. There is good in everyone I philosophised sagely, studiously ignoring my own bad attributes.

I wrote every day to Lily, keeping her amused with the comings and goings at my school. Knowing this was my last year gave me a sense of nostalgia. My student years were nearly finished and though we pledged eternal allegiance I knew that my close group of friends and I were bound for different journeys. Because of this, I think we made more of an effort to spend our spare time together, hiking, playing games, star-gazing. The camaraderie was warming and we had shared many adventures over the years together. This was to be our last innocent summer and the feeling was bittersweet. The weeks passed and summer marched on and watched us shaking hands and patting backs in mutual respect and melancholy at our parting. We resolved to keep in contact before going our separate ways yet again.

London blustered and blew at me on my return but I was immune to its aggravation. My father stayed at Fenton Estate, but had already arranged my lodging and had presented my key. I trudged through the barrage of noisy cacophony letting the sound bounce from my armadillo shell of contemplation. All I could think about was Lily. It had been several weeks since I had last seen her and the absence had elevated her to my fondest yearning. I thunked my gigantic trunk step by step up to the lofty room that was my lodging but had the luxury of tranquillity once I had finally ascended the stairs, as there was only a small deserted butcher's shop underneath. The view was admirable and I knew my writing would envelope the sights and smells of my fellow Englishmen below ferreting away at their business called life. My creativity would abound in this juicy environment. But not before I had secured my Lily. My responsibility and duties remained to adhere to the Fenton business but my nights would soon be peppered with joyous frivolity. Tomorrow, the season would begin and I would see her again.

Cloud Nine

The scene was set and I knew tonight I would see lovely Lily again. Even without my mother and Meg's help I had miraculously groomed myself enough to be considered a dapper, handsome prospect. The sultry heat tried its best to thwart the crispness of my white shirt yet I refused to bow down to it. With the address securely embedded in my mind I set off on a casual stroll to the venue. The Londoners were out in force and I kidded myself that more than one person turned to admire my appearance. There was a distinct feeling of being watched and though generally it was with appreciation, there were occasions that I sensed a more sinister scout skulking in the shadows. However every time I swung around the figure would disappear into the dark. Berating myself for being such a superstitious creature, I endeavoured to ignore the sensation and focus on my destination.

The ballroom was spectacular. The room was filled with glorious birds of society, tittering and fluttering their fans. The male peacocks strutted around importantly, talking loudly and engaging the young ladies with their magnificence. I knew a few faces and nodded graciously as I skimmed the crowd. Where was my beautiful Lily?

Twins were always a little bit special, but the arrival of the Whittle twins caused a wave of excited hubbub. They were a stunning pair and they highlighted each other complementing the differences and the similarities they shared. They oozed a magnetic field that drew everybody in, wanting others to make their acquaintance and bask in their unique quality. As they were well-bred girls they made polite enquiries and comments appropriate to the subject being expressed before them. Carla bloomed in the attention and the peacocks melted and flashed their feathers all the more in vain attempts to garner her favour. She radiated desirability and was soon whisked away for dance after dance, each man vying for a place on her dance card. Lily was more demure, content to watch her sister dazzling the crowd and smiling complacently. Though she chatted to each attendant, she involuntarily scanned the room from time to time. It gave me the greatest of triumphant joy to see her light up once her eyes hit mine. The love arrow thrust deeply within my heart yet again and I nearly stumbled in its power. We looked at each other and became the only two people in the room. I staggered towards her, pushing through the paraphernalia of humans. I kissed her gloved hand and bowed.

'You cannot know the pleasure I have to once again see your lovely face, Lily.'

She curtsied.

'The loveliness you see is a reflection of my joy in seeing you again, Charles.'

You are my wondrous Lily.

'Would you do me the great honour of this dance?'

'I have denied all others to ensure we danced first together. I could not bear any man but you.'

'Then we shall dance on cloud nine tonight.'

I escorted her to the dance floor and held her in my arms. The music flowed around us and we floated deliriously in love. She was in perfect harmony with me and the others on the dance floor could only watch in envious wonder. We were oblivious to them and our eyes locked and spoke the secret language of true soul mates. I drowned in her eyes and she in mine. We were kindred spirits and mutual devotees that no man could put asunder. I noticed her mother watching on from the corner, seeming to smile with maternal satisfaction. The Fentons were held in high regard in Warwickshire and were of good stock; perhaps Mrs Whittle was considering such things, happy that it would be a good match, while Lily and I danced on, innocent to any calculating musings.

When the song ended it was a physical wrench to part from each other's arms and dutifully escort another onto the dance floor. Pure politeness and societal necessity demanded this from us, but as soon as any opportunity arose we would return to each other jubilant at being together again. One could almost pity any other contenders for their dejected state.

The champagne flowed down thirsty gullets and the buffet supper was nibbled upon but we were nourished on love alone. Alas, the time sprints quickly away when you are in love. It was merely a blink before the night was over and the guests departing. I beseeched my Lily to see me again the following afternoon and take the air at Hyde Park. She agreed instantly, coyly adding that Carla may be our escort. I kissed her hand dearly and reverently and bowed, watching her, her mother and Carla glide away to their carriage that would carry my beloved to her fortunate bed.

The next day and the next and the next were saturated with Lily. We walked, we danced, we cheered at the cricket matches, we gambled at the races. All with a chaperone in tow but still managing sneaky kisses whenever the scrutiny lapsed. Other men tried and failed to ensnare my wonderful Lily, but soon it became obvious that we had an understanding. They would dally with the capricious attention of Carla, who wounded battered heart after heart with her guileful ways. She dangled them on her string and they danced and skipped for her just so they could receive a small nugget of her praise.

Every now and then the sneaking fleet of someone

trailing my shadow would enter my senses but I would soon be lost again in the glory of my Lily. I was exhausted, with my day commencing early, working hard at my father's London office, attending court summons, dictating, filing, interviewing clients and building my knowledge base of criminal and best law practices. When the day was over I would race home to bathe and change, ready to do whatever my Lily desired until the night would fall and me with it, collapsing onto my pillow late at midnight, feet aching from an evening of dance. On the odd night that there were no evening activities I would strive to write, scribbling furiously magical tales of goblins and fairies, of caves and mystical waterfalls. I would use the faces and characters of working-class people I saw every day and warp them into magic folk and elves, knobbly faces and wispy wings. I knew instinctively that the day-to-day burden of being poor and downtrodden made them crave an escape to magic lands and fantasies. My inspiration was everywhere and my hand struggled at times to keep up with the rampaging torrent of words gushing forth. Though I had promised to show Lily my work, I kept deferring her request, not wanting my novel to see the light of day until its entirety. I protected it as a mother hen would her newborn chick.

The summer was my most wonderful time of my life and it was drawing near to the end when I would have to return and complete my last term at school, but more catastrophically, I would be parted from Lily until the end of year. I felt the dark clouds forming and dreaded this time fearfully. It would be a calamitous drop in fortune, of that I was sure, but I never, ever could have predicted how far my fall would be.

The shadow

With the social programme complete for the summer, Lily and Carla were resigned to returning back to Warwickshire. My father was arriving soon to look over the books with me and any errant legal paperwork. I had two more weeks left before I returned to Rugby and now that my Lily was returning I faced a quiet and sombre time of it. We promised to continue our correspondence, feeling as if our hearts were ripped in two at this loathsome separation. It stabbed me deeply to see the little crystal tears forming and trickling down her perfect face as she waved wretchedly from her departing coach. Even in sadness she was exquisite and I stood watching the coach long after it had disappeared from view. It would be the sandiest desert of despair before I could drink in her loveliness again.

Without Lily there I concentrated solely on my work and my writing. I filled each day with purpose and drive, knowing every moment I burned brought me closer to her eventually. I wanted to make her proud of me and be able to provide her with everything she deserved. I punished myself for any wandering thoughts during the day, re-focussing my efforts to the task at hand. Only at nights, when I slumped into bed did I allow the luxury of recalling Lily and all the wonderful memories we shared that summer. Each letter I received from her was read line by tender line and then re-read to elongate the pleasure. Once I had sucked every delicious drop from her orderly sloped handwriting I would gently add it to the ribbon-bundled pile tucked away in my trunk, kissing it lightly with love. I was in the process of reading one of her letters when someone knocked at my door.

'Who is it?' I called, annoyed at the disturbance so late at night.

Silence. Then they knocked again. Really, this was just too much. Who would be calling now? It couldn't be Father; we had already arranged for an early morning visit as I knew him to be more of a lark than an owl. I grumbled and swore under my breath, unlocked the door and opened it.

'Hello Charles.'

It was Lutka. She stood before me like a ghost, a heavily pregnant ghost. A lump formed in my throat and solidified. I don't believe I moved an inch.

'Aren't you going to let me in? It's the very least you should do, don't you think?' She pivoted, displaying her belly to me as if it were a pot roast. I stood back, still holding the door handle to give her room to enter.

'Of…of course. Please come in.'

She sashayed in and studied my room.

'Would you care for a cup of tea?' I enquired, trying not to stare at the bulging stomach.

'No, thank you. I find I am up all night if I drink anything after dinner. The baby presses on my water-works you see.' She smiled and sat down.

I started at the mention of baby and her discomforts. A lady should never talk of such things. At a loss as to what to do next and with legs quavering, I sat down awkwardly on my bed. My head was swirling with thoughts. How did this happen? What does she want? What do I do? Oh my God, oh my God. Help. Help. Help. She sat watching me grapple with my dastardly discovery.

'You seem ill at ease, Charles.'

'You could say that.'

'It's been a long time.'

I squirmed.

'I know. I was meaning to find you but things became very busy at school.'

'I'm sure they did.' She knew I was lying.

'You are with child.'

'I always thought you were a clever one. It's yours, of course.'

'Of…course. How did you find me?'

'It was not easy. After you became "busy" I found out I was in the family way. I knew it wouldn't be long before Mr and Mrs Montgomery noticed it and would want me gone. So I remembered you saying you worked in London during the holidays. I stayed with them, covering my sickness until the baby grew bigger, and then I ran away to London. I had a little money put away, which I have been using to stay here and there in different places, not staying long enough to raise questions. I have been looking for you and catching glimpses every now and then, but you appeared to be "busy" yet again. Not wanting to cause a scene, I have watched and waited until I found out where you lived so that I might be able to see you. So now, here I am waiting for you to make an honest woman of me.' She finished her story and placed her hands one on top of the other over her stomach.

The blood rushed from my face and I would have fainted if I hadn't already been sitting down. This was a complete and utter disaster of the unthinkable kind. I was floored. She wanted me to marry her. Her, the pig-trotter, pickled-egg-eating, gypsy girl who lifted her skirt at the sight of a bit of tucker! She was practically a prostitute, except probably cheaper. I was disgusted not only with her but also myself for being so stupid and blind in a moment of desire. I was stupid, stupid, stupid and my life was ruined and for what? All I got was a tumble in the hay, for which I gave her food with money from my own pocket. Willingly too, so blinded I was by lust. I cursed myself, berated my foolishness and lack of judgement. What about Lily, my beautiful and perfect Lily? Am I to turn my back on my one true love? The love of my soul and mind, the love of life that I was going to grow old with? What about her? Am I to toss her aside for this piece of…strumpet?

'How do I know it's mine?'

'Fie on you, Charles Fenton; you know it's yours. We were stuck together like glue all winter, and you weren't questioning anything then. Any spare time away from the farm I spent with you, or can't you remember?' she said.

'I remember,' I sighed.

'So that's enough of that sort of chat, thank you very much. Now I want to know what you are going to do about it.'

I buried my head into my hands and groaned. This could not be happening. My whole life, all my dreams and ideas, were wiped in a puff of black smoke. I have nothing. I am nothing. I am tied forever with this rancid little Lutka. I felt sick to the stomach. It took all my resolve not to break down and sob like a baby.

'What do you suggest?' I looked up at her desolately.

'I suggest that seeing how our baby is not far from coming into this world, we travel back to your parents immediately and let them know the most wonderful news that not only you are about to be married but you are also going to bring them a baby to carry the Fenton name.'

'That will ruin them. I can't do it.'

'You can do it and you will. You have no choice. Do you really want the mother of your child to be swept out with the swill and giving birth in the gutter?'

No matter how much I loathed the situation, I could not honestly say that even I could stoop that low. I had been raised to cherish children and give them love and support. How could I turn my back on my own blood? This baby had a right to a name and security. He would be born into land and title and given every opportunity as I had. Who was I to make him a bastard, never realising his worth?

I hated her. I hated her with a passion. Her rapacity to not only suck me dry of everything I owned but also to destroy any future happiness I had with Lily. Any good memories I had of her when we'd first met were swept away into oblivion. She sickened me with the way she felt the world owed her its services just because she got knocked up. I looked at her so assured of my meekness and obedience. I had followed her around with my tongue dragging on the ground, lapping up any attention she had thrown me in the hay barn. Of course she considered me a weakling, so would have I in her shoes. She sat there picking at her nails and casting a covetous eye over my belongings. She would strip me to the bone and put my family into bankruptcy. It was a helpless situation and I needed time and advice before being cudgelled into matrimony. I stalled for time.

'No, of course I don't want you to suffer. You carry my child, the blood of Fenton. But my parents are elderly and I need to be cautious in my approach. Please let me see them and break the news alone. I beg you.'

She tapped her ponderous belly, thinking.

'And what of me? Do I just sit and wait while you run out of the country?'

'For God sakes, woman! I have honour! Can't you see what you have done to me?' I cursed her.

'Not as much as you have done to me, Charles. Don't forget that. I don't want you to be "busy" again and disappear.'

I sighed.

'I will see my father tomorrow and explain the situation and then I will secure two tickets back to my home town. I will go tomorrow evening and arrange your ticket for the following day to be left at the station. This will give me time to deliver the news to my mother and prepare her for your arrival. Is that acceptable to you?' I said rather bitingly.

She nodded. 'Agreed. But I need some money now. I am starving. You will give me some to cover my journey home and fill my stomach. Plus I wish to stay the night here; you have a bed and I am tired.'

'No. NO. This I cannot do. I will give you some

money and you can stay at a nearby inn. You go too far.'
I was suffocating and if she stayed any longer I would
not be able to control myself. I scrambled around and
found some coins for her accommodation, which she
took unblinkingly. I walked her to the door, urging her
to leave, but she stopped and turned.

'Don't worry, Charles. It won't be that bad. We can
do plenty of rumpty bumpty and I won't even make you
wait till the wedding night if you want.' She reached out
to put her arms around my neck and plant a kiss on me.

I recoiled and impulsively pushed her away. I pushed
too hard.

Murder most foul

Her hands spread wide in dismay and desperation, trying to snatch at my shirt. A small button was ripped from its place and thrown against the wall. She wavered and toppled, unbalanced by her enormous stomach and uneven footing. The first step was too close for her to regain her equilibrium and we both knew she was going to fall. Unthinkingly I grabbed for her, knowing it was hopeless but trying anyway. Her eyes were fixed onto mine, a wide eyed, bulging harrowing stare burning into my corneas. She knew I was conflicted. She knew that deep, deep down in my darkest soul I had wanted this to happen. I had pushed her away in antipathy when she was at her most vulnerable and she realised in that split second that I had forsaken her.

In abject terror she fell backwards, arms flailing searching for anything to grip and save her but there was nothing. She impacted fully on her back in bone crunching nauseating finality, her neck whipping back and her skull fracturing on the first step. She slid backwards down the stairs, her spinal cord now severed and her two bottom teeth, already rotten, breaking off from their roots and dropping back into her throat. She was bouncing macabrely with each step as she rolled down without any bodily control. I watched a spirited woman turn into a bag of shattered bones before my eyes.

The fall was mere seconds but was also an eternity. The shattering sound of bones breaking on her descent made my skin crawl and turn to old wet leather. I was witness to and origin of the decimation of not one but two living souls, one being my own child. Standing there from the top of the stairs, looking down on her moribund state ripped my innards to shreds. I had not only committed murder of a woman, but the execrable act of feticide. Or had I? My unborn baby was due any day according to Lutka. Could there still a chance for him and the saving of part of my soul?

I dashed back into my room and searched for the sharpest knife before sprinting down the stairs and ripping up her clothing in maniacal state. I ripped each layer to get closer to her swaddled inhabited abdomen. My absolution lay in bringing up my child in the way an heir of Fenton deserved.

I ignored her empty face and concentrated on finding the baby. Tears streaming down my cheeks were not felt but dripped onto her body. I soon had the stomach with its tight rotund mound peering at me in suspicion. Taking a deep breath I raised my knife high. I could see the wriggling writhing mass moving under her skin fossicking for an escape from its placental jail. A cold sweat erupted from my pores drenching me and making the handle slippery. I must not hesitate or all would be lost. With eyes grim in concentration I hacked into her flesh. Blood oozed out, pouring rivulets of red over my hands and onto the floor. I tore apart the incision I made concerned I might cut the baby if I used the knife again. I reached into her hot wet stomach and groped and tore through her body. Pieces of organ, unrecognisable to me, squelched out and slurped in protest to my disregard. A small limb appeared to my hand and I grabbed it, using the other hand to reach for a more substantial hold. I pulled steadily, watching the emerging form of my child with the most diabolical look on my face. I kept pulling and pulling until its tiny form was in my hands and wriggling, mewing tiny noises and covered in blood and entrails. The umbilical cord pulsated and quivered anchoring the baby to its mother in final demand of ownership. It was a girl, a tiny, minute fragile girl. The eyes remained closed and it spasmodically twitched in a gory fashion. Now that I had my daughter in my hands I was at a loss what to do next. I stared at her, willing her to tell me what to do for her survival. The blood dripped between my fingers, plopping indiscriminately onto what used to be known as Lutka. I looked at the baby and then the body and then back again, wishing for a mystical midwife to appear and wondrously make the gore go away, returning with my daughter cleaned and wrapped. It didn't happen and I was struck senseless, watching my daughter die in front of me and unable to stop the deathly and vile calamity. With my monstrous unthinking act I had only delayed the inevitable and desecrated her mother in her final moments. The blood-shed was appalling and unforgiveable.

My baby daughter perished in my guilt-ridden hands and was still. Gently I laid her down on her mother and I sobbed. I sobbed for the death of my daughter and the senseless murder of her mother: a woman for whom I had once picked ripe blackberries. A woman I could not keep away from. A woman I had rescued from a drowning death. I had killed them both. I could not leave them. I wanted to die too and be unable to think concise thought. To exist now was inexcusable for a heinous monster such as me. I lay down slowly next to them, uncaring of the sticky clotting blood I bathed in. My concluding thought was one of certain death by pure will and doggedness and I would then be free of this odious horror. I closed my eyes and went to sleep with the metallic smell of blood in my nostrils.

Paternal protection

'Sweet Jesus. No. No. Please God, no. Oh God. Oh God!'

My father, wondering why I hadn't made my appearance at the office had come to find me. When he opened the bottom door and saw me lying in a pool of blood senseless, he assumed I had expired and he had lost his only son. The haggard sound of his voice stirred me unfortunately back to consciousness, a place of which I no longer wished to be part. I moaned in bitter disappointment at the fact. How could God have failed me now and made me live? I realised this was the most horrid punishment that I could bear. On hearing me groan, my father rushed to my side and checked me over.

'Where are you hurt, my sweet boy? Who did this to you? Show me the wounds.'

He patted me down and turned me anxiously this way and that, baffled at my seemingly intact shell. I rolled as if I were a sack of potatoes, unable to use my limbs in a complete shutdown of self-loathing. I could feel his fear but couldn't reassure him, so mind-blighted I had become. I hated myself even further for this apathy and the pain I was giving my father but there was nothing I could do about it. I wished to no longer exist.

He checked me thoroughly and when he was satisfied that nothing physical was wrong with me, his attention then swept to the bloodied heap of mother and child strewn beside me. I can only imagine the torture going through his mind, speculating what could have happened to not only his son but this sad creature and her baby. I was saved by his quick thinking legal mind that worked through the potential scenarios and most likely explanations. Any other person happening across this scene would have run screaming and terrified into the street, calling forth the law, the people, the shopkeepers to come and rescue or condemn my pitiful form. It was my father's intellect and protective spirit that stayed his hand and kept him quietly squatting by me.

'Did…did you do this, Charles? Did you, my son?'

He spoke softly, aware I was in a state of shock but trying to understand. I groaned and with a Herculean effort I managed a small nod. He fell back, a devastated sound escaping from his mouth, which he covered in horror. He rested back against the wall no longer able to support himself. There he sat with one hand on his mouth, which was agape and the other on his brow, staring at me in pure disbelief. The silence was thick with black murder, swirling around my father and me and menacing our sanity, waiting for us to crack under the choking pressure. I had nothing in me. I was replete. It was completely up to him to move forward and deal with what lay before him. The time waited and watched.

He sat there thinking for a long period before making up his mind about what to do. He stepped gingerly over us and clambered up the stairs, each leg weighed down seemingly with anchors. He emptied out my large school trunk and added newspapers, a bowl of water and several rags, and then came back down to me. I had not moved but remained curled in a foetal position, covered in blood. He opened the trunk, lined the bottom and sides with the newspaper and hoisted Lutka in with the baby still attached. He scraped as much blood and tissue up with remaining paper and pushed it down around the coiled body now entrenched in its makeshift coffin. Next he undressed me, removing every article of clothing and rendering me stark naked. The soiled clothing was also pushed in and around the bodies as a form of repugnant packing. He worked quietly, having removed his own shirt and trousers in fear of tainting them with the blood. He plunged his bloodied hand into the clean crisp water and reddened it with the rag, mopping and sponging the floor, the outside of the trunk and myself. He emptied the bowl over and over, refilling with clean water and rags. Finally dragging me up the stairs, step by heavy step, he poured me into my bed and tucked me in, before coming back down to finish. He scrubbed the floors and steps with sand and then scoured with a brush and lye caustic soda. A final once-over with a clean wet rag ensured him satisfied that all traces of the murder had been expunged. Each filthy red rag and sand was packed into the trunk with the lid closed and locked carefully. Once he had cleaned himself thoroughly, he redressed and stared at the trunk.

With a small prayer and looking up towards my room, he set off into the streets with the cursed trunk on his trolley. He kept his eyes down but maintained a neutral face, refraining from his normal polite greetings. He walked briskly, belying his age and kept true to his course, using his knowledge of the streets to its best advantage. Everyone was too busy with their own day of business, their own will to survive, to notice a middle-aged man and his luggage. The noises and the smells battered around him and swept away to the next person.

He continued on, walking not too fast or slow to attract attention. The sun was high in the sky now, throwing its sultry heat on his head and simmering the fetid flesh in the trunk. He worried about the smell and steered clear of people as much as he could. The odour merged seamlessly with the foul stench floating up from the dumped raw sewage in the river. The stink was decaying and of human waste but not as putrid or cadaverous as his own malodorous package. He struggled to keep the bile from spewing forth from his mouth and swallowed hard. Despite the smell he kept close to the river, keeping an eye out for an opportunity to dump the dreaded trunk and its contents. Whenever he felt the moment was advantageous, he waited only to be saved from discovery when a lone beggar or dock worker strode past, unaware of Charles Fenton senior and his abominable plan. Patiently he stood close to the shadows, keeping as unobtrusive as he possibly could. All he needed was a few clear minutes to allow the body to sink and forever be destined to its watery grave. He prayed whilst he waited, praying for the mercy of God on his son and the poor unidentified souls in the trunk. He apologised and begged forgiveness for what he was about to do and swore on his life to make amends to the church and this poor girl if only his son could survive. The pain and grief pounded inside him causing a near physical ache and cramping in his stomach. What had caused his son to behave in such an abhorrent way? He prayed for the strength to bring his son back to him. Both he and Elizabeth had fought so hard to bring young Charles into this world and it just couldn't be all taken away from them now in the autumn of their years. He simply would not be able to bear it, Fenton or not. This was his blood, the blood of his heirs, the blood of the future. He loved him no matter what his son had done, and no man was going to take that away.

Eventually a pause came and without hesitation he rolled the trunk over and into the river. The censorious splash reverberated in his ears as he hurried away, worrying now only for his son.

Housebound

How long he was gone I will never know, but the sun was rising when I heard his key in the lock. He entered the room unsure what to expect but found me exactly how he left me, tucked into my bed. He walked slowly and quietly up to the bed and sat down, touching his hand softly onto my shoulder.

'Charles. I'm back, son. Don't worry, everything will be all right. We will deal with this together, as Fentons. I will never leave you, my son. I will take care of you and we will get through this. Just trust me.'

I heard the words but they sounded far away, in a void. He lifted my head and poured small trickles of tea in, wiping my chin with any dribbles. I was a baby again and nestled in his strong familiar arms inhaling his scent. He rocked me gently and continued until I had finished the cup, then he gradually laid me down to fall back into a slumber.

Whilst I dozed, he wrote messages addressed to the school, Lily and his wife. He informed her not to worry, that we would be staying on in London and that we would explain on our return. He signed and sealed each letter and found a delivery boy to deliver the letters to the general post office at St Martins-le-grand. He sent a separate note to Sophie, his office maid, informing her that she would be now required to clean and cook at my lodgings until further notice. She arrived promptly at midday, providing a hot meal and cleaning the small room. She must have stared at my pathetic form, but knew her place and didn't ask. She watched my father over the days and then weeks as he mollycoddled me, feeding me broths and custards, beef teas and arrowroot puddings. He forced me to walk, stumbling around the room twice a day, gave Sophie my chamber-pot to empty, read to me and rubbed my limbs out of atrophy. He also wrote daily to my mother and to my darling Lily, assuaging their worries, writing pacifying letters of hope and hinting of a re-acquaintance in the very near future. I was oblivious to all of this until he told me much, much later at my insistence. We prayed together nightly and he reminded me often of God's love and forgiveness. He spoke of the Fenton fortitude and of the hopes both he and mother had for me. He praised Lily, telling me how wonderful a bride she would be and how happy I would make them feel to see us wed. He refused to listen to my guilty rants and after briefly explaining how he'd disposed of the bodies, rebuffed any further discussion on that. After I told him, with racking sobs, of the events from that day, he declined to discuss it further. He brushed it all into the past, to be left there and kept unsaid. No one else would ever know what happened that night. In this, he was obdurate. The devil had momentarily overtaken me and now I was back with God and would be ready to stand in his light again. God was forgiving and almighty and only God would decide on my fate. It was my duty to live for the sake of myself, Lily and my family.

I began to hope. I began to believe that my father might be right. I had been given a second chance to prove myself worthy of life and to repay my father's love and protection. He nourished me and brought me out of my cocoon, emerging weak and ashen, blinking painfully at the cold reality of day. It was time for me to come home.

On the final week of my recovery, Sophie arrived at her usual time hauling in a steaming pot of chicken pot pie. She sat it down on the table and retrieved our plates and cutlery.

'Here you go, sirs, a lovely hot pot pie.'

We had grown used to Sophie's culinary skills and had even agreed she would give our cook a run for her money. My father may have nursed me back to health, but Sophie had definitely contributed. It would be sad to have to say goodbye. I realised as I chewed rapturously on the fare, that I knew nothing about her. Ashamed, I tried to make up for it on this final day.

'Sophie, you've outdone yourself yet again. Did your mother teach you how to cook?'

Sophie bowed her head. 'No sir. My Ma is a lush. She has been since Pa was killed.'

My father and I stopped eating; almost every day the newspaper was printing funeral notices of the latest workers killed on the railway. Was that how he'd met his end?

'I'm so very sorry, Sophie. May I ask what happened?' my father asked softly. She squared her shoulders and took a deep breath.

'He was a member of the Sheffield Chartists and part of the rebellion. He had been a carpenter and I remember him making me a little cart to pull my doll around. I was his special girl and I was so proud when he told me that he was going to fight and make the world better for us. I didn't really know what that meant, but it sounded exciting to me. My Ma didn't want him to go and I didn't know why, but it may have been 'cause she was going to have another baby.'

My father and I looked at each other quietly. He had been instrumental in ensuring at least ten of the survivors from the resistance were jailed and subsequently transported to Australia. They were destined never to see their families again. We listened, subdued.

'He went anyway and told me he would be back in a few days with a present if I was good and helped Ma.

So I waited and waited, looking down the path every day for Pa but he never came back. It turned my mother something bitter. She took to the gin and when my sister was born, they sent her away to the home. My Ma didn't even care.'

Sophie smiled grimly. 'But I got little Rosie back and worked hard to look after her. She's all grown up now and is going to be married to a collier,' she finished triumphantly.

My father looked at Sophie and then lowered his eyes. He reached into his wallet and gave her an extra pound on top of her weekly wages. Her face lit up and she pocketed it quickly.

'Thanks ever so much, Mr Fenton! You are a real gentleman!'

My father coughed and curtly dismissed her, advising her we would be leaving tomorrow and she could return to her usual cleaning duties at the office. She nodded and left with a spring in her step.

Humility

The train and coach ride home was long and tortuous. I felt every eye upon me silently disgusted at my audacity to breathe in their world. I kept my head down to avoid the attention of the fellow travellers and thereby attracting it to my wretchedness. My father noticed and clamped his hand on my knee, muttering to me to keep my head up and explaining to those who enquired that I was recovering from the fever. This was a likely explanation as I looked gaunt and sallow, lacking all signs of robustness. We were left alone after that until we reached the Fenton Estate. Things would not be so easy there, and my father took a deep breath for strength when he spied my mother marching out the front door.

'Charles! What has happened to our son? He can barely stand!' She cushioned my face between her delicate hands, examining me in horror.

'I did not want to worry you, dear. He has had a slight touch of the fever again and we felt it judicious to stay in London until he was well enough to travel.'

'The fever!' She gasped and touched my brow. 'You should have told me, Charles. How could you?'

My father looked chagrined. For all I knew, this

might well have been the first time in his married life he had knowingly lied to Mother. His guilt must have stabbed inside, but from the outside he looked resolute. She must never know the true reason of her son's demeanour. Never. I staggered in with a parent on each arm and was shown back to my room. They laid me down and I fell into an exhausted stupor.

'We will have to inform Lily immediately. She has been asking daily when he would be returning and has been most troubled.'

'Agreed. But I feel Charles might need a bit more convalescence before she should be allowed to visit. He might find the reunion overwhelming and have a relapse.'

Elizabeth frowned worriedly and nodded in agreement. She wrote a short message and gave it to one of the servants to deliver to Lily. They sat in silence, concern etched on their faces. Charles Senior spoke at last.

'I think that Charles returning to school would be unwise. He has taken this very hard and I don't want to risk any undue stress on him.'

Elizabeth was surprised. Education was always a strong point of necessity wherever a Fenton was regarded. For her husband to speak thus showed how dreadfully ill their boy was. She shivered and felt very sombre.

'Once he has recovered I will send him my accounts and papers to put to order here at home. He will be able to work at a pace not too demanding of him in my office.'

Elizabeth approved of this, knowing she would now have her beloved son under her roof indefinitely. She kissed Charles gently on the cheek.

'You are a most wonderful man, Charles.'

'And you are a most wonderful wife, Elizabeth.' He kissed her back and pulled her onto his lap to cuddle, drawing comfort from her and realising how much he had missed her through the last traumatic weeks. He was home, his son was safe and everything would be all right with the gentleness of love and time. He hugged her tight.

Reclamation

My nights were long and filled with blood. Whenever I dropped off to sleep I was bombarded with nightmares of Lutka's death. Sleep became the enemy to be battled with. I woke most nights drenched in sweat and sobbing. I could feel her swirling around in dark clouds under my bed, in my closet, just waiting to drag me into the abyss with her. The dark circles under my eyes negated my quiet protest that I was fine whenever my parents asked. They looked at each other anxiously and kept silent.

The household drew together and determined to cure me. At their insistence I was forced to walk outside daily with Meg and her daughter, to keep company with Jack in the stables and to read the bible to my mother. They were all horrified at how I looked and cursed the dreaded fever for what it had done to their beloved son again. Lily asked to see me daily, but I couldn't look at her face knowing what I had done. It was my mother who finally gave her permission to visit, much against my wishes. She waited in the parlour for me, my mother sternly warning me to be on my best behaviour, before retreating to leave us alone.

I sat and looked at the rug, feeling so miserable to be

so presented to my beloved. I heard a small gasp escape her mouth at my appearance but no words were uttered. She rose quietly and stood in front of me touching my hair. This kindness was too much to bear. I fell to my knees, her sweet scent floating around me whilst I sobbed uncontrollably and clutched at her.

'Oh Charles, my dear sweet Charles. What has happened to you?'

Small tears trickled down her face silently as she watched me fall apart in her arms. She kept quiet and held me, her love flowing through to me as a panacea to all pain. I hated my affection for her but couldn't think how to surrender my love. I did not deserve her at all, no matter what my father said. I had to give her up. And yet she wouldn't let me.

She refused to listen to my remonstrations, grew angry with me whenever I highlighted my failings and embraced me when I was glum. She would sit for hours on end, reading the adventurous Robinson Crusoe by Daniel Defoe. We would lose ourselves in the story, fearsome of the cannibals and admiring of his tenacity and adaptability. It was a welcome haven from my self-loathing and I came to look forward to her visits daily. I was no match against the combined efforts of my friends and family, who plunged me into their welcoming arms of love and care. My father was able to travel to London more often, discreetly listening for any discoveries of the murder or bodies and gratefully hearing none. He had been able to save his son from the hangman's noose; a fact that became more certain as each week passed. We never again discussed that night and he remained firmly fixed on the future of his family, in particular, Lily's and my future.

At Christmas time my good friend Henry Felldon came to visit. He brought me up to date with Benjamin Roberts and Arthur Mannings. Our school cricket team won the college school competition and, he humbly added, both he and Roberts were already tipped for the Warwickshire cricket team next season. I congratulated him heartily, knowing how much of a dream it was to him and promising to come to every match and cheer. He mumbled I may have had a chance too if it hadn't been for my dreadful illness, even though we both knew I was not at the same skill level, but I nodded seriously to appease him.

Arthur Mannings had lost an aunt, who'd slipped on a river bank and drowned, weighted down by her voluminous dress. Her husband was devastated and had gone to live with Arthur's family where he deteriorated further and had to be admitted to the lunatic asylum. His six-year-old son now lived with Arthur's parents and was likely to remain so. They were in the process of considering formally adopting him and thereby giving him a more secure upbringing. Henry Felldon and Benjamin Roberts went to visit Arthur Mannings on the death of his aunt and found the child to be very similar in looks to Mannings himself, especially the ears. Mannings had, with the financial assistance of his parents, opened a photography studio and was doing very well from it. His spare time was still spent staring at the stars but now he had a companion in his fiancée, Sarah. They planned to marry once he could afford a place of their own.

I resolved to immediately write to Arthur Mannings after Henry was gone to relay my condolences for his departed aunt and apologise for my absence. He wrote back soon after and expressed a joy at hearing from his long-lost friend again. He had heard of my ill health and hoped I was feeling much better. He wondered how my story writing was going as he was very keen to see me accomplish my dreams I had talked about so long ago on the banks by Rugby School. It felt as if that had been a different lifetime to me, the age of innocence and brashness. I now had a much quieter and more reserved nature to what he would have remembered.

Lily was less reserved.

'I think it's a marvellous idea. You are a wonderful writer and have a real flare for capturing the essence of a character. You could do a fairytale about your goblins and other mystical creatures.' She became even more animated. 'I will draw the pictures for them! You have always thought highly of my paintings. Drawing elves and goblins sounds positively thrilling!'

I had no rebuttal to her stubbornness and acquiesced unenthusiastically.

We discussed it with my father, who was thrilled to see an opportunity for his son to revive further. He set aside a room for us both to write and paint and we set to work the following day.

The book was dark and courageous, exciting and macabre with cave-dwelling goblins battling against the wood pixies to avenge the death of a goblin king. He was poisoned by the pixies, who detested anything ugly, their silly scatty heads filled with thoughts of mischief and mayhem. The goblins captured a female pixie called Astra and dragged her back to their cave to torture her for information. However Zeneca one of the warrior goblins fell in love with her and she with him, so she was released, choosing to stay underground. The pixies refused to believe that a pixie would ever wish to live with a vile goblin, instead telling the woodland folk she had been kidnapped and tortured in a most evil way. This riled the river fairies, who normally kept their distance from the air-headed pixies but could not tolerate such a foul act happening in their forest. They joined ranks with the pixies, ignoring the forest animals that had visited Astra and knew the truth. Therefore, in respect for their hard-working and often maligned friends, the small creatures claimed loyalty and honour to the goblins and prepared to battle against their old friends until justice was done.

My fingers flew across the page and the book was made more magical by the creative hand of Lily. She painted gallant goblins with brave rats and proud hedgehogs. She turned the usually beautiful fairies into a more sinister being, the little pixies snarling with pointed teeth. The battlefields were large dewy lit forests, a clearing by a stream, a wintry night. All beautifully coloured and expressed to make the reader feel a part of the enchantment. Nothing was what it seemed in the mythical world we knew so little of and it was all conveyed in a way that grabbed you and wouldn't let go until the last page was turned.

It took six months to complete and we sent it to two publishing firms in London and waited with impatience. Charnells and Co publishers accepted it, stating how refreshingly vibrant the story was. The book would be printed and bound just before Christmas.

My nightmares were still there but less frequent. I continued to pray every night and go to church every Sunday and religious holiday, with the added pleasure of Lily accompanying me.

I was invited to and attended the wedding of her sister Carla, to a debonair tradesman by the name of Daniel. He was strikingly handsome, with jet black hair and an almost buccaneer proudly hooked nose. Carla was in a fit of hysterics and clung to him, delirious at the thought of their honeymooning in Paris before moving to India and seeing the world. The wedding was elaborate and, I thought quietly to myself, a little garish but it was well suited to the exotic pair of peacocks. Carla was never meant for a life in our quiet little town and I for one wished them well on their journey.

Lily cosseted and cooed over her sister on her wedding day but I could see she was out of sorts when she thought no one was watching. To her, the loss of her twin sister was a loss of part of herself and she felt the break keenly. Her mood rapidly declined once the happy couple gaily waved from their coach and she held the tears back no longer, her tiny face turned away from mine to hide her tears. It distressed me greatly to see her upset and I wondered how I could ease the pain for her after everything she had done for me. It has never been my fortune to make wise and sound judgement. My life was peppered with ill-conceived foolish actions rushing into disaster and decline, but for that one afternoon, as we watched the departing couple, I had an epiphany that I knew to be absolutely impeccable. But for once I would be cautious and mature as it was the most important positive step I could ever make. I was going to ask Mr Whittle for his daughter Lily's hand in marriage.

Mr Whittle

Meg knew something was afoot when she saw how carefully I had groomed myself on the morning of the planned visit.

'Charlie, you look rather spectacular. Is it for anyone in particular?'

I knew she knew by the barely repressed excitement in her question. I smiled and kissed her on the cheek.

'You know me so well, Meg. But please, not a word to Mother. She will be in my ear filling my head with 'do's' and 'don'ts'. I can't afford any distraction.'

'Oh Charlie! You are doing the right thing, I just know it. Lily adores you and has brought the light back into your face.'

'I adore her. She is my salvation and my one true love. I could not imagine living without her in my life. She has made me whole again and I plan to spend the remainder of my days doting on her and keeping her happy.' I nervously checked my reflection in the mirror. 'But I have to do this right. I can't barrel in like I used to in the days of old. I want her father's blessing first and if he can't give it, I will make it my soul objective to convince him otherwise.' I shuddered at the thought of

Mr Whittle's dismissal. My fragile heart would shatter. Meg brushed my coat down and gave me a hug.

'No man in his right mind could ever say you are not good enough for their daughter. I have looked after you since you were just a babe in my arms and I know you are a very, very special young man. Now go out there and make Mr Whittle a happy father.'

I headed out to the Whittle household. Normally, it was Lily I came to see but this time I presented my calling card and asked to speak to Mr Whittle. I was brought into the parlour and provided with a cup of tea while I waited.

The time was stretched with every second eked out in a miserly fashion. I drank the tea but it could have been puddle water for all the taste I noticed. I looked around the very familiar room and recalled the numerous chats I had endured with Mrs Whittle before being allowed to walk with her daughter. Her cook was not of the same proficiency as ours and it took many swills of brewed tea to be able to choke down some of her crumbier attempts at cake. Her sickly sweet walnut slice still made me nauseous to think of it. I now hated walnuts, but I ate every piece, pasting a smile over my face and complimenting its delectability. It was no wonder that Lily and Carla were so slim.

Mr Whittle walked in and shook my hand.

'Greetings Charles. How nice to see you again. How is your father?'

'Well, thank you, sir. He is in London at the present time.'

'London? Dreadful place. The air is positively poisonous.'

I wholeheartedly agreed.

'And your mother is well?'

'Yes. She is currently visiting Mistress Magda Williams. Her herbal teas are highly sought after.'

Mr Whittle frowned slightly at the mention of Magda but quickly recovered. Magda Williams seemed to have that effect on the Warwickshire men.

'I'm sure they are. Now what is it I can do for you today?'

I looked at Mr Whittle and cleared my throat.

'Mr Whittle. I have been spending a great deal of time with your daughter Lily. We have been kept very busy with my book.'

Mr Whittle nodded. 'Yes, so you have.'

'And…she is a wonderful artist, really very good.'

'Agreed. She has her mother's gifts.' He nodded proudly.

'Well…it's just…that…'

'Speak up, man.' He was getting impatient. It was now or ever.

'Well, Mr Whittle…I…I… would like to formally ask your permission for her hand in marriage.'

He sat back, a bit nonplussed. My shift from the book

to matrimony had him somewhat mystified. I stared at him and silently cursed my hasty stupidity. The carefully prepared speech I had rehearsed repeatedly on the way over had disappeared from my brain. In my anxiety to receive his approval, my mouth stumbled over the speech clattering in my head and drove straight to the heart of the matter. I watched him regather.

'Well. I see. And where do you propose to live?'

I understood his concern. He had already lost one daughter to the veiled world of India and Lily was all he had left. I had thought of this too.

'We would live at my parents' estate until we had built a dwelling on some land by the river. My father had earmarked that land for me when I came of age. I assist my father with his business at home therefore it is not necessary for us to move to London. We would stay right here and we could visit you as often as you would like.'

Mr Whittle's face brightened at the thought. I know he loved his daughters dearly and though she would no longer live with him, he had to accept the reality of her leaving home soon. He looked at me, making me want to squirm (but knowing I daren't) under his steady gaze. I was holding my breath and my chest felt tight. This was the moment.

'You are a fine young man, Charles. My wife tells me that Lily is besotted with you. It is only natural that this was going to happen one day.' He pulled out his cigar box and clipped an end. 'I give you my blessing. You may ask her hand in marriage.'

I breathed out deeply and shook his proffered hand, smiling weakly. 'Cigar?' He offered, one hand reaching to his box. I politely declined and made my excuses leaving him phlegmatically smoking alone.

I asked a maid to call on Lily and enquire if she would care to take a walk with me. She was down immediately, her cheeks flushed with pleasure. My heart caught in my throat as I stared at her loveliness. I adored her and couldn't believe she might soon be mine. I smiled at her and offered my arm for her to hold as we stepped out.

We found a bench in her parents' superbly manicured garden. What they lacked in cooks was well compensated for with their gardener. I had often admired the fusion of colour and structure that allowed small pockets of privacy and stolen kisses with Lily when I visited. The romance was in the air with the soft perfume of roses wafting around us. She held my hand and looked at me. I went down on one knee and looked back at her. Her spare hand went to her mouth.

'Lily Mavis Whittle. I have loved you ever since the day I first saw you at primary school. You caught my eye and my heart when we were only children. I have always thought of you when I was at Rugby and you were the endless light in my darkest days. You have brought me back from the brink of nothingness with your gentle affection and dedication. I am not worthy of your love, but if you will have me…I promise with all my heart, that I will never let a day go by, without letting you know how much I love you and what you mean to me… Lily Mavis Whittle, will you marry me?'

I watched her, feeling my heart pounding. She touched my cheek tenderly.

'Charles. My darling Charles. I love you too. Yes, I will marry you. I will be your wife.'

I swelled with joy and took her in my arms for a lingering kiss. She was mine, all mine! I felt euphoric and happier than I could have ever dreamed possible. This was love. This was my future wife. Oh glory, glory be!

Whirlwind

My mother was in her element. The vague notion of a long engagement was quickly dispelled with a flick of her stately hand. She visited the Whittles the following day and after much mutual fussing and congratulations, arranged a dinner for the two families at our house. My father was dutifully called home and a sumptuous feast appeared and was appreciatively eaten by the Whittles. I took Lily into the jeweller's without Mother's knowledge and we peacefully looked together and chose a diamond ring for her to wear. It met the approval of both mothers who paused briefly before reminding us to send word to our relatives of the impending marriage. We were barraged with multiple letters and cards sending their well wishes and many visits were made to admire the happy bride-to-be to inspect firstly her ring, and then me. Mrs Whittle was immediately at the newspapers announcing our engagement for all to see and it felt as if the whole town knew we were betrothed.

We bounced from shop to shop nodding dazedly at the merchants, who quailed when they saw my mother enter the door. Lily and I did not want a fuss and we both bravely stood up to our mothers' unwanted advice.

The wind flew out of Mrs Whittle's sails a bit until Lily asked her if she could have the honour of wearing her mother's old wedding dress. Immediately maids were sent scurrying to the attic to reverently produce the delicate white-lace gown. Carla had refused to wear it, saying it was old-fashioned and preferring a pearl-laden affair sent from France, but the classic elegance of the dress needed only small adjustments to suit my darling Lily.

We agreed to a church ceremony followed by a wedding breakfast at the Whittle household. Only a few very close family members and friends attended – a great contrast from Carla's gregarious cacophony of guests. My mother was frustrated at our insistence of a humble get-together but with a gentle word in her ear by Father, she agreed, on the proviso that the Whittles would allow our cook the honour of baking the wedding cake. The Whittles accepted the kind offer much to everyone's relief.

The day was a whirlwind, with speeches and presents from virtually every guest who attended. It wasn't until late afternoon before both Lily and I were able to say our tearful goodbyes to our parents and get on the carriage taking us to a quiet inn in Rugby. Meg and Jack had already packed my luggage and Lily's trunk was firmly attached at the back. We arrived as husband and wife, the fact of which I proudly informed the inn-keeper.

She smiled and winked at me before showing us to our room. Once the luggage was unpacked and brought in and fresh water provided we were finally left alone. We looked at each other, suddenly feeling shy. Our courtship up till then had been mere kisses and holding hands, all done with the sense that someone was close by watching for any impropriety. This would be our first night together without restrictions or expected behaviours. It was a daunting feeling for both of us.

'Mrs Fenton.'

'Mr Fenton.'

We smiled coyly at each other and kissed tenderly.

'How would you like to do this?' I asked, watching her blush and look down.

'If…if perhaps you could help me out of my dress? My maid usually does it and I can't untie the laces myself.' She reddened further. 'But keep your eyes closed.'

I wondered how I would achieve this as I studied all the ties and hooks, but I closed my eyes just the same and fumbled my way to her back. My hands scrambled and fossicked in a vain attempt to do as she asked but I had been working for nearly ten minutes without success. Eventually her modesty was overcome by her concern for my efforts.

'Perhaps it would be more sensible if you opened your eyes after all,' she offered, feeling flustered.

I breathed a sigh of relief and got to work straight

away, the task only slightly easier with my indelicate hands. I laboured with a great deal of concentration and was able to release and untie first her dress and then, not one but two, petticoats. A small sense of satisfaction was snuffed out when I saw the corset. The white feminine ribbon could have just as easily been a tangled fishing line, and I took it on as such. Start at the top and slowly unwind and pull your way down. A small bead of sweat appeared on my forehead and I became engrossed with finding out how it came off. Lily kept quiet, moving with every tug of the evil corset. I gave a small hurrah when it finally could be unclipped and removed. This left only the chemise and drawers, a small slither of linen between me and Lily's naked skin. My emotion changed from self-congratulatory to nervous anticipation. She turned bashfully and faced me.

I could see the outline of her breasts through the sheer white fabric. The room became very warm and I loosened my tie, removing my jacket and vest. She stood watching me while I debated removing any more of my own clothing to make her feel more at ease with her near-nakedness. I went down to my drawers and, slightly puffing, stood again in front of her. My hand moved automatically to her breast. She was startled and I moved it quickly away again but she placed my hand back with her own and tip-toed to kiss me on the lips. She was trembling but so brave and I kissed her back as gently and intimately as I could. She responded back, her arms curling around my neck, deepening the kiss. We broke apart and stared intensely into each other's eyes. We kissed again before I moved to her neck, trailing light kisses down to her shoulder. I picked her up and carried her to the bed, lowering her down as if she were so fragile she could break. I got in too and put the cover over us before modestly removing my drawers. She lay still, her eyes wide and anxiously watching me wriggle and throw my undergarment to the floor. It was the first time she had been in a room, let alone the same bed, with a naked man in her life and she was frightened. My heart sank a little at her face and I moved cautiously towards her to kiss her lightly and tenderly until she relaxed a little. We continued to kiss and I caressed her, softly touching her arms and then breasts, moving slowly and retreating whenever she tensed. I had all the time in the world. I did not want our first love-making experience to be one she regretted. I loved her so much, never thinking that such raw emotions such as these could be possible. I would never, ever let anyone or anything come between her and me. She responded to my loving embraces and emboldened, I moved to her drawers and pulled them down. There were no hindrances between us now and I lay on top of her, resting my weight as much as possible on my elbows.

'Are you okay?' I asked her softly.

'Yes. I love you, Charles.'

'Can I put it in?' I said. She nodded nervously.

I gradually entered her, feeling a slight resistance, then a warm wetness of blood coming out. She flinched slightly and I stopped, waiting for her signal to continue. She kept very still and was almost relieved when I ejaculated and it was over.

'Did it hurt?'

'A little.'

'I'm sorry, my love.'

'It's all right. It will be better next time. Carla told me so.'

Trust Carla, I thought, but then I silently thanked her for her sisterly information. We spent the rest of the night entwined together and woke refreshed, though still somewhat shy in our nudity.

My mother was mortified that we only wanted a few weeks' travelling around England, turning down her enthusiastic offerings of a long extended sojourn through Europe. We were not travellers like Carla and Daniel, who were sending back occasional letters filled with spices and perfumes, adventures and exploration. Our excitement would be the train ride taking us to different parts of our country and stopping wherever we felt the urge.

I knew we were close to Arthur Manning's hometown and on an impulse, asked Lily if it would be all right to visit him and his fiancée. She had heard so much about Arthur that she was more than a little intrigued and agreed immediately. We cheekily decided not to send a calling card announcing our impending arrival, but just jauntily stepped up to his photography studio and walked in.

'Charles Fenton! How marvellous to see you! Come in. Come in.' He shook my hand enthusiastically and turned to look at Lily. 'And you must be the most beautiful Mrs Lily Fenton. What a pleasure to finally meet you.' He kissed her hand and bowed. She curtsied slightly and smiled.

He showed us through the back where his studio attached to his lodgings. Tea was offered and poured and we sat in mutual appreciation. Lily liked him and the conversation flowed as he reminisced about school days. He convinced us it would be an honour to have us stay for dinner and he would invite Sara to join us. We agreed and found a nearby inn to stay at and refresh ourselves before returning to his house promptly at six. We found Sara already there. She was not what I expected at all. She had long curly gloriously red hair which defied the multitude of bobby pins endeavouring to restrain its freedom without luck. Tiny ringlets feathered down and bordered the most exquisite green eyes I had ever seen. The emerald colour flashed out from under long brown lashes and considered us. Her lips were generously pouted and sensual and her nose perfectly proportioned to make her face an inspiration to the arts. When she smiled, her teeth were blindingly white and we both looked at her dazzled by her beauty. I would have fallen in love instantly if my heart had not been already taken.

'This is Sara, my fiancée,' Arthur announced with his arm casually around her waist. We looked at my good friend Arthur, standing tall and gangly with his inglorious wings for ears and I know, without doubt, both Lily and I were wondering (somewhat guiltily) how he managed to become attached to such magnificence as Sara. We made our greetings and followed them to the dining table, rather baffled.

If beauty was sometimes sullied by vapidness, then it did not apply in this circumstance. She was intelligent and thoughtful, prompting us to talk about our book that was now selling at the stores. She listened assiduously and I don't mind saying that Lily and I both felt a small crush for her and we spent the evening vying for her attention. She was also an animal lover and enthused about her pet cat Duke, a furry grey moggy that proudly brought her dead mice every day. Knowing Lily's childhood penchant for rodents, I took a sideways glance at her and worried she would be upset at this daily slaughter, but she was completely captivated with Sara and appeared not to notice. Arthur filled the table with roast saddle of mutton, green peas, fresh dinner rolls with sweet cream butter and pickles. This was followed by fresh blackberries and a lemon-balm cake with a custard sauce that Sara had baked. There was no end to her perfection and we marvelled again at this creature. It was a delightful evening and we stayed late, sipping port and becoming dear friends with each passing hour. When it was finally and regretfully time to retire, I took that opportunity to congratulate Arthur on his beautiful bride-to-be.

'My word, Arthur, you are a dark horse. She's absolutely stunning! Why didn't you tell us how beautiful she was?' I enthused, shaking his hand. He looked at me a bit perplexed.

'Is she? I hadn't really noticed. Beauty is more than the skin that holds the bodily organs inside, Charles,' he remonstrated. 'However, I must admit to being positively fascinated with her passion for technological improvisation. We have spent many joyous hours debating over the optimal application of the wet collodian plate process with regards to photographic spectrograms of star processes.'

I stared back at him, not really understanding what he was saying but deciding he really was quite unique. The ladies arrived at the door and Lily and I made our fondest farewells to them both, promising to visit them in the very near future. We looked at Sara, hypnotised like moths around a bright light and it really was an effort to pull away from her glowing splendour. We were deeply envious of Arthur receiving all of her devotion and lingered at the edges in hope of a few scraps coming our way. We hung onto every word spoken from her sweet lips and nodded in profound agreement to all statements she uttered. Any passing glance was hooked in by our hunting eyes, straining to hold her completely to ourselves. Arthur remained relaxed and Sara seemed unfazed by our adulation. Finally and regretfully, we turned to leave. Star-gazed, we walked home chattering animatedly about our new friend.

That night, I had my first nightmare since being married to Lily. I thrashed around in the sheets, wailing and covered in sweat. Lily shook me awake, staring at me with wide eyes, frightened at my suffering and anguish. I denied any memory of the nightmare when asked and pretended it had never happened before. She held me close and stroked my hair, whispering that she loved me and would never let me go. She kissed my brow and cheeks and held me to her bosom and with time, my trembling stopped and I calmed. I felt sick at lying to her and sicker still that my murderous past gnawed away at my future happiness. I cursed anything that ate into my precious memories I was collecting with my darling Lily. There was no way of knowing how precious my memories with her would be, or how short.

Married Life

We returned back to Fenton Estate after several weeks of leisurely travel around England. We took secret delight in visiting every bookstore and hunting for our book 'The Goblin Wars', written by Charles Augustus Fenton with illustrations by Lily Whittle. At Lily's insistence, I even bought a copy which we hungrily read through with contented pride. We entered the store in full acting capability, pretending to 'chance' upon the most fascinating piece of literature (our book) we had ever seen. Our delight was second only to a dipsomaniac discovering his gin bottle was not yet empty as he had previously thought. We may have laid it on a bit thick, gripping the book wondrously waiting to drink of its magic. The storekeeper certainly looked at us sideways and I couldn't help thinking, as he wended his way through the incommodious clutter, that he was rather brisk with removing the treasured book from our hands, wrapping it and taking our money. His face warranted no invitation to begin a desired and detailed conversation about this amazing literary find we now owned. We brooked our resentment and held the parcel nestled under my arm for that evening's private crowing.

My parents had set up our furniture in part of the estate, organising the delivery of Lily's clothing and toiletries becoming of a lady. We settled in and began almost immediately to concentrate on the building of our very own home.

My father had already marked out the land for our future abode. He had an architect friend in London called Mr Trevor Boltside, who kindly agreed to meet us and discuss what our vision might be. Lily was very keen to introduce the gas light to our home and avoid candles as much as possible. As a child she had the unfortunate ability to knock things over in her quest to recapture her escaping pet mice. She wished to avoid her mother shrieking and trying to stamp her cherished babies to death. On one such occasion, she had upset a hallway candle, which not only scorched her dress but poured hot wax onto her arm, burning her terribly. My very own mother had given HER mother a soothing balm which Mistress Magda Williams had concocted and she healed without scarring. I was not surprised to hear this and swallowing a lump in my throat, I extolled the healing ability of my mother's dearest friend. Lily was naïve to my awkwardness.

We met Mr Trevor Boltside that autumn. He was of small stature, elegantly dressed and festooned with a most luxuriantly full moustache. His black beetle eyes scuttled around our parlour, searching and devouring the room's character and assessing what needed to be done in his professional opinion. His nose curled over the moustache in defence of its existence, almost daring us to breach its stronghold. He spoke briskly and wrote just as quickly, leaving the eloquence and poetry to the socialites. I could see why my father enjoyed this no-nonsense man.

'And the nursery? Have you considered where you would like that?' he asked us in his forthright manner. Lily blushed and looked down at her hands that were pretending to lie still on her lap. She looked at me to speak.

'Ah… I guess we hadn't really thought about it. We have barely returned from our honeymoon, so it is still very early days for such an eventuality.' I smiled at him in an apologetic way to cover for our discomfort at such a personal question. He looked at me and raised an eyebrow, before looking again at my wife and then back at me. He seemed to be disbelieving of our innocence and I was rather taken aback at the scrutiny. Had I missed something? I looked back at him affronted and prepared to cross swords if he dared speak any derogatory comment regarding my wife. Mr Trevor Boltside kept quiet and we moved on to the guest rooms. Before long the details had been sketched and he returned back to his office to commence the process of building our home.

The weather was crisp and the grass crackled under our feet in the early morning. All visitors were drawn to our generous fires dotted throughout the house. Our cook was widely appreciated after the creation of the wedding cake she made for Lily and I, and the Fenton Estate became a very popular place to call on for delicious afternoon tea. No one was disappointed. Their eyes lit up when the tiered stand arrived, cascading with angel cakes, moist date loaf and pikelets suffering under the weight of rich blackberry jam and whipped cream. The cook was in seventh heaven, beating and whipping, layering and slicing her masterpieces to be celebrated with oohs and aahs heard from the parlour. My mother would have been horrified if she'd known how many cards of enquiry were surreptitiously given to Cook as to whether she could be convinced to work for them. She ignored them all, tossing them in the fire. She had virtually grown up with the Fenton family, arriving there as a domestic servant at the tender age of seven and would stay here until no longer required. She had no fear of being cast out. Charles Senior and Elizabeth had already decided long ago that they would provide a generous pension and room for her until her demise, rewarding her loyalty and years of dedicated service.

This was the Fenton way. Our household staffs were among the happiest in the town. Any dissenters were quickly weeded and tossed out; all those that endeavoured to work hard and live a clean life were rewarded richly by my parents. We had a good reputation as employers and vacancies were rare. On the odd occasion that we advertised in the newspaper for staff, the applications were numerous, leaving my father to painfully short-list and select the lucky applicant. My mother found the job too heart-breaking and would retire to her room or visit Mistress Magda Williams to avoid the pleas of starvation and misery directed to Charles Senior. Occasionally she would bustle down to Cook and whisper to her to give away a day-old loaf or a few vegetables when her husband wasn't there. He detested begging and vowed everyone could work for his supper and not drain the nation's economy by leeching at the elite. Ironically, when he thought no one was looking, he too would smuggle small bags of food to the more pitiful that turned up at their door. He would hand the bags to grateful peasants threatening them with hellfire if they should ever mention the benefactor of their goods to others. They would take the bag and run with sideways glances, thanking him in dulcet tones and nodding their silent promise to his demand.

We were fully staffed and nestling down to the wintry season in front of the fire. The plate wore crumbs signifying there once presided yet another of Cook's illustrious projects. Mr and Mrs Whittle were visiting and regaling us with the sordid details of Queen Victoria and Prince

Albert's son, Edward. He had been sent to Ireland with the Grenadier Guards to curb his waywardness and bring discipline to the future king of England. It was during the summer and the 12,000 soldiers had drawn the attention of some sixty-odd prostitutes, euphemistically named the 'Curragh Wrens'. They had been called after the feathered birds on account of their nearby abodes being constructed within a thick perimeter of gorse. The rooms were sparse with no windows or chimneys, but the walls were impressively solid and incorporated mud and gorse branches, making them surprisingly strong. It was to this dubious nest that Edward flew in and made his acquaintance of one Nellie Clifden; supposedly an actress, but we could all see through that disguise, Mrs Whittle smirked in scandalous glee. The 'affair' was discussed through all the gentlemen's bars and eventually reached the ears of Baron Stockmar, one of Prince Albert's trusted advisers. He informed the long-suffering father of his son's latest misadventure and young 'Bertie' was swiftly returned to England to be kept under unofficial guard until a suitable wife could be found. Prince Albert had just returned from reprimanding his son and was currently laid up in bed following another gastric attack.

'Children can do that to you,' muttered Mr Whittle, who had just that week received correspondence from Carla, informing them that they had been trapped in a sandstorm of several hours in Persia. She delighted in writing how 'terribly exciting and romantic is was to be stranded against nature, protected only by the camel and rustling cloth'. It was only the experience of the natives that had saved their lives with their prompt actions and disregard for their own safety, making sure the hallowed Englishmen were firmly barricaded before attending to themselves. All that Carla had noted was the snug 'camel tent' where she and Daniel marvelled at the enormous sound and buffeting of wind. They emerged some hours later and watched the camels shake the dust from their coats and wait patiently while the people followed their lead. The fact that they could have died did not enter in their equation and Mr and Mrs Whittle were shaken that their beloved daughter had been exposed to such danger. Mr Whittle needed Magda's tonic powders to soothe a stomach ulcer.

I listened avidly whilst my wife raised her cup of tea to her lips. She paused and sniffed the brew, frowning.

'The tea might be stale, Charles. It has a funny odour to it.' She offered the cup to me to study and smell.

'It smells fine to me. There is nothing wrong with it, Lily.' I carefully corrected her, as she had been a bit short with me lately.

'You are mistaken, I'm sure. Mama, please tell me what you think.' She handed the cup to her mother, who hesitantly agreed with me in finding no fault, though adding it had a perfume that was unsuited to more delicate tastes. I considered this an appeasement to Lily, who was frowning at her usually supportive mother, completely disputing the fact.

She continued to sniff the cup and declared it undrinkable, placing it down firmly. This was completely out of character for my polite and decorous wife but I dared not say another word. I just sat and speculated on her strange behaviour.

Prince Albert

Just a few weeks later, Prince Albert was declared dead. The bells of the churches tolled in mutual solemnity. The country was in the blackest mood and the shock was on everyone's face. It was declared to be caused by the 'fever', typhoid fever, my nemesis. My mother relived the scenes of my own battle with this disgusting disease and prayed more fervently that night for the gift of her son and the passing of her queen's husband. She was most distressed, as was my Lily, who reacted violently. On hearing the sad news, she rushed from the room holding her mouth and was fiercely sick. Her pallid face on her return announced to us all how affected she had been and she was absent from supper that night, preferring to lie on our bed and recover.

The country stopped, in mourning, and my parents travelled to Windsor to stand as the funeral parade passed through the streets. All shops were closed, curtains drawn and people draped themselves in black to show the deepest respect for beloved Prince Albert. He had suffered many years of ill health and it was rumoured that the behaviour of his son, Edward, was the final straw to break his back. Queen Victoria was strongly advised to go to Osbourne for fear her grief would not bear the service.

Lily and I attended the evening church services and spent the remainder of the night sitting in silent sorrow for the great man. It affected me deeply with our kindred tie of the typhoid fever and I barely noticed the white pallor of my usually admired wife, so lost in my own deep musing. Christmas was a sombre affair with many staying at home behind darkened curtains and smothering any festivities as poor taste. It wasn't until a few days after Christmas that my eyes truly opened and I saw Lily in a clearer light. She looked ghastly; her skin was white and her cheeks hollow. She complained of ongoing nausea and fatigue and could barely be roused from bed, refusing anything but peppermint tea. Alarmed, I talked to my mother who had already sent word to Mistress Magda Williams to visit as soon as possible. I sat holding her hand and died a thousand deaths before Mistress Magda arrived.

'Charles, could I please have a moment with your wife?' she asked in a manner that needed no response. I moved meekly out and hovered by the door. My mother was allowed to stay, a point that rankled a little. Magda conducted a full examination of my wife, quizzing her on different aspects of her health, asking about dietary intake and general wellbeing, before I was graciously allowed to return.

'Please, Mistress Williams, what is the matter with her?' I asked.

'She is with child. You are going to be a father.'

Time stopped and I stared at Magda in pure disbelief. 'How could this have happened?'

My mother ignored me and happily kissed Lily on the brow. 'You darling girl. I wish you all the best in this glorious journey of life. Congratulations.' Lily grabbed my mother's hand and kissed it before also kissing Magda's hand. Smiling weakly, she reached for me and hugged me, rousing me from my state of shock. 'I love you, Charles,' she whispered into my ear and she settled back into the pillow.

I looked at her as if it were the first time I had seen her. Lily, my wife, was going to have a baby. Lily, my wife, was with child. The news was slowly sinking in and a surge of paternal pride rose inside of me, pressing my heart to beat strong and fast and my chest to swell. I was going to be a father. I, Charles Augustus Fenton, had created an heir. A grin lifted to my face and stretched from ear to ear. I stood up and hugged and twirled my mother around the room. She laughed and pulled my ears playfully before kissing my cheek. I even hugged Mistress Magda in a spontaneous show of gratitude for bearing such wonderful news. She hugged me back, congratulating me and warning me to take care of Lily. She left us with various herbal teas and tonics to soothe Lily's nausea and advised her to ensure she took small walks every day in the fresh air to keep her blood well oxygenated and healthy for the baby.

My father was elated. There was an heir to the Fenton fortune. We celebrated with the Whittles, who came over immediately on hearing the news. Lily sat pale but smiling at the table, watching us devour roast meats and gravies, wine and cheeses, whilst sipping at her tea and beef broth that Cook had made especially for her. The tonic powders helped immeasurably and her health improved as each week passed. We dutifully took a small walk daily, only staying inside when the weather was particularly foul. The necessity of having our own home became of most paramount importance to me and I bothered Mr Trevor Boltside constantly. He bore the impatience with grace and had the autonomy now to discuss freely about the nursery I had previously rejected. The work was progressing, but never as fast as I had hoped and in the end, for my own peace of mind, I avoided the construction site and focussed instead on my father's papers and accounts sent from his legal firm in London.

Occasionally, and at the behest of my wife, who refused to be flapped about, I was sent to my office to work on a new book called 'Fenton's Bedtime Stories for Children'. We had enjoyed moderate success with 'The Goblin Wars' and Lily thought it would be very special indeed to be able to amuse our own child with words and illustrations created by us. She would often sit and paint a most detailed picture with pumpkins and pixies, giants and toadstools that inspired a new story. It did not seem long before another book was produced and duly accepted for publication. We could not have been happier than we were right then.

The catch-up

It was the following March that we were sent word of Arthur and Sara's wedding. They had a private ceremony at his parents' house. He had sold the photography studio and purchased a new one with living arrangements more suited to a married couple. He wrote and asked if we would care to visit, adding he had also invited Henry Felldon and Benjamin Roberts to complete a merry get-together.

I was very excited. Henry and I kept in contact regularly and he featured regularly in the newspaper with his cricket prowess in the Warwickshire county team. It was only a matter of time before he played for his country as far as we were concerned.

In between playing cricket in the summer and rugby in the winter, he had managed to attach himself to a young lady called Harriet. She was quiet and mousey and completely infatuated with the mighty Henry. I'm sure she spoke, but I could barely make out what she said when she did. Henry must have the auditory sharpness of an owl because he would smile and laugh on completion of every whisper. It frustrated both Lily and me to be missing potentially amusing narratives but we did not wish to appear rude so we smiled and laughed on cue with Henry. Up to this point our subterfuge remained undetected and the system worked well.

We decided to share the carriage with them to the train station and then proceed onwards to the newly-weds' marital home. Henry had not met Sara yet and had been driven mad with our blathering about how beautiful and fantastic she was. He held doubts, but we were reassured all would be revealed on introduction.

The noise on the train made conversation with Harriet impossible so we spent the journey talking to each other. Lily now had a baby bump and I was forever cossetting over her. This would be our last trip before sharing each other with a baby. The house would not be ready for another six months, despite my pleas, so we resigned to the fact that my mother would lay siege on our little one until we escaped. Between her and Lily's mother we had our heads filled with thoroughly important facts on baby rearing and the only proper and correct way to do it. This would have been valuable if the points they made didn't contradict each other. My nightmares continued, but I accepted them as part of my life and tried my best to keep them from Lily. There were long periods of uninterrupted sleep that did occur without rhyme or reason for which I was grateful.

We arrived at Henry and Sara's and found Benjamin Roberts had beaten us there. He was as athletic as ever, strapping and single. I hadn't seen him since I'd left school and we hugged and slapped each other's back laughing. Henry, Harriet and Benjamin all instantly fell in love with Sara as we did and she took the group adulation with style, making sure we were all given equal and fair attention from her. Arthur remained his usual conundrum of relaxed self-reliance. We settled in to a night of conversation and fine food.

'Henry. I hear you are a great sportsman. What do you do when the field hasn't claimed you?' Sara asked, her eyes twinkling magically. Henry lit up.

'I am an accountant. Numbers have always been my game. I am a straight-up man who likes facts and figures. There's no deception or distortion and the numbers arrive in obedient clarity. I strike my ledgers like I strike my cricket balls; with surety and strength.'

'I am sure you are a wonderful accountant in that case.' Sara smiled, and we all sighed and felt bitter at Henry for this sought-after accolade. He puffed out just a little and looked smug.

'And you Benjamin? Is there no young lady waiting to catch your eye?' she asked, offering him a plate.

'Sadly no. But if you should have a sister...' He waggled his eyebrows.

Sara laughed and it was musical to our ears. 'Unfortunately, I only have two brothers, but I will keep an eye out for you.' Benjamin nodded appreciatively. Arthur raised an eyebrow and looked at us all hypnotised by his wife. How very odd we were.

Harriet spoke and Lily and I drew closer to prepare to catch the words. It seemed she too, was clambering for Sara's benevolence.

'Would you like to hear a song I have written?'

Once again, I thought we'd misheard her. I could have sworn she was contemplating singing, but that would have been ridiculous. This time, I had to clarify.

'Pardon?' I asked politely, and we all leaned in together, except Henry.

'I said, would you like to hear a song? I made one up and sang it to Henry just the other day.'

'Yes! It was beautiful! You sing like an angel.' Henry enthused. With that endorsement, and some misgiving, we settled back into our chairs and watched her stand and collect herself. This would be interesting. I focussed my ears to high alert and cocked my head slightly for improved listening. My friends adopted the same posture of high concentration. Her mouth opened and out exploded the most euphonious sound I had ever heard. The room filled with her voice and resonated around the walls, pushing us back to sink in complete surprise and amazement. We felt the power of her singing and were captured with the poignancy of her lyrics. She took us on a journey of passionate aspirations, yearning to lift us higher and threatening to break our walls down under the intensity. If Arthur'd had the ability to capture our faces on his camera, he would have caught a sea of open-mouthed guppies lost in the moment. Henry sat through it and watched her lovingly. Her attraction became tenfold and I swore never to judge a person so quickly again. Sara, for that brief moment, was swept into the shadows as we sat entranced with the song bursting out of Harriet's mouth. The last haunting line glided into our ears and sat there weighty in its luxuriance. After the song had finished, we rose and applauded little Harriet, the mouse, and offered our newly found respect. Both Sara and Lily had tears streaming from their eyes, and I think a speck of dust irritated mine enough to quickly be swept away. Looking around, it appeared the room was dusty enough to catch us all and the men coughed and shrugged it off to regather themselves. She sat down next to Henry and smiled demurely, her voice returning to a murmur.

'That's my girl,' was all Henry said and kissed her lightly on the cheek. She blushed and squirmed at being the centre of attention. Henry picked up on this and began recalling the famous game when his good friend, Charles Fenton, saved the day with a winning tackle against the terror of Rugby. The way he spoke transformed me into a super hero sure and true, when the reality was that I ended up with a mouthful of dirt and an injured shoulder; but it would have been rude to correct him. Henry and Benjamin joined in, adding feats that no mere mortal could have done, until the girls were holding their sides in laughter and all pretence of admiration towards me was obliterated. I sat pretending to preen and even demonstrated the finer points of tackling to the delight of my guests, using Arthur as my prop. He role-played the beast well, trying to puff his slight frame into a menacing rugby player, deepening his voice and thumping around the room in primate fashion. He even thumped his chest and stuffed a cushion under his shirt to reconstruct the scene more accurately. We finished with a flourish, with me pretending to tackle him and him falling face down into the lounge chair, making the girls squeal. We stood up and bowed dramatically, accepting the applause given for our performance. It was a fabulous night of merriment and we were unwilling to leave when the time came to return to our own homes a few days later. I looked at my happy friends and my beautiful wife and wondered why God had blessed me so after all that I had done. I prayed and gave thanks to him every night before going to sleep to have, or have not, my vivid and disturbing dreams.

My son

My wife was enormous. It was now summer and the heat was making her irritable and unpleasant to be around. This is a fact that I kept to myself as I cherished my head. She fidgeted, moaned and farted in her sleep. When I, in a moment of madness, laughingly told her this, she denied it hotly and refused to speak to me for the remainder of the day. She slapped my hand away when I reached to touch the baby and then in the next minute, demanded I feel the baby kicking, annoyed if I didn't leap up immediately to catch the precious moment.

I spent long periods of time locked away in my office, using the remorseful excuse of pressing work to do, when really I was hiding from her. My father would keep me company, nodding and smoking his pipe while I babbled on about this strange woman that was once my delicate flower. His own advice was, 'It will pass.'

Meanwhile Lily was fretting and telling both my mother and hers how unthoughtful I was, how I avoided her and didn't listen enough when she was complaining of aching feet or a pressing sciatic nerve in her back. The pain would shoot down her leg and nearly cripple her when it happened and she expected me to take it away; after all, it was my entire fault. The mothers consoled her and plumped her pillows, rubbed her hands with lavender cream and her feet with peppermint oil. Whenever I made an entrance into this room filled with oestrogen, I was glared at by all three, and upon hastily retreating, I declared to make it my focus to get our house built and move out before all control was gone. My father agreed that would be the best thing to do and poured me another port, sucking sagely on his pipe.

Finally. Finally. Finally. The day came that she went into labour. Her initial contractions were mild and she walked around, breathing deeply as her mother had shown her. She even smiled at me and seemed as excited as I was that the day was now here and she was going to be a mother. The happiness did not last long, however, before her contractions grew stronger and stronger, and soon I became the man that had done this to her and I was to get out of her sight. Magda was called in as soon as her waters broke and I was scurried away by the women, with the door firmly shut behind me. I went pale listening to her cries of pain through the door and might have made the mistake of re-entering if my father hadn't happened to walk by and rescue me back to our familiar den.

The waiting was far worse than I had imagined. Hour upon hour crept by, only broken by the occasional plate of food brought in by the maid. My father read his newspaper in an unruffled manner, telling me snippets here and there that he thought might interest me. I fumed inside at his obvious collected calm and paced the floor wondering if I should go see how she was getting on. Each time I voiced this opinion, my father firmly shook his head and counselled against it in his most austere manner.

'That would be MOST unadvisable son. MOST unadvisable.'

The door opened and my mother walked in. She was beaming and came up to me, hugging me and whispering into my ear those dream-like words: 'Congratulations. You have a son.'

'A son? I have a son?' I repeated her words in wonderment. She nodded and watched proudly as Charles Senior shook my hand and congratulated me heartily. I had a son. I had to see him immediately and despite my mother's remonstrations I strode up to our room and walked in. Lily was breastfeeding our son and talking quietly to Magda who looked askance when I entered the room but kept her peace. She drifted out silently and left us alone.

'Charles. I'm so pleased you're here... I love you so much. Come and kiss me.' She was still flushed from her delivery and damp with perspiration, but she was the most beautiful woman in the world at that moment. I kissed her on the brow, tasting salt from her sweat, then I gave her a longer kiss on her lips. She was the mother of my child, the love of my life and my heart was bursting with joy.

I could hear the snuffling of our son suckling away on her breast and I admired him and loved him instantly. He had been cleaned and wrapped by Magda in a little white cocoon. Lily handed him to me once he was sated. His milky breath and puffed tiny lips were exquisite to me, and his belch was an achievement proudly praised by us both. He stared at me with blurry eyes, contemplating the strange man staring down at him. I knew from the moment the pregnancy had been announced, what my son would be called.

'I name you Arthur Henry Benjamin Fenton.'

My mother used to tell me when I was growing up that I would be a famous name who would one day be a proud father, but I had always doubted her, until now. As an emerging author and now a parent, everything she said was becoming true. Too quickly, my doubts vanished. I should have known better and realised nothing would ever be as it seemed or should be.

Fairy tales

'The Goblin Wars' was moderately successful so we were completely taken aback with the nation-wide triumph of 'Fenton's Bedtime Stories for Children'. The stores could not keep up with the demand of the book. The publishers were high jigging with joy and kept busy printing more copies to supply the furious demand by the public. It had gone global and countries from all over our Commonwealth, even as far as New Zealand, were scrambling for a copy to read to their beloved children. This had a waterfall effect and created renewed interest for our earlier effort, 'The Goblin Wars', which doubly delighted Charnells and Co, making them and us a substantial wealth.

They brayed for another book. We were contacted regularly and reminded to strike while the iron was hot. All protestations were brushed aside and long conversations were had with Lily and me. We both loved working together and the partnership of her pictures and my writing was a winning combination. However, it would mean that something had to give, and my legal work for my father was suffering. I never really had the heart for law and had only persisted at his behest. Knowing how much he had already done for me, I was very reluctant to broach the subject of quitting my studies to him. He took it remarkably well.

'Charles. You have grown before me to become a man of your own means. I always knew you would be great at whatever you did. Both your mother and I have only ever wanted what was best for you, therefore you have my full support.' He shook my hand and accepted my resignation with aplomb.

We never looked back. 'Fenton's Forest Fables' was published with lightning speed, in between caring for little Arthur and moving into our brand new home. It was a busy, busy time for us and we loved it.

Arthur was a happy baby, smiling and laughing within weeks of his appearance. We took him with us everywhere and Lily even used his cherubic face as inspiration for one of her pictures. We worked on our book whenever the mood took us, and thankfully for the publishers, we were always motivated by our son for new and inventive tales to tell.

We had a nanny called Vadoma whom Lily had selected after advertising in the paper. She was a quiet and efficient girl, who had been brutally abused by her former employer, Mr Weston. Lily took pity on this little skeleton immediately and refused my remonstrations of caution. One look at the bruising on her arms and jutting ribs was enough to march her down to the local authorities, prompting them to arrest the villain. The village was in an uproar that one of their shopkeepers could have been capable of such cruelty. She had been fed weevil ridden grains and scraps and kept behind doors to hide her injuries. Hardly anyone had known she existed until the story came out, and we were all deeply upset that something like that could happen in our neighbourhood. The shop was closed down amidst cheers from the sanctimonious mob. He was made penniless with the monetary penalty and driven out of town to everyone's delight.

Vadoma rewarded our actions by being a caring and gentle nanny for Arthur. Nothing was too much trouble for her and she tended to his night-time feeds happily, bathing him and presenting him fed and giggling to us every morning. He pulled on her dark curly hair, weaving it around his fingers in delight and yanking away in the hope he could keep it. It must have hurt her but she would just unwind the fingers and carry on as if nothing had happened.

Our cook was never going to be as wondrous as my old cook, but she came close. She made it her life mission to put beef on Vadoma's bones and settled in to creating mutton stews with dumplings, vanilla custards and rich plum puddings. With such offerings, Vadoma had no choice but to eat and grow healthier and more confident before our eyes. We grew to depend on her in a very short time and I even convinced myself that it was me, not Lily, who had stumbled across this godsend.

Our hearts opened to her when she let it slip where she had come from. Her mother had disappeared when she was very young and she had been forced to go to the poorhouse with her older sister. The conditions there were bleak and as soon as they were old enough they had been forced to work twelve hours a day. It came as a blessing when her older sister found gainful employment on a farm only a few months before Vadoma was hired to work at the now-banished local grocer's. This was going to be the start of a better life for them both. They never heard from each other again, but she knew in her heart they would one day reunite.

Lily, whose sister was on the other side of the world, felt the yearning keenly and prayed that this would be a pleasure they could both share. I, on the other hand, was happy to keep Carla at a distance. Her adventures filled the letters sent erratically back to Lily and each story made Lily worry incessantly about her safety. I wished Carla would have the tact to keep some things unspoken but that was never her style.

With all the household staff interviewed and employed and the rooms furnished and filled with all sorts of paraphernalia that Lily had acquired, we were now looking like a proper home. We settled in to our house, away from the meddling mothers, and started our family life, not realising what lay around the corner waiting in the shadows.

The unexpected visitors

'Charles, I wouldn't let Arthur do that if I were you,' my lovely wife called when she saw her nappy-free baby clamber up on my knee.

'Nonsense Lily, he's a lad. All boys love climbing, it's good for their bones.'

'It's not his bones I'm worried about,' she responded.

On cue, a pungent smell wafted up to my nostrils. I sniffed and grimaced, looking down at my son, who had thoughtfully soiled himself before using my trouser leg as a ladder. The soft brown faeces smeared down each side of my thigh and his little white bottom twinkled at me and wriggled. I now understood why he was eager to remove the nappy and come and see his father. I would have done exactly the same in his situation.

'Oh, that is disgusting, Arthur! Get off!' I growled, hastily handing him to Lily, who held him at arm's length and called out for Vadoma. Arthur kicked his legs in frog-like fashion and laughed merrily at being passed from parent to parent. He was completely unapologetic and was even more ecstatic when Vadoma appeared to take him away for cleaning. Lily laughed.

'I did try to warn you.' I made to grab at her and

rubbed my trousers against her, but she was much too fast and ran away squealing. I looked after her fleeing form, smiling before returning my attention to the trousers and heading to our bedroom for a fresh pair. The housemaid was given the offensive-smelling clothing and she went straight to the copper tub to set to work. Her face said it all.

Jack and Meg visited from time to time, bringing their little daughter Rachael along. He was leasing some of our land and had spent every spare moment taking care of his cows. He sold the milk, butter and even cheese to the village and had nearly enough to place a deposit on the land to buy from us. Their calm and experienced voices were sought after whenever young Arthur prevailed to test our youthful innocence. We never realised how much a baby would alter our life-style and how much we would treasure having a nanny like Vadoma. I was mystified how Jack and Meg had managed their duties and taking care of Rachael without one. They usually visited in the afternoon and the knock on the door not long after the nappy affair had me ready to expand the now-funny story to them over a cup of tea. I chuckled in expectation of their faces as I opened the door. Instead of Meg and Jack however, there stood two sober-faced men. They both wore identical uniforms of a dark swallow tail coat furnished with eight brass buttons and a thick leather belt. A shiny top hat on their heads gave the impression of height and the crisp white trousers on the bottom hinted pious cleanliness both in thought and nature. They may have been twins except for the presence of a fulsome beard on one, whilst the other was clean shaven. I stared at them dumbly. The bearded one spoke.

'Are you Charles Augustus Fenton?' he enquired.

'I am he,' I responded, a bit perturbed.

'Mr Charles Fenton, I am Constable Jacob White and this is Constable Stuart Brown. We have come to take you to London, sir.'

'Whatever for?'

'We have found your trunk.'

Statements

I gave Lily a hastily written note to deliver to my father and kissed both her and Arthur goodbye, bidding them not to worry. She stared at the constables, who watched me and me alone, unfazed by the distractions of Arthur who, now clean and clothed, was attempting to pull at their wooden truncheons.

We travelled to London chatting civilly about general day-to-day topics, patently skirting the main issue at hand. It was a surreal experience with my inner turmoil carefully masked with an outward calm. It occurred to me that they had done this all before many times. How polite in the face of calamity we English are! It is our crutch to hold us when we wish to belong, when we falter, when we are lost, when we are offended. Our manners are our rulebook that never fails to inform others of what to do in any circumstance. We must never lose that stiff upper lip and nobility that makes us proudly British to the end. My father had taught me that as a child and it had held me through the most challenging of times.

We arrived at London and I was brought before the magistrate. He sat behind his desk and adjusted his glasses before peering down at the document held in his hand. He read carefully through the article first, his eyes belying nothing, and took a moment to dip his quill in ink before writing a small note on the margin. I stood between the two constables and looked at him.

He spoke: 'Charles Augustus Fenton, you are advised that on the morning of April 26th during the construction of sewer pipes along the Thames, a worker by the name of Elijah Goble, did discover a trunk partially covered by refuse at a disused docking station. It was in an ill state of disrepair and appeared abandoned. As the area was required to be cleared for further work he prepared to pull the trunk free. In doing so, the trunk broke apart and two decomposed bodies were found. He called for the police immediately, who, on further investigation, were able to determine the name of Charles Augustus Fenton etched on the brass within the trunk. They were able to ascertain your whereabouts and collect you for your statement. I now require you under oath to make your statement with regards to this discovery and your confirmation of ownership of the aforementioned trunk.'

My knees buckled and I would have fallen to the floor if not for the burly strength of the constables flanking me. I had known this day would come, in my heart I had known it; but there was nothing I could have done to prepare for it. I nodded and was frog-marched over to a desk where ink and paper lay waiting for me. In the corner was a large mound covered with sacking. Constable Jacob White and Constable Stuart Brown brought the item into the middle of the room. For a sickening moment I thought I was to be exposed to the putrefying remains of Lutka and our baby and my eyes rolled in anguish.

'Remove the cover,' the magistrate ordered.

They kept their eyes on me, watching my every move. I sank within myself and could feel my chest caving back towards my spine in an effort to self-destruct. An icy cold wave flowed over me, chilling my bones, stopping my heart and my ears began to ring a high-pitched squeal. This was the moment. This was my nightmare relived over and over for all these years. Lutka had come back to me and was going to get her vengeance.

They lifted the cover and revealed an empty decrepit trunk void of any human remains. It was musty but not overly unpleasant in smell and looked benign, if one did not know what it had been made to conceal. I began trembling all over and felt faint. The magistrate poured a snifter of brandy and handed it to Constable Jacob White.

'Give him this; it will restore his colour.'

The brandy was poured into my mouth, and I spluttered on the fumes. A dark curtain was drawing over my eyes and I started hyperventilating.

'He needs more, sir.'

The magistrate harrumphed but poured another nip, which was passed down and dribbled into me again. He stepped back and gave me room to breathe. I propped myself up on the desk and sucked in oxygen, willing myself to breathe slowly. The darkness paused and lifted and my body began tingling pins and needles. My reactions were noted by the trio and the magistrate scratched away with his quill, making lengthy notes.

The constables had stood together in front of the trunk, thereby partially obstructing its view to me, but as I regained my sensibilities they withdrew back to allow me full visual access once again.

'Mr Fenton, could you please inform us as to whether this is your trunk?'

I recognised my brass plate immediately. My mother had it inscribed before my first day at Rugby School all those years ago. It had been polished till it shone and the trunk rubbed in the finest conditioning creams to protect and fortify it. At the time, the trunk represented the love and pride they had for their son. It was strong and solid and would keep my clothing and important articles safe from harm. Now, because of her love, the trunk stood firm and had lasted much longer than most would have done. If it had been used in flippancy as most luggage was, it would have disintegrated and released the bodies to stagnate and rot away without compunction. However the conditioning cream, so lovingly lavished by Meg, had partly water-proofed the trunk and made it buoyant enough to find a resting place further down the fetid river. There it had sat with its grim contents, nestled under bracken and refuse, waiting for its owner to reclaim it, the bold brass plate now tarnished but stalwartly bearing my name to hang me with its irony. I stared at my trunk.

'Yes…this is my trunk.'

'And the bodies inside? Who were they?'

'She was called Lut…Lutka, and the other was my daughter.'

The collective intake of breath was a vacuum to my spirit. I sagged despondently on the chair and wept. Unsure what to do next, the constables recovered the trunk and moved it to the side. They looked at the magistrate, who took control.

'Please be advised that you are to be held in custody for further questioning. You are to make a statement for the disposition hearing and then a decision will be made as to the formal charges brought upon you. Gather yourself, young man. You will need all of your faculties to prepare for what lies ahead.'

I wrote my statement regarding ownership of the trunk and identification of the bodies. It was duly filed and I was dismissed. The two constables escorted me to Newgate Prison, where I was then led through a labyrinth of bricked walls and gates so contrary to the outer solid austere fortification that even if I was of sound mind, I would never have made my way back out without a directory. The officer unlocked and locked gate upon gate automatically selecting keys to breach each cell. He seemed uninterested in my state, talking instead to the constables about the sublime art of bare-knuckle boxing.

I was brought to my cell. It was a small rectangular brick room, lit only with the barred arch window on one end. Near the window was a water tank and basin, which were befriended by a shelf containing standard plate, cup and bible. My bed was not a feathered and plumped nest of comfort as I was used to at home. It was almost apologetically rolled away and secured in a barren corner, making space for daytime pacing. The width of the mattress assured me of an intimate connection with the hard unsympathetic floor and thus promised a long night of meditation ahead. The door was closed and I was alone.

My first night

I shared my insalubrious inn with the barbaric and bedraggled. Voices called out through the night, cursing the legal system that had taken their freedom. The brick walls leaned oppressively towards me, taunting the newest fodder for Newgate. I rested on my mattress, a term I use loosely, and stared at the ceiling, listening to the city scum and the deplorable poor call out to let the world know they still existed and still breathed the same air as the free. We are here! Don't forget us. Oh, woe is me! Hardened criminals goaded first timers who may have only been incarcerated for the uplifting of a loaf of bread, or some fruit to appease their grumbling stomachs. The air was pungent with violence and desolation, malevolence and hopelessness. The aggressive and quarrelsome roared out threats into stale pockets of the prison, ordering quiet even as they disturbed it themselves. They sat bellicose and combative, the feverish anger turning them red with unrequited violence. I lay thinking of the victims they would line up tomorrow to quench their thirst with fists. Sleep had never come easy to me as it was, but that night evaded all promise of it and I was given no quarter of blissful slumbering.

My thoughts whirled together and sank without peace, only to be picked up again and hurtled into the melee of worries spinning around and around in my head. My wife, my child, my parents, my friends; all destined to infamy by their relationship with me. Once the newspapers got wind of the owner of the trunk they would be in raptures knowing it was someone of moderate fame. My fellow countrymen lived for such atrocities, lapping it up in minute detail and forcing as much drama into their voice for maximum effect on the avaricious listeners. We cried how shocking, how disgraceful, but we clambered for more the next day. I was as guilty as the next man, reading the dishonour being disgorged from the court reports. The enthrallment came partly from applauding the punishment and the removal of such evil doers from our community and partly from being gratified that it wasn't oneself. I cramped and held my stomach at the imminent exposure of my life to all and sundry.

I was formally interviewed the next morning. A clerk took shorthand, sitting unobtrusively in the corner. I was led into the office and faced a burly, coarsely featured officer, who bristled with guarded alert. He indicated the seat and I sat down bleary-eyed from lack of sleep.

'My name is August Tripp. I am here to advise you that whatever is said in this formal interview will be used in a court setting. Once the interview is over, the clerk will provide you with a written record to review and sign as correct. Are you ready to begin?'

I nodded.

'I require you to answer all questions orally rather than by actions for ease of translation by the clerk. I therefore ask you again; are you ready to begin?'

I looked at the clerk poised with quill in hand. 'Yes.'

'Let us begin. What is your full name for the records?'

'Charles Augustus Fenton.'

'And what is your occupation?'

'I am an author of children's stories.'

August Tripp paused and looked at me closely.

'What are the names of these stories?'

'"The Goblin Wars", "Fenton's Bedtime Stories for Children" and "Fenton's Forest Fables".'

August Tripp sat up and rubbed his chin smiling. 'I know these books. I have them at home. I read them to my daughters. They particularly love "The Goblin Wars".'

'Thanks,' I responded glumly.

He looked at me for a moment longer before returning to his questions.

'You have already confirmed that the trunk found on the April 26th is your own and have identified the victims within as a woman named Lutka and your daughter. What was Lutka's surname?'

I faltered. I was ashamed to admit that I hadn't bothered to ask.

'I…I don't know.'

'Interesting… And what was the relationship you had with Lutka?'

'We were…intimate during my senior school years at Rugby.'

'When you say you were intimate, by that do you mean you had sexual relations?'

'Yes.'

'And how long did this relationship last?'

'Only a few months.'

'And what ended the relationship?'

'I went home during the holidays and was re-acquainted with my present wife.'

'So on your return to school, you sought Lutka out and advised her that the relationship was over?'

'No. I did not… I avoided our old meeting places and didn't hear from her again.'

'I see.' He glared at me silently. I squirmed in the chair, knowing how heartless I sounded.

'And when did you see Lutka again?'

'I was working in London for my father. She knocked on my door late at night some months later.'

'And were you pleased to see her?'

'No, I was not. I had been seeing my now wife Lily and had no intention of seeking Lutka again.'

'What happened next?'

'She was obviously pregnant and told me it was mine. She insisted we get married and that I introduce her to my parents. I was horrified.'

'So you killed her, to make everything better again?' he asked his tone cutting. I flinched at the barb.

'It didn't happen that way at all. I talked with her and we discussed our options. Even though I had already fallen in love with Lily, I eventually agreed to marry her and we decided that I would see my parents first to break the news.'

'How honourable of you. And so you told them?'

'…No. As she was leaving, she missed the top step. I lived on the top floor lodging and the stairs were precarious. She turned to try and embrace me…but I was repelled. You have to realise that all my dreams were gone and that I faced a future not only with a woman I didn't love but I would lose the love of my life that I had planned to marry. To me, my life was in ruins. I just wanted her to go and let me get used to my new situation.'

'Did you consider that maybe Lutka was also unhappy with the "situation", as you so eloquently put it?'

'I guess she would have. But she seemed to me to be very self-sufficient up till then.'

'So you resented her?'

'No! …Well initially maybe I did, but I had come round to the responsibility required of me!'

'Let's return to the scene. So she went to embrace you and missed the step.'

'She fell down the stairs, rolling over and over before stopping at the bottom.'

'Was she still alive at this stage?'

'No. Her neck was broken and on a funny angle. She wasn't moving at all.'

'You said you were repelled when she tried to embrace you?'

I paused. Could I have stopped the descent? Would she have lived if she had only let me be?

'I...I...did not want her to kiss me, so I pushed her away.'

'And that's what made her fall?'

'Yes... Because of me, she fell down the stairs.'

August Tripp and the clerk looked at each other meaningfully. I slunk down into my chair and bowed my head. I had said what could not be unsaid. I had admitted to murdering Lutka.

'After her fall what did you do?'

'I was devastated. I hadn't meant to do it. I ran down the stairs and thought about the unborn baby. I had it in my head that I might yet save one life. I ran back to my room and retrieved a knife, which I used to cut her stomach open and remove the baby... It was a girl. She was alive for only a few moments...but then she died in my arms.' I wept, recalling the moment; it was burning in my head. My nightmares had been filled with the image of her tiny innocent form that I had snuffed out. The room was silent except for my sobs.

'You mutilated Lutka's corpse with a knife?'

'Yes. But it was in the desperate hope of saving another.'

'There would have been a lot of blood.'

I prayed my father had not been to the authorities yet. This tragedy was of my own doing, and I would be damned if he should take any of the blame. I braced myself to break the law again and commit perjury.

'There was, but I worked like a madman and cleaned all morning. I packed the two bodies into my trunk and deliberated on the quickest and easiest way to dispose of them. I ended up throwing it into the river and watching it sink. I swear it had sunk when I returned back to my lodging. I thought that I had got away with it.'

'The truth will out eventually. It may have taken us some time to discover your little secret, but we've got you now. Murder is a capital offence; you know that don't you?'

'I do. But please believe me when I tell you that it was never my intention to hurt her. It was an accident, a terrible, terrible accident.'

'We will let the judge decide, you piece of scum – don't put that in the records – and accident or not, you will see justice.'

The clerk read back the interview and I signed the document as correct. I was led back to my cell to reflect on what had just happened. The blackness settled over me and made every movement thick and heavy. I struggled through this depressive state to respond when an officer advised me I had visitors. He had to drag me up by the elbow to make me follow him and greet the waiting guests of Newgate. I dreaded the moment.

Visiting hours

I was led towards a passage with a section of bars. Between the bars sat an officer drinking a steaming mug of tea. On the other side, at a distance of about five feet were my family: my mother and father, my wife Lily and my nanny Vadoma, holding onto Arthur. I faced a sea of grim faces awash with shock at my enforced subjugation. I stared back at them, numb to the point of dullness, still in my dark stupor. It took the voice of my father to jerk me into the present world.

'Charles! Look lively, man. We have only limited time to speak, so pay attention. Are you all right? Have you eaten today?'

I really couldn't remember but nodded to appease them. I shook my head and tried to clear my thoughts. I had to let my father know not to get himself entrenched in my sticky web and thus incriminate himself. I prayed he would understand my double tongue and not give away our oath of silence. It had to be done quickly and in a manner that stifled any argument. I ignored my wife's pleading eyes and focussed on my father.

'I am fine, Father. They have treated me well here.'

'Good, good. Now listen to me, don't say a word until

I can arrange for my good friend and colleague, Richard Flitcroft, to have an interview with you. He is…'

'It's too late. I have made my formal statement that I and I ALONE was responsible for the death and SUBSEQUENT HIDING of Lutka and our daughter.'

Lily fainted clean away. She was saved from serious injury by my mother grabbing at her arm as she fell to the floor. She urged Vadoma to fetch a nurse and began fanning Lily's face. Vadoma plodded off, encumbered with my son, who was crying loudly. My father gripped the bars.

'Tell me it's not true. Tell me you haven't done this! Ohhh, my son, my son. What have you done?'

I took my callous opportunity to speak frankly whilst everyone else's attention was on Lily. I stared at him, willing him to understand me.

'Father, I know what you know. You have protected me and cared for me since my birth. But please listen to me. I want no interference or discussion from you with any of the legal representatives. I need you to be strong for me and take care of my family. I plead with you that if you love me you will do as I ask. This is my only hope of peace.'

'Do you realise what you ask of me?'

'It is something I should have done long ago. I see that now. This was bound to happen eventually and my only regret is the pain I have caused you and my darling Lily.

I am so very sorry for that. You must believe me, but you MUST NOT do anything more than take care of my family. Please, Father, please.'

Lily was slowly coming to. My mother propped her up and with the help of my father, was able to hoist her into a chair. A prison nurse had arrived and was in the process of laying cold compresses on her head and administering brandy. She was ashen and weak and I ached to hold her in my arms. Arthur kept crying and Vadoma was trying her best to soothe his wails, hushing and bobbing him in her arms. She shot a glance at me of pure hate and I physically stepped back stunned at her virulent animosity. Then, just as quickly, she transferred her attention back to Arthur, crooning softly until he became more settled. Taken aback, I returned my attention to my father and was gladdened to see after a lengthy deliberation that he had nodded his compliance to my pleas. His face was dark and I felt the torture he was going through, but he knew that a Fenton must take care of his own and honour the word of his kin, even his own beloved son. I nodded back and placed a hand over my heart in gratitude. He moaned softly but repeated the gesture too. I bit my lip to keep in control and stay the tears threatening to expose my weakness.

'Lily, Lily? Speak to me, Lily.' I asked anxiously, watching her dazed face. She looked at me, pallid and bloodless, not appearing to recognise my voice.

'Charles?'

'Yes, my love, it's me, your Charles.'

'So…you killed a woman…and your own…daughter?'

'It was an accident, a sad sorry accident. I never meant to do it. You must believe me.'

'I believe you, I do. I'm so sorry, Charles.'

'Sorry? What could you have ever done to be sorry for?'

'I'm sorry I can't be there with you to take the hand of the man I love. I know you would never have intended to harm anyone. I know you. You are the man I will love forever.'

I reached a hand through the bars and stretched out to her. She stood, supported by my father, and reached towards me, our fingers touching at the tips. We stood this way, looking into each other's eyes until the officer warned us to stop. My heart was breaking; I couldn't take the pain my actions had caused to my family. My mother began crying, trying her best to smother the sobs into her lace handkerchief, her other hand wrapped around her midriff, holding herself as if in pain.

The officer looked at his pocket watch and declared our time was up. I was almost grateful as I couldn't have stood there for much longer without falling apart. I bade them all a wrenching farewell and they promised to visit again as soon as they were allowed. I followed the prison officer back to my cell and banged the wall with my fist until it bloodied and I had settled somewhat. Then I held my head in my hands and let the room darken again.

My prison officer informed me that my appointed lawyer, a Mr Richard Flitcroft, was coming to visit that evening and he punctually appeared as advised, after supper. After shaking my hand, he got straight to business, perched awkwardly on the stool provided.

'I have already reviewed the signed statement you made in front of the magistrate without my prior knowledge and before being asked to represent you by your father. This was ill advised but there is nothing to be done about that now. We shall move on. The next step is the bill of indictment. It will be put before the grand jury for declaration in one week. Once approved, you will be brought to court and formally charged. Then you will have to wait for the holding of the Assizes which is late July. During this wait, I will arrange a list of witnesses who can vouch for your character and organise a psychiatrist to interview you and state you were not of sound mind during the incident. We might still be able to impress on the jury that in a momentary lapse of sanity you were not in control of yourself and had pushed her without sound thought.'

'It was an accident.'

'I'm aware of that, but the extenuating circumstances leave a very suspicious tone of the affair. Man faced with a pregnant woman with whom he no longer desires to be in a relationship, determines to be rid of her in one fell swoop. Then he hides the body and tells no one. It doesn't read well at all, Mr Fenton.'

I sagged. I knew this; of course I knew this. I cursed the day I had ever laid eyes on Lutka. I was such a foolish, silly boy in lust. I would never have realised this could happen in a million years. Mr Richard Flitcroft continued to interview me, asking me to repeat over and over what happened that morning. The disposal of the body was covered so many times, I almost felt I had done it myself, much to my own relief. I had to convince the jury of my innocence whilst lying through my teeth. I only prayed my father would not break. My dark humour was tickled enough for me to snort, much to Mr Richard Flitcroft's surprise; of course he wouldn't break. He was a Fenton. I chided myself inwardly smiling.

Prisoners

As forewarned, my bill of indictment was declared to be a 'true bill' or 'billa vera'. I was brought to the court and formally charged with knowingly and deliberately performing the act of wilful murder on one 'Lutka', surname unknown and infant.

There were a couple of newspaper reporters there taking notes, whose ears pricked up at the announcement of my name and my charge. They knew of me, and had even had my books advertised in their local rags. Those that had helped my rise to fame would now be the ones to bring my sordid past out for all to see and scorn. Loyalty was a word with no meaning for these buzzards and I hated them for their malleable allegiance. By that evening my name and details of the murder would be blazing out of the papers and selling by the hundreds to Londoners, rippling out to the surrounding towns by sunrise.

I was returned to the ward, where men were lounging about, some whom I had recently seen at court with me. We were a motley lot. Some were scrawny with the tenacity of a Jack Russell on a scent of a gnarly rat. Others were fidgety but trying their best to keep a low profile and avoid confrontation, yet attracting the attention of a brawny pugilist determined to assert his dominance and become top dog. The more cunning used their wiles to manipulate the fighters to their advantage. They watched on carefully. It was a seditious cabinet filled with the most opprobrious specimens and destined to explode into a fracas at any moment.

I scanned the room and spotted a slightly built, well-dressed man smoking by the fireplace. He seemed to be calmly perusing the room and had caught my eye at the same time as I saw him. He smiled in a friendly way and I determined to make his acquaintance and fill in the long days. There was strength in numbers too, which would help in this volatile atmosphere. I walked up and offered my hand to shake.

'Charles Fenton. How do you do?'

He looked at me unhurriedly, starting from my shoes, up my legs, delaying a little around the groin before travelling upwards from my chest and finally (to my relief), finishing at my face. He smiled demurely and clasped my hand in his.

'Jasper Hudson. I do fine, thank you very much. Would you care for a cigarette?'

'No thanks. I don't smoke.'

'How very odd. It's the best way to kill the infectious vapours before they enter your lungs you know.'

'So I hear, but ever since an unfortunate incident with a cigar as a child, I have kept well clear of them.'

'Pray, do tell me more.'

I gave him the full and uninterrupted story of my vainglorious attempt to be a man during the Great Exhibition. I held nothing back and by the end of the story had him guffawing with laughter, a rare sound in such chambers.

'My, my, aren't we just the fool?'

'So it would seem, Mr Hudson.'

'Please, call me Jasper.'

'In that case, I insist you call me Charles.'

'Delighted to, Charles.'

'And where do you hail from, Jasper?' I asked.

'I have spent most of my adult life right here in London, but I grew up in Redditch.'

'Never! Well, we are practically neighbours, my friend. I grew up in Warwickshire. How marvellous… Which college did you attend?'

'Rugby. A very manly place it was too.'

'Rugby! I went to that school too! What a mystery we have never met before.'

'Perhaps not quite a mystery. You may not believe it to look at me, but I am all of 32 years of age. I suspect you are a more youthful model.' He twittered.

'So true. I am 24 years old. That certainly explains it, though I never would have guessed such a difference of age between us.' He looked smooth skinned and sported a fashion mainly seen on the Bohemian clan. His neck-kerchief flounced out in a spotted silk vibrancy that was only donned by the most stylish of the social set. His hair, on closer inspection, seemed suspiciously dark and coiffed for a man of his substantial age. But I kept this observation to myself, noticing how flattered he was with my comment.

'I do try to keep up with the latest trends, though it is a struggle to retain my joie de vivre in a place like this.' He flicked his hand around haughtily as if to underline his aristocracy against such philistines. He sighed dramatically and I nodded in sympathy to appease him. In a more crepuscular corner an unkempt, squat little man was contenting himself by delving into each of his nostrils and methodically clearing them of their contents. He examined each bogey on the level of scrutiny not dissimilar to a scientist's, before flicking it between thumb and forefinger to whoever was within his parameter. This worked in a very effective manner as the area around him soon became uncluttered of human presence, with the not-so-quick muttering dark words if a missile came too close and needed to be brushed off. I say muttering, but not one dared to back it up with a threat. His face was heinous to look at and he glowered at anyone foolish enough to meet his penetrating eyes. Even the battlers amongst us avoided his corner, some-how sensing that he was a nasty piece of work, and that was saying something to be sure. To me, he was not the heroic goblin I had written about in 'The Goblin Wars', but the evil goblin of earlier days that thrived on torture and suffering. Jasper and I shrank back simultaneously.

We resumed our discussion on Rugby and I was astonished to hear that Jasper had, up until his incarceration, maintained regular visits to Reverend Fleet. He alluded to his nasty herbal teas and hoped that I had avoided them, to which I nodded, stating that they left a funny taste and had only tried them once. I was delighted to hear he was so devoutly religious, in so much that he kept faithful towards our school priest. He pursed his lips slightly and replied how it was always a pleasure returning to his old mentors, a point I wholeheartedly agreed with. I was saddened at never really making my farewells to the professors that had taught me so much. He smirked.

'You do realise what the good Reverend was?'

'What do you mean?' I asked.

'Well, my dear sweet man, he was a paedophile. He liked to fiddle with the boys.'

My reaction amused him deeply.

'But that's outrageous! I went to him for lessons regularly and he never "fiddled" with me!'

'But you drank the tea. Tell me, did you truly suspect nothing?'

I remembered how woozy I had been that night and how my clothing was dishevelled, but he was a man of

God! They are above suspicion. Suddenly it hit me. The pieces were coming together. James McDonnell. The boy I had found hanging in the church. It seemed all too clear to me now what his fate had been and why he had taken his life. He was always called to see Reverend Fleet and the first time I met him was when he was extremely upset but refusing to tell me why. How could I have been so stupid? Now I saw what must have occurred. I felt sickened to think the Reverend could have caused the demise of the young Scotsman with his repeated abuse. Reluctantly I pondered on the fact that I might meet my end in the very same way that James McConnell had. I did not want to imagine what the vile Reverend may have done to me as I lay on his couch. I paled and Jasper looked concerned.

'Sit down, Charles. It's a bit of a shock to you, I know. I really can't believe you didn't realise.'

'I...I suppose I didn't think.' I kept silent about McDonnell. His death lay even heavier on my guilt-laden head. I sat quietly, musing on my shortcomings. Jasper shifted away, and we didn't speak again until the following day. I had another sleepless night in the cell and looked worse for wear when we met again. He politely ignored this.

We chatted quietly, studiously ignoring our prior conversation, until lock up. It gladdened me to have made a friend, albeit a temporary one, to pass the day.

Every friend in here was one less enemy. We had mutually decided not to talk of the reasons why we were confined at Newgate, preferring to pretend our situation did not exist. It helped to digest the indigestible and the days dripped by, coming ever nearer to the end of July and the beginning of the Assizes.

The blessing

Magda glided through the streets of London under the blanket of night. She moved freely and without hesitation towards the main cemetery where Lutka and her baby daughter had been buried that day. The ceremony had been attended by a prison guard, the grave digger and a priest. On the dirt a small cross showed where their pathetic forms now rested.

She looked at the freshly dug earth now mounded high, disturbing the uniformity of nearby graves. She kneeled on the dirt and placed a small posy of flowers at its peak, muttering softly under her breath. She grabbed a handful of the dirt and smeared it on her cheek, before opening her hand and staring at the small pile there. Then she sprinkled the dirt back onto the pile and, reaching into her pocket, pulled out a small vial of liquid. It shimmered in the moonlight and seemed to move at a slower speed around the container. She popped the cork off and carefully nicking her finger, she dripped two drops of her blood into the vial, turning it deep red. She rolled the vial between her palms, closing her eyes and raising the vial towards the moon. Her voice muttered; she began chanting and swaying with the potion, dancing to her lyrical sound. She spoke so deeply that only the wind picked up her prayer and bent it down towards the bodies lying deep within the cold earth. She was merely fogginess and haze to anyone happening along at that darkest hour of the night, with only the stray cats and stealthy rodents as her company. She wailed keenly at the end and after kissing the vial, scattered it over the gravesite.

She sat there for some hours, motionless and brooding, before the shimmering grey dawn warned her of sunrise. Rising wearily, she whispered into the breeze before clutching her amulet hanging from a long silver chain and tucking it back under her dress. She walked past Newgate Prison, gesticulating with her long agile fingers before scuttling down an alley.

That night I had the most vivid nightmare; I felt as if a hundred rats were crawling over my body nibbling at me and I was paralysed. I couldn't do anything, not even call out for help. They sniffed and probed through my clothing, finding tender flesh to bite and chew. Where the clothing was thick, they gnawed and gnawed until the material was decimated and they could see my skin. One rat, bigger than the rest, climbed over my face and began scratching at my eyeball, piercing the eye with its unclean nails digging deeply. The ocular jelly oozed out and seeped down the side of my face while I lay agonised and in abject terror. It delved deeper, burrowing into my eye socket and ferreting out my soft lobular brain. I could feel it all; it was so real to me, that even when I woke I jumped madly around shrieking and hitting my face and body in revulsion. I could still smell their fusty coats in my nostrils and I could hardly believe that it hadn't really happened. I whirled around in my cell, searching wildly for the furry scurrying creatures, so convinced that they were hiding and biding their time. I found nothing and I wondered if I had finally gone mad. I couldn't wait to be released so I could join my jovial friend, Jasper, and purge the nightmare from my consciousness.

I had to wait some time as his court case was held that morning. He returned unusually irate and I hesitated to ask what the matter was.

'I got two years, Charles. They plan to lock me in here for two whole years! You were lucky to catch me. I was only back here to collect my belongings. I am moving to the general ward now to begin my sentence. I guess I should be grateful I wasn't hanged! It wasn't that long ago they did that to people like me.'

'What do you mean, people like me?' I asked innocently, deeply upset that my only friend inside was leaving.

'Charles, you simply are too glorious for words! Let's just say I am a keen follower of the Uranian love, something I think you might have found quite pleasurable.'

I screwed up my face and stood in confusion. I had no idea what he was talking about. He laughed and shook my hand warmly.

'Good luck with your trial. Who knows, we may even become cellmates. Now that's a delicious thought.'

I could only agree, but knew the likelihood was slender as I bade my fond farewells to Jasper. I caught the eye of the goblin (a nickname Jasper and I had given our bogey picking man), and he grinned evilly, his rotten teeth barely holding the eel tongue in his mouth. He looked at the departing back of Jasper and snickered, then back at me, before smacking his knee and roaring with glee, his phlegmy throat reduced him to a cough after a glob of spit catapulted from his mouth and landed on the table. I looked at him and looked away sickened, making as much distance between him and me as I possibly could.

The ward grew busier and more crowded as the date of the Assizes came near. The goblin was unperturbed and maintained his corner to the detriment of any newcomer unaware of his firing range. We crammed in and I spent my days communicating with my lawyer, a psychiatrist and most cherished yet painful of all, my family. The newspapers were filled with detailed accounts about me and the charge of murder. My family bore it all with a stoic silence, refusing to talk to any reporter who discovered their identity. I was the millstone around their neck, dragging our name through the mud. Even my picture, though crudely drawn, was plastered on all the tabloids. I was now famous for all the wrong reasons. And there was worse to come – the trial.

The Assizes

I was as ready as I'd ever be on the morning of the Assizes. Living in limbo, not going backwards, not going forwards, keeping my family dangling in a city far away from home, was maddening. I had reached the point of facing the charges, telling my story and wanting the verdict as soon as possible so they could all move on. I didn't care about me at all and though I intended to plead not guilty, it was an accident when all was said and done; I knew the case was hopeless even if my family refused to believe it. They insisted on attending the trial against my wishes, to show their support for me. I walked into the court.

The air was thick, heavily beleaguered by debauched criminals, underpaid clerks and melancholic families. The perspiration staled and dried under the dim caliginous lights, languishing in each corner. If their purpose was to brighten and illuminate the room, then they had failed spectacularly. They only managed to highlight the musty stench rising into the nostrils of the supercilious judge and associated lawyers. Not that they were innocent of smell, but theirs was of a more organic kind, not steeped in fear.

The trial began with my charge been read out in court by the clerk. I entered my plea of 'not guilty' and the prosecutor presented his case followed by my lawyer, Richard Flitcroft. As I listened to the prosecutor, I cringed at his vile description of me.

'This man is a monster that should never see the light of day again. He brutally SLAUGHTERED not only a pregnant woman but then BUTCHERED her as she lay broken, and RIPPED the baby out with his own bare hands. He had done this dastardly deed to rid himself of a responsibility he didn't care for, that is, to be a father and husband to this innocent waif. She had nowhere else to go, she could no longer work and when she found out she was pregnant, believed that the DEFENDANT (here, he pointed at me) would take care of her and their baby. And this was how he took care of her – by PUSHING her down the stairs and DEFILING her body with a KNIFE. Over the course of this trial I will show you, beyond any reasonable doubt, that THIS IS a self-centred villainous man with no capacity to care for the weaker sex and who only could took care of one person – HIMSELF.'

The jury and people in the court, apart from my own family and lawyer, glared at me in antipathy. If they could have free rein, they would have ripped me to pieces then and there and felt the community was much better off. I looked at my father who had squared his shoulders and raised his chin. I mirrored him and tried my best to be strong in his eyes. I knew this was killing him and it would have finished him to see me unable to uphold the Fenton pride and courage. Thankfully it was Richard Flitcroft's turn next.

'The prosecutor is trying to incite a lynch mob. He believes that the jury is incapable of sound and logical thought. He thinks that this public,' he swept the crowd with a benign smile, 'would like nothing better to do than to inspire a crazed blood frenzy on my client without even hearing the facts. Emotive ramblings, impassioned twaddle, do not hide the simple facts. This was an accident, a sad, tragic accident. My client is an upstanding, successful author of CHILDREN'S stories. He is a kindly, God-fearing man, married with child and has a clean bill with no prior brushes with the law. He should not be made to suffer because of a momentary loss of reason in his youth. Look at him; does he really look to be the vicious killer that the prosecutor wants you to believe he is?'

I stared ahead, not willing to face the sea of eyes assessing my capacity toward ferocity. No one could see madness or villainy in my open features. They all remembered the sweet fairy stories they had read to their children, words that I had written, that could never have originated from a heartless fiend. I was well dressed and from a family of high esteem back in

Warwickshire, with a reputation of fairness and hard work. The mob turned and the blood lust so recently filling their expressions was replaced with a more thoughtful and considerate one. How fickle we are!

The prosecutor shuffled his notes and called in his witnesses. First was Elijah Goble, followed shortly after by Constable Jacob White and Stuart Brown. They explained under oath the initial whereabouts of the trunk and subsequent finding of the decomposed bodies. They talked about the plaque with my name engraved on it that led to my arrest, and how I had confirmed the trunk's ownership and identity of the bodies. They added my reaction to the appearance of the trunk and how I needed to be revived with the magistrate's brandy. This was confirmation of my formal statement that had been read out earlier and shocking though it was, it gave no surprises.

The prosecutor moved on and called Mr Montgomery to the stand. He looked familiar to me but I couldn't remember why. It soon became apparent.

'Mr Montgomery. You own a farm just outside Rugby School?'

Mr Montgomery was pulling at his ill-fitted suit. This was clearly not a place he felt comfortable in, but he pulled himself together.

'Yes, I do.'

'Could you tell the court what your relationship with the victim was?'

'She worked for my wife and me as a farmhand.'

'And she was a good worker?'

'Very good; we never had any troubles. She was like a daughter to us after our sons died of the fever. We were very upset when she disappeared and we even advertised in the papers trying to find her and bring her back home. We had no idea what had happened to her but we never stopped hoping she'd come back to us.'

'Did you know of her relationship with the defendant?'

'No, we did not. She never spoke of him.'

'So he never came to the farm?'

'I wouldn't say that. I recall seeing him spying through my window once. It gave my wife and me a right scare. He had no business being there!'

'That must have been very frightening for you. What did you do next?'

'I went outside and tried to catch him. He yelled at me and kicked me several times before running away in the direction of the school.'

The courtroom gasped. I was a peeping Tom, sneaking around, trespassing and attacking people on their own properties. It looked very bad. I recalled the day in my head and remembered the scalding hot coffee that Mr Montgomery had poured over me and the way he'd wrenched my shoulder back. He neglected to add that part in, I noted a little bitterly. The prosecutor looked tellingly at the jury before deferring to the judge. No further questions were asked and he was excused.

Next was the prison doctor who had performed the autopsy on the bodies prior to burial. He was asked what injuries and cause of death could be determined from the examination. He listed the multiple fractures on Lutka's skeleton, surmising that the broken vertebrae in her neck were the most likely cause of death. He added that never before had he seen such a multitude of injuries in the twenty years he had been practising medicine. It would have been more expedient to list the bones not broken rather than the ones that were. However he did concede, on questioning, that some of the fractures could have been sustained after the bodies had been thrown into the river and also due to the rough handling of the trunk. He concluded that my statement of falling down the stairs correlated with his findings but could not conclusively advise of how firmly she had been pushed. The violence of the injuries, however, was suspicious of more than mere 'tumbling'. After a few technical questions asked by the judge and with the approval of the prosecutor, the defence lawyer was then asked to state his case.

Richard Flitcroft called the first of my character witnesses. I was heartened to see my good friend Arthur Manning approach the stand. He was sworn in and after a brief introduction was asked to describe my character.

In his special and idiosyncratic way, he gave a complex definition along with objective examples as to why I was a truly upstanding and trustworthy individual, a reputable author and fine family member. He then, surprisingly, showed his more personal emotions and advised the packed courtroom of how much he appreciated and cherished my friendship and loved me like a brother. I was deeply humbled as this sentiment was echoed by Henry Felldon, Benjamin Roberts and Jack Sloane. My headmaster, Mr Goulburn, my Latin teacher, Mr Wiseman and even my rugby coach, Mr Campbell, came to London to attest of my good character. They all added their own personal opinion of what a fine student I had been at Rugby College and how much of a contribution I had made both to the school and in assisting other students who needed help. Mr Campbell made a stirring speech in recalling how mature and caring I had been when an unfortunate student was found dead in the school chapel. Mr Wiseman advised that though I had initially struggled with Latin, that with help from Reverend Fleet, I soon not only excelled but then went on to help others to improve their grades. Our class was one of the more successful ones, thanks to me, according to my Latin teacher. I cringed during these interviews, and was relieved when they finally left the stand. I wanted no further association with Reverend Fleet and what he now stood for. Richard Flitcroft must have drilled them well, because I sounded angelic, hard-working, dedicated and faultless. How could anyone, listening to the accolades presented, even consider that I was capable of murder?

After my character witnesses had finished, Richard Flitcroft called in his expert witness, Mr Leland Fox, the psychiatrist. He advised that I had experienced a TEMPORARY moment of insanity and had possibly behaved in this way due to the extreme duress I had been put under. It was his professional opinion that I was now of sound mind and was a threat to no one. Richard Flitcroft reminded the court of the McNaugten Law of 1858 where Daniel McNaugten was found not guilty of murdering Robert Peel's secretary, Edmond Drummond. The ruling was that at the time of committing the act, the accused was temporarily insane and unaware of the nature and quality of the act that he was doing. He repeated this statement slowly and deliberately, looking at each jury member as he spoke. Not-guilty-by-reason-of-temporary-insanity. He let them digest that information before both he and the prosecutor made their closing statements.

After the judge's summing up, the jury filed out of the court to consider the verdict: Guilty or not guilty. My trial had been the lengthiest one on the Assizes schedule, partly because of the fact that I was considered a 'famous' author and was to be given every opportunity to a full and extensive defence. Most of the other trials had averaged a mere fifteen minutes and were spat out in brusque efficiency, moving from case to case and ignoring the stunned looks of the crestfallen. Even so, we had barely filled a day and the jury appeared to be in keeping with the rapidity of the Old Bailey, filing back in after only an hour had passed. I looked at my family and saw the trepidation filling their faces. My life was about to be decided.

The verdict

Each juror's face maintained a carefully blank expression, knowing full well that we were all analysing every nuance, tic or squint for a hint of which way they leaned. They avoided all eye contact and looked studiously at the wall ahead, marching like an army of sleepwalkers, then turned and sat on their respective chairs. We had all risen then sat on the behest of the court official, once the judge had reclaimed his official throne of omnipresent power. The buzzing press, buffeted by the public behind them, practically squirmed in their seats with the impatience of worker bees frantic to return to the queen with their trifles. As soon as the verdict had been read, they would be racing back to deliver the story of the year. Was Charles Augustus Fenton, author of the famous children's stories, guilty of murder? Stay riveted public, buy the next paper, and get all the delicious details of this man's downfall. It will disturb you, it will shock you, to see how the words you lovingly spoke to your adoring children at night, were fuelled by the mind of a murderer!

I knew my family and friends were watching with me but I couldn't turn to face them. All of my energy was drawn towards the head juror, watching him stand and knowing my fate was swirling knowledgably within his brain. He knew this was his moment in the limelight and a sage and seemingly wiser man could not have acted as well as him. The theatrics of the courtroom were made all the more spectacular because it dealt with real lives and real murders. And yet, even with all the genuine sombreness of this man, I knew he would retire home to his loving family and regale them with the trial, act by scintillating act. They would applaud his sagacity and admire his judgement, for he was the man who had led the jury and kept their streets safe from people like me. Bravo sir! Bravo!

'Charles Augustus Fenton, please stand.'

I used the desk in front of me to prop myself up onto my legs. They felt spindly and weak to me. I looked at the judge.

'Members of the jury, have you reached your verdict?'

'We have, your honour.'

'What say you?'

'We the jury find Charles Augustus Fenton…'

My heart was pounding. This was it.

'…GUILTY of murder.'

A collective gasp swept through the courtroom. The door flew open and the verdict was spread like wildfire to the public waiting outside. Runners ran delivering the news to the gentlemen who had employed them, feeling it would be unseemly to linger themselves. The news was accepted with surprise. One of theirs was going down. The protective supremacy of the upper class had been chinked away at today, which didn't sit well at all. One might even have detected a slight shudder of the elite backbones as they sat smoking cigars. Dreadful state of affairs all round.

I could hear both my mother and Lily crying softly. My friends sat in stunned silence, stupefied at what they had heard. I collapsed back into my seat, disintegrating. Everyone around them was hustling and bustling, anxious to let the people know what they knew. The judge raised a hand calling for silence. The bustle simmered away and was thinly covered by a sense of propriety. The scene wasn't finished yet.

'Charles Augustus Fenton, you have been found guilty of murder by the grand jury. Before sentence is passed I will now give you the opportunity to address the court. Please rise.'

I drew in a deep breath and recovered. This would be the only opportunity I would be given during the court process and I needed to speak my mind. I breathed again and spoke.

'Thank you, sir. I would like to say that I deeply, deeply regret what I have done. I have lived with this shame for many years and the burden has been heavy. I apologise to my family and friends for my actions and to…Lutka and my daughter. I have spent all of these year's praying to God for forgiveness and trying my best to be a better man before him. I want to thank those around me who have stood by me in this darkest day and I know I can never repay you, but I feel honoured at your belief in me… Thank you.'

I sat down and waited for my sentence. The judge nodded in appreciation of my heartfelt speech and then donned his black hat.

'The court doth order you to be taken from hence to the place from whence you came, and thence to the place of execution, and that you be hanged by the neck until you are dead, and that your body be afterward buried within the precincts of the prison in which you shall be confined after your conviction. And may the Lord have mercy upon your soul.'

The court cleared and I was led back to my cell to collect my belongings. I followed the officer, clinging onto my meagre collection of possessions, as he locked and unlocked gate after gate, turning and finally climbing a flight of stairs to my new abode: the press-room. I shared this apartment with approximately twenty other convicted felons and was disconcerted at seeing the goblin had transferred there too. His eyes sparkled at seeing me enter and he took particular delight at my discomfiture. He chuckled, but not in a jolly way, in a way that made the men around him take a sideways glance whilst making more distance between them.

I had found out during my incarceration why he was

here. He had been caught raping a mother and child, and forcing them to watch during the act. He had beaten them insensible, kicking them and punching bare fisted at their faces. Nobody knows why he had started his unconscionable attack. A baby had lain in his cot and had begun crying at the disturbance. He had picked it up and bashed his brains out against the wall, swinging him at the feet. It was only the bleak cries of the woman that had alerted the neighbours. They entered the property to investigate and found the alarming scene. What was more horrific was that these poor bloodied sufferers were his wife and step-daughter. They had been physically and mentally abused for as long as he had laid claim to them. His coercion of marital fidelity to the now-battered woman had been supposedly to save her from the poorhouse when her first husband had died, leaving her heavily in debt. The baby had been his but that had not saved him. He had shown no remorse at the mutilated body of his son. The mother and child survived but were disfigured for life, though it was understood that a wealthy widow had taken them under her wing to live with her after she'd heard of the story. This vile monster was to be my last companion on earth. He sickened me.

The date of execution was set for two weeks' time. There was nothing more I could do but wait.

In limbo

The press-yard was at the corner of Newgate running alongside Newgate market. There was a double grating by the gate on one end that allowed for visitors. It had the same restrictions as before with an officer standing between the grates preventing any passing of illicit goods. This time, the visiting was more an act of farewell, though many prisoners still waited for the recorder's report and the crown's mercy. I had no such optimism. Even though Richard Flitcroft had not given up, I knew the cause to be hopeless and, through prayer, had found peace and acceptance. Where I had dreaded the visitors, I now looked forward to wringing every last vision of them into my final days. I determined not to wallow in self-pity but to celebrate our times we'd had together before the trial.

'Arthur Mannings! And the beautiful Sara. It is always a pleasure to see your faces.' I watched the odd pair near the bars. Sara looked as if she had been crying but she was still captivating and the guard straightened up and sucked in his stomach, an effort for one so portly. He was wasting his breath and after realising she was ignorant of his existence, he exhaled and returned the buttons to full stretching capacity. They were now Mr and Mrs Mannings and Sara had the full bloom of pregnancy flushing her face. It would have seemed impossible for her to become any more beautiful but here she was more radiant than ever. I soaked in her exquisiteness and sighed.

'Charles. You are looking well. We just had lunch at The Anchor as you recommended. It was quite spectacular.'

'Did you try the pork sausages? They come with a tomato and apple chutney that zings.'

'Yes, I did. If I keep that up, I'll be fatter than Billy Sedgwick.'

I laughed. 'No one is fatter than Billy Sedgwick.' Having said that, both Arthur and I stole a glance at the guard. He was pretty darn close in size to our rugby playing prop from Rugby School. He sensed the scrutiny and rustled his newspaper open in defence. Arthur and I looked at each other and laughed again. Sara tried her best to smile and I smiled in gratitude towards her.

'What's old Sedgwick up to now?' I asked.

'Billy Sedgwick works with the railways. He's overseeing a new line heading up North. We will have to put a stop to this soon or I'll be tripping over tracks wherever I put my feet.'

'Especially with your two left feet.' We laughed again.

'Feet should be firmly planted on the ground and

eyes firmly raised to the stars. That is where the future belongs.'

'Do you still have that telescope you showed me on the first night at school?'

'Funnily enough I do, but I have upgraded to a Grubb telescope with an equatorial mount and declination circle split into two quadrants, which gives a superior visual quality. The mount assembly allows a vast range of astral visualisation and the locking nut stabilises the telescope for easier use of the pinion focuser... Of course, I will always cherish that first telescope and it will be handed down to little Charles when he is born.'

I looked at them both, a bit stunned. Sara nodded gently and smiled at me patting her swollen abdomen.

'Yes, Charles. If it's a boy, Arthur and I will call him Charles,' she said softly.

'Well. I am honoured, deeply honoured. Thank you, my friends. Thank you.' Tears pricked at my eyes and I blinked them away. The mood changed. It hit me that I would never see their son being born, never be a part of his life. I pushed my hands into my pockets and squeezed them into tight fists, willing myself to regather. Arthur and Sara pretended interest elsewhere as they also struggled to keep their own emotions under control. My allocated time was nearly up and this was going to be their last visit. I had already said my good-byes to Henry Felldon and Benjamin Roberts and had ordered them not to attend the public execution due now in two days.

Meg, Jack and Rebecca had made their last visit yesterday and despite my remonstrations, Meg had sobbed and cried throughout the whole visit, trying to cling to my hand and collapsing in a heap wailing and beating her chest. This had made Rebecca upset and she couldn't understand why I had to be kept behind bars and not telling her fairy stories like we used to back on the estate. Jack had apologised over and over again, trying his best to be strong and comfort his girls at the same time. The meeting was a disaster and he had to carry Meg and Rebecca away, leaving me in the gloomiest anguish. 'My Charlie, not my Charlie!' were the last words I heard from her as she howled.

'I have something for you, old chap.' Arthur Mannings reached into his pocket and pulled out a photograph. He addressed the guard. 'Is it all right for you to give this to my friend?' He handed the photograph to the guard, who studied it a little sullenly before handing it to me. It was a photograph of all of us: Me, Lily, Arthur, Sara, Henry, Harriet and Benjamin. He had taken it on the night that Harriet had amazed us with her first song. She had sung several times since, but she had caught us unprepared for the vibrant notes that first night and swept us away. It had been a wonderful night and I studied the photograph reminiscing of one of the happiest memories we shared. It was a perfect gift.

'Thank you. I will keep it with me always. Could you…could you let my father know that I wish to be buried with this photo?' I croaked out, struggling to keep control.

Sara held her handkerchief to her mouth, smothering a sob. Arthur nodded grimly.

'Of course. You can consider it done.'

'It will be in this top pocket.' I put the photograph carefully in the pocket and pressed it.

We looked at each other for one last time. No one could speak or move. I did not want them to leave and they could not do it anyway. It was the guard who took control.

'Times up.' He stood up and beckoned them away. Another officer came to lead me away and with one last painful look, we parted for the final time. Tomorrow was my last visiting day before I would be transferred to the press-room below. Tomorrow was going to be my last time with my parents, Lily and my son Arthur. I didn't know if I could endure it.

Final Call

I pulled the photograph from my pocket several times that night. Sleep eluded me and it was my saviour from the brink of lunacy to remember the good times and pray for each and every one of my friends and family. I leaned heavily on God at this time and my religious belief held my spirit up like a blessed crutch. My last visitors would be my most challenging ones to say goodbye to and I prayed with the fervour of the damned, that I would be given strength enough to withstand the pain of separation. I trudged to the visiting grate, using each step to mentally prepare and suck in the air of bravery. My eyes hit first on Lily holding our son, Arthur. My parents were standing either side as a support. We stared at each other and I couldn't bring myself to speak. My father took control.

'Hello son. How are you keeping up?'

I dragged my eyes to his face and raised my chin. 'I'm fine, Father, just fine. How are you all?'

Mother sobbed and quickly covered her mouth with her lace handkerchief. Lily wobbled and a chair was hurriedly brought in for her to sit on. Mother put Arthur on the floor and he immediately tried to squeeze through the bars to get to me.

'Papa?' His fat little body turned sideways and his arm and one leg were flapping through the grill, trying to transform into jelly and ooze towards me. His head, try as he might, was adamantly solid and only a little pearl-shaped ear joined the quest. 'Papa!'

Lily gently spoke to Arthur and coerced him to sit on her lap. He sucked his thumb and frowned at the bars preventing him from grabbing his Papa. He struck out with his fist towards the grill angrily. His frustration and anger then turned to tears and a slow wail began that moved rapidly to a deafening roar. His mouth was wide open and his head tilted back, eyes were squeezed shut and his hands turned into fists splayed out on each side.

'PAPAAAAA!'

The guard cringed at the sound and sourly watched Lily's attempts to pacify Arthur with little success. 'WAAAAAHHHHH! WAAAAAHHHHH!' I jigged up and down and tried to distract him with funny faces, a game he loved at home, but he was determined to roar the prison down. My father and mother joined in the effort, looking sideways at the guard whose patience was wearing thin and worrying he might cut our visit short. Reluctantly, Vadoma was called over and carried him thumping and kicking away, with me yelling after him, 'Goodbye little Arthur. Be good. I love you!' Tears pricked and I blinked them away, not wanting to blur my last vision of my son. The sound abated and I had no doubt that the other prisoners would be wondering what the cacophony was. The whole episode flustered us and all well-thought-out speeches and terms of endearment rattled. Only the guard appeared more relaxed and at ease. My mother spoke first.

'Charles. I love you, Charles. You have been the son we have always wanted and dreamed for. You could never know how much and how desperately we fought to bring you into this world and keep you with us. I want you to know that all our love, all our hearts' worth, is flowing towards you and…no son could ever be as cherished and as adored as you have been.' She trembled, but continued. 'May you walk eternally in Heaven's sunshine and wait for us in God's light to join you there in the afterlife. We pray for you and feel his warmth on you to keep you strong until the end… Goodbye my son. Goodbye and God's speed.' With that, she shakily walked away, her shoulders hunched over as if in pain but resolutely refusing to turn around. I called after her, 'Thank you, Mother, thank you. I love you too.' Her body stiffened but she kept dragging one foot ahead of the other and disappeared around the corner.

This left my father and Lily. I had to make sure that he had talked to Arthur Mannings about the photograph; it was very important to me. I patted my pocket and raised a questioning look at him. He nodded grimly.

Both he and Jack were going to be at the execution. My father had paid a large undisclosed amount of money to ensure that they could take my body afterwards and return me to Fenton Estate to be buried in my family cemetery. There was a deal of risk involved as the obligation of the executioner was to carry out the judge's orders and bury me within the prison walls. The coffin had already been ordered and was arranged for transporting me back that very same day. Even though I would be no longer aware, this information gave me peace of mind that my family could still visit my grave. I realised how painfully hard it would be for both him and Jack and I would have given anything to let others take charge of retrieving my body but they both refused to risk that sacred duty to anyone else. I had to respect their wishes. My thoughts turned to Lily.

'Lily.' She was shivering all over with her head stooped and her frame seemed to have shrunk within itself. I ached a dark deep pain inside at seeing her so forlorn. This was all my own doing. I spoke again, in a softer tone. 'Lily. We haven't much time. Please look at me.'

She raised her head slowly, her face ashen and gaunt. She had lost so much weight and I feared for her health. Her head seemed too heavy for her neck and it was such an effort for her to keep it up. She sucked in a deep breath and pushed out her chin, trying her best to be strong for me. The anguish and torment that I had given my loved ones was too much to bear. Lily, my beautiful, spirited, creative Lily. How could I ever forgive myself? My love, my love.

'Do you remember the first time we met? We were only children then, so innocent.' She nodded. 'I stole your pet mouse, do you remember? I thought that if I had your mouse you would agree to marry me...I'm sorry about little Albert.' She smiled weakly.

'I have so much to apologise for... You must be so very ashamed of me.'

She stood up, her nostrils flaring with anger. 'Don't you DARE say that! How could you even THINK that I would ever be anything but proud of my own husband? I would NEVER EVER be ashamed of you or regret ever loving you... Never.' She breathed heavily and regathered her control before speaking again in a calmer tone. 'I will wait patiently for God to let me know when we will meet again. I will bring our son up to be PROUD of his father and to defend his name with honour. You have nothing to be sorry for!' She sat back down, her indomitable spirit that I adored so much, cowing me into submission. I stood corrected.

The guard looked at his watch and got up. Our time for farewells was over. My father spoke. 'Be strong, son, be strong. I'll be there for you tomorrow.' He put his arm out for Lily to hold.

I couldn't speak; all the words I had planned to say

had vanished. All I could do was look first at my father and then my wife. I gripped the bars to steady myself as my legs were weakening. This was our last good-bye. I would not see my wife ever again in this life. A single tear flowed down her cheek and she bit her lip as it wobbled. She leaned heavily on my father and he brought his arm behind her back to hold her up. 'Come now, Lily,' he murmured, egging her to use her reserves of courage.

The guard came to take me away and I looked back at my father and wife. I could only say one more word.

'Lily.'

My last day

The goblin and I were transferred to the press-room below. We were the only condemned men present and it sickened me to be spending my last hours in his vile, contemptible company. He was unrepentant and showed no sign of distress. He took great pleasure in sitting with his pants down and masturbating in front of me, grunting like a pig and trying to catch my eye. His filthy hands were rubbing away at his crotch not for his sexual pleasure but so he could wring every last drop of dignity from my final hours. He crowed with sadistic triumph when I glanced over at him and caught him in his offensive act. I quickly turned my head and faced the other way, but the vision was burned into my retinas. His putrid raspy voice rose in volume to sear my eardrums, escalating in pitch and tone as he reached his foul climax. The rusty chuckle of pride afterwards turned my stomach and I retched holding my stomach.

To be in the same room with such a beast was made only worse by the realisation that we shared the common ground of killing our own child. I was basically no better than him and in fact, his outward appearance was probably more honest than mine. My rottenness lay within and I had fooled everyone into thinking I was a good man; but what man would kill a woman heavy with his own flesh and blood?

It was a relief when five o'clock came and the guards moved us to our final cells. This was my last resting place until I was taken through to the scaffold tomorrow. It was small, barely six feet wide by eight feet, and was sparsely adorned with a bench, a wrought-iron candle-stick and a bible. The air was sour and wafted down the stone walls from a tiny heavily barred opening up high, but I was happier, as it was away from the goblin and my own uncomfortable comparisons with him.

The night was long and sleep was impossible. I spent the hours reviewing my life and the people I had grown to love. The memories cascaded one on top of the other, strangely making me smile for my younger years. When I wasn't thinking, I was praying; the prayers becoming a soothing balm for my troubled soul.

I could hear the hubbub of the crowd as they filed in from around the city. Not a room could be found for love or money with all visitors booking everything as soon as my execution date was confirmed. It had been a long time between hangings and it was made all the more alluring by the thought of a famous author meet-ing his doom. The newspapers containing my story were sold by the bundle with every detail lapped up and talked about avidly. I was a real cash magnet that had made many vultures rich from my impending demise. There had been a flourishing trade in 'The Illustrated Police News'. This publication was packed with comprehensive facts of the crime, the trial and even included a farcical copy of my last true confession. The fact that I had never put pen to paper to write this confession was a trivial detail and the more frustrated writers in the tabloids were given free rein to write whatever overly flowery prose they wished. If that wasn't tantalising enough, the whole package was dotted liberally with artistic drawings showing my face, the trial and even the hanging to come. Supply could not keep up with demand and no sooner was the ink dried, than the publications were swallowed up and others were chirping for more.

The volume of the voices grew with excitement and a festival feel bounced around outside my cell. Little children squealed with delight and looked up to wonder at the sumptuously dressed ladies delicately holding their opera glasses to their eyes to afford a better look. They were stationed on the roofs, with their gentleman friends present, sipping at port and smoking cigars as if it were an opera about to begin. The price they would have paid for the good vantage points would have been enough to feed and house a family of four for a year in the poorer classes, but that notion did not enter their head.

The street vendors were selling refreshments on the edges of the growing crowd and trade was fierce. Baskets of freshly baked pies were the more popular choice and hordes of people could be seen merrily munching the crisp pastry and licking the gravy from their lips. As the hour drew closer, the mob squeezed in closer, endangering the smaller and slighter frames amongst them who were unable to push back against the power of numbers.

It was with a thinly restrained keenness that my guard came into my cell, trying his best to maintain his expected dignified professionalism. He must never have seen such a gathering of voyeuristic countrymen before; there were literally thousands just waiting for HIM to bring me and the goblin out. He ordered me to put my journal down and turn around. This was it.

Conclusion

Magda looked down at the rapacious throng with loathing towards her own species. She was perched on top of a large wooden crate, flanked by two baying women. The thrilled cry for 'Hats off,' began when the prisoners appeared. Hats were removed in a hypocritical show of respect towards the condemned, yet the wolves drooled in anticipation watching the pair climb unsteadily up the stairs. Charles had his hands manacled behind him as he was pushed through the cell door towards the scaffold. He looked very scared. The goblin was revolting to the end, spitting hard on the closer spectators much to their dismay. This led to an angry roar from the crowd, booing at him and hissing. He yelled back, pouring obscenities from his mouth and causing mothers to cover their young ones' ears in delicate censorship. The irony was not lost on Magda. She turned and looked at one of her neighbouring woman, who sensed her watching and returned the gaze. Magda kept silent and didn't move but the woman was soon trembling and pushing people to move out of her way. The last Magda saw of her, she was yelling at the spectators to let her through and looking over her shoulder fearfully at

Magda. Magda smiled grimly and returned her attention to the crowd.

She scanned the mob and spotted Charles Senior and his farmhand Jack Sloane being bustled about. They were anxiously watching Charles Junior and trying their best to keep close to a guard who had agreed to the access of his body afterwards. They stood out in their misery amid the celebrations and cheer. She gazed on them with some sympathy before returning her attention back to Charles Junior.

The hangman stood them both behind their nooses. He put the white hood over their heads followed by the heavy rope, which was checked and tightened slightly, tilting it under the ear to ensure no accidental slipping off. He was a professional piscator of criminals' necks and had an unblemished record of successful hangings; this was not going to change now, even with a celebrity in front of him. He sniffed with judicial pride as he adjusted the rope and placed them both evenly on the trapdoors. He frowned at the guard, who had simmered with excited energy when he brought the prisoners in. That sort of behaviour was completely unprofessional and reflected badly on Newgate. He made a mental note to have a talk with the guard afterwards and run by him again the importance of decorum. This reminded him of the taller man's father, who had approached him earlier. He saw no conflict in interest there as he was a parent himself and had hungry mouths to feed. The money he was promised to be given on transfer of the body would enable him and his family to move to a cottage he had his eye on, with its own back garden neighbouring a farm. He could finally move away from the filthy slums of London town and start on his own vegetable garden, maybe even get some chickens. He looked over at the squat man on his left and grimaced. No one had claimed him at all. He would be disposed of once a cast had been done of his head for future study and speculation later.

He positioned himself by the lever and waited for the chaplain to deliver the final prayer.

'O most merciful Jesus, lover of souls, I pray thee by the agony of thy most sacred heart, and by the sorrows of thy immaculate mother, wash in thy blood the sinners of the whole world who are now in their agony, and are to die this day. May the lord have mercy on their soul. Amen.'

The crowd went silent. Magda held her breath. The hangman watched the chaplain, who bowed his head and kissed his bible. He nodded at the hangman who nodded back, placed his hand on the lever and pushed forward hard. A sudden jolt and the trapdoors opened dropping both men instantaneously. There was a second of stillness, and then the mob celebrated and roared as one. Charles Augustus Fenton, who was a living breathing man only minutes ago, was now dead.

She watched his dangling figure, having known all along that one day this would come. He was famous – a man that everyone knew and would forever claim some small connection to, with or without substantiation. Only his son had the ill fortune of keeping his name alive. Magda could never have realised at what cost this foretelling would be to her. That knowledge cut her deeply and, however futile it was, she would have sold her soul twice over if it could have changed the outcome. It had never been her intention to give Elizabeth false hopes or trick her when she told her that Charles would be famous. The divinations were open to the interpretation of the person. The reality had been painful for them both. She could never have predicted when they first met as children all those years ago, how their futures would be so entwined with perfume and pain. But a life without Elizabeth was untenable and Magda could not part from her even if she wanted to.

Magda turned and walked away from the bustling throng of rabid enthusiasts. She clasped the amulet in her hand tightly and muttered a small prayer – lost in thought and regret; how could it have all gone so wrong with her so closely linked to the family? All these years, watching and waiting, all for nought. She sighed and squeezed her amulet in a comforting gesture, determined not to fail in her duty EVER again.

Charles Senior and Jack Sloane pushed desperately

through the cheering swarm, anxious to retrieve Charles Junior's body. In the rush to the corpse, neither of them noticed the photograph slipping out of his top pocket. It came to rest in a muddy puddle of water. The photo of the sunny group of friends so filled with hope and joie de vivre that night, was soon trodden on and destroyed by the foot traffic.

The faces vanished. Happy faces from happier days. They were in the past and forgotten. It was all down to Charles Senior now to ensure his son would be brought home one final time and that his grandson, Arthur Henry Benjamin Fenton, would continue the Fenton name and make it a source of pride again. He determined not to fail his son and pushed harder towards his body.